PRAISE FOR REED FARREL COLEMAN
AND THE MOE PRAGER MYSTERIES

"Among the undying conve_____ ____n is t__
that requires every r_____ co_____ _____aun__
Reed Farrel Colema_____ _____ _____ _Valk
Perfect Square with _____ _____ a__
skin . . . a true coup." _____ *_ne New Yor__

"*Walking the Perfect Sq____ __s perfect pitch in the key of NYC.*"
—*Rocky Mountain News*

"Reed Farrel Coleman goes right to the darkest corners of the human heart—to the obsessions, the tragedies, the buried secrets . . . Through it all he maintains such a pure humanity in Moe Prager—the character is as alive to me as an old friend . . ."
—Steve Hamilton, Edgar Award–winning
author of *Blood Is the Sky*

"Moe Prager is a family man who can find humanity in almost everyone he meets; he is far from a perfect hero, but an utterly appealing one."
—Laura Lippman, Edgar Award–winning
author of *The Sugar House*

"[Coleman] makes us care about his characters and what happens to them, conveying a real sense of human absurdity and tragedy, of the price people will pay to get ahead or hide their true selves."
—*Publishers Weekly*

"Coleman writes in a way that seems absolutely right. Interesting, honest, and worth reading."
—*The Mystery Review*

"[A] witty, elegant, and quirky book, filled with delightful details, smart takes on relationships, politics, and life in general."
—*The East Hampton Star*

Reed Farrel Coleman was born and raised in Brooklyn, New York. He is the author of *Walking the Perfect Square* and *Redemption Street*, the first two books in the Moe Prager series. He lives on New York's Long Island.

In the Moe Prager Series

Walking the Perfect Square

Redemption Street

THE
JAMES
DEANS

Reed Farrel Coleman

A MOE PRAGER MYSTERY

PLUME
Published by the Penguin Group
Penguin Group (USA) Inc., 375 Hudson Street, New York, New York 10014, U.S.A.
Penguin Group (Canada), 10 Alcorn Avenue, Toronto, Ontario M4V 3B2,
Canada (a division of Pearson Penguin Canada Inc.)
Penguin Books Ltd., 80 Strand, London WC2R 0RL, England
Penguin Ireland, 25 St. Stephen's Green, Dublin 2,
Ireland (a division of Penguin Books Ltd.)
Penguin Group (Australia), 250 Camberwell Road, Camberwell, Victoria 3124,
Australia (a division of Pearson Australia Group Pty. Ltd.)
Penguin Books India Pvt. Ltd., 11 Community Centre, Panchsheel Park,
New Delhi – 110 017, India
Penguin Books (NZ), Cnr Airborne and Rosedale Roads, Albany,
Auckland 1310, New Zealand (a division of Pearson New Zealand Ltd.)
Penguin Books (South Africa) (Pty) Ltd., 24 Sturdee Avenue,
Rosebank, Johannesburg 2196, South Africa

Penguin Books Ltd, Registered Offices: 80 Strand, London WC2R 0RL, England

First published by Plume, a member of Penguin Group (USA) Inc.

First Printing, February 2005
10 9 8 7 6 5 4 3 2 1

Ⓟ REGISTERED TRADEMARK—MARCA REGISTRADA

CIP data is available.
ISBN 0-452-28650-6

Printed in the United States of America
Set in Horley Old Style with News Gothic
Designed by Daniel Lagin

PUBLISHER'S NOTE

This is a work of fiction. Names, characters, places, and incidents either are the product
of the author's imagination or are used fictitiously, and any resemblance to actual persons, living or dead, business establishments, events, or locales is entirely coincidental.

for Rosanne

ACKNOWLEDGMENTS

I would like to thank Wendy, Trena, Ryan, Jake, and Brant. Thanks also to my friends the Schares and the Lights. But as important as all of these folks are, none of it would mean anything without Rosanne, Kaitlin, and Dylan.

CHAPTER ONE

THE RECEPTION WAS AT THE LONESOME PIPER COUNTRY CLUB.
The piper was so lonely because no one could afford the membership
dues. Situated on a twenty-four-karat parcel of Long Island's Gold
Coast, the clubhouse, the former manse of a railroad robber baron, sat
on a tree-lined bluff overlooking the Sound and Connecticut beyond.
One peek at the place and you immediately understood why Old New
York money had claimed this piece of the island as its enclave.

I had to admit that even if the marriage didn't last the honey-
moon, Craig and Constance would have a hell of a wedding album.
As the photographer clicked away—"That's right. That's right.
Groom, turn a little more to your left. Good. Smile. Perfect. Perfect. Hold it. Just one more . . ."—I couldn't help but be curious
how Aaron and I had wound up on the guest list. Considering the
social status of our fellow invitees, my brother and I had a lot more
in common with the help.

Constance had worked for us for about six months while she
was finishing up at Juilliard. That was over a year ago, and it
wasn't like she was employee of the century or anything. True, we
liked her well enough, as did our customers, but we never fooled

ourselves that she'd stay on. Constance was a wealthy, handsome, and talented young woman who was more playing at work than working. It was as if she were fulfilling some sort of missionary obligation to teach the children of the Third World how to read.

Frankly, I didn't care why we were invited. All I knew was that Katy, my wife, was in better spirits today. Smiling, even dancing with me a little, she seemed almost her old self. She had taken time with her makeup, fussed with her hair, worn a dress that accentuated her curves. She had kissed me hard on the mouth for the first time in months, making a show of wiping her lipstick off my lips with her fingers. It was as if she had awoken from a coma.

"Excuse me, sir," a red-jacketed waiter said, just touching my shoulder. "Mr. Geary, the bride's father, would like a word. He's waiting for you in the East Egg Room."

It wasn't up for discussion, and I was curious anyway.

The East Egg Room was a private space on the other side of the clubhouse, away from the dining area and close to the men's locker room. It was all walnut paneling, green glass ashtrays, and nailhead chairs, and smelled like the ghosts of my father's cigars. This was the place where members played poker, drank scotch or cognac, made private deals. Mr. Geary smiled at my entrance, but with proper restraint. Six feet tall and square shouldered, he was a man of sixty with the weathered good looks of a cowboy. A cowboy with a North Shore dentist and a personal trainer. He looked perfectly at ease in his surroundings and gray morning coat.

"Mr. Prager," Geary said, offering me his firm hand. "A pleasure to meet you. Connie tells me you and your brother treated her very well during the time of her employment. I trust you and Mrs. Prager are enjoying yourselves."

"Very much so. Thank you."

2

He cleared his throat. The prepared text or pretext out of the way, he was ready to move on to the real business of the day.

"Do you know Steven Brightman?" my host asked, picking up his Manhattan off a green-felt-covered card table.

"Should I?"

"Come, take a stroll with me, Mr. Prager."

We stepped through the pro shop, toward the practice putting green and along the driving range. Several of the members nodded to Geary; a few took a moment to congratulate him. They regarded me with suspicion, some scowling as if I were one rung up the evolutionary ladder from silverfish.

"Do you follow politics, Moe? May I call you Moe?"

"No and yes. I'm an ex-cop, Mr. Geary. Cops don't have much use for politicians, though politicians got lots of uses for cops. None of 'em any good as far as I can tell. And yeah, you can call me Moe."

"Though I sometimes find them as distasteful as you do, a man in my position inevitably makes the acquaintance of several politicians."

"No doubt."

He pointed out to the first-hole tee box. "Do you play?"

"Some. Brooklyn isn't exactly a hotbed of great golfers."

"You know why they call it golf?"

"Because all the other four-letter words are taken."

"Exactly."

I suppose he thought telling me the oldest golf joke on earth was meant to show he was just a regular Joe, that we weren't really that different, he and I, in spite of minor details like wealth, religion, breeding, schooling, and career. Did he have a career? I wondered what he had time for besides being rich.

"You should play more, you know," he continued. "It's a real

thinking man's game. Chess with sticks is how I view it. The unini-
tiated believe ball striking is the talent, but it's the ability to manage
the course, to think your way around it, that makes a good golfer."

There was a message for me in there somewhere.

"No offense, Mr. Geary, but what's this—"

"A young woman named Moira Heaton, the daughter of an
ex-policeman like yourself, was working as an intern for a state
senator. She left his office on Thanksgiving Eve 1981 and never
made it home. She's been missing ever since. Not a dissimilar story
to that of your brother-in-law, Patrick."

"Do you research all your wedding guests this thoroughly?"

He laughed, but not loudly enough to disturb anyone's back-
swing. "No, Moe, not all my guests."

"This is where I guess that the missing girl worked for Brightman and that you think I can help find her, right?"

"Actually, Moe, I was hoping you would have heard of this
and saved me the trouble of the background details. Short of that,
yes, I think you might be able to help."

"Sorry, Mr. Geary, I really appreciate having been invited here
and I have had a good time, but I—"

He shushed me politely. "Moe, a wise man listens before making up his mind, and all I'm asking is that you consider taking this
on. If, when all is said and done, you choose not to get involved,
then we'll shake hands and part amicably."

This guy was good. Never had the promise of a friendly hand-
shake sounded so much like a threat.

"Let me think about it, okay?" I parried. "At the moment I'd
like to head back to the reception and dance with my wife a little."

"Absolutely. Pardon my taking you away from her. Convey
my apologies, won't you?"

4

"I will. Again, congratulations."

When I got back to the reception, things had changed, and not for the better. Aaron was pacing a rut in the cart path outside the pro shop.

"Where the fuck have you been?"

"Getting a lecture on philosophy and the art of golf. Why?"

His lips turned down, anger changing to sadness. "It's Katy."

"What's Katy? What happened?"

"After you left, I was dancing with Cindy."

This was remarkable in itself. Aaron and my sister-in-law danced about as often as Siamese cats went scuba diving.

"Yeah, you were dancing and . . ."

"One of Constance's cousins walked by our table carrying her newborn, and Katy asked if she could hold the baby."

"Oh, for *chrissakes!* She was happy today. Where is she?"

Aaron shrugged. "Still in the bathroom with Cindy."

Needless to say, my presence was less than welcomed in the ladies' room. Anyone who could flee did so at the sound of my voice. Only the attendant, a wrinkled old black woman in pink polyester and a silly frilled hat, protested. I chucked a twenty in her tip basket and her squawking came to an abrupt end. I nodded for Cindy to wait outside.

"Just tell everyone the toilets are flooding."

Guilty, wounded, Katy couldn't look at me. She angled her legs and chin toward the stall wall, her chest heaving as she tried to suppress her tears. I knelt down in front of her and held her hand. Her face was a mask of trembling embarrassment.

"It's okay, kiddo. You've gotta stop punishing yourself like this. You didn't do anything wrong."

A month, two months ago, these words would have been

magic. *Abracadabra! Presto chango!* She would have stopped crying immediately, for I would have pushed her rage button. First she'd aimed her accusing finger at God, then at herself, then me. Initially, I hadn't minded. I'd almost welcomed it in a martyrly fashion: if it helped Katy, I could take it. But eventually it left us both exhausted and bruised. No, the rage was gone, and in its place were only guilt and pain.

Our baby was dead. Had it been someone else's, someone I'd read about in the paper, I suppose I could have retreated into the comfort of cold philosophy. I could have played the semantics game. *Was it really a baby at five months? A fetus? What?* At least we still had Sarah. At least we had been spared the trauma our friends Cisco and Sheila had been forced to endure. Their son had been stillborn. What's worse, when Sheila's labor was induced, they knew their son was dead. Of course I'd been philosophical about it, spouting the usual bullshit about how it was better this way. What way was that? Better for whom, exactly? We haven't seen Cisco and Sheila for over a year now.

I realized I'd been punishing myself, the way Katy had punished herself, the way she punished me. In spite of my Jewishness, I know only the guilty deserve to be punished, and even then, not always. Given the randomness of things, it's a miracle any of us get born at all. But that knowledge doesn't stop my mother's words from ringing in my ears: *When things are good, watch out!* In the world of her creation, we were always one breath short of disaster, one nightfall away from the sun's refusal to shine. My mom lacked perspective. Now I had all the perspective I could stand.

"Life is hard for us all." That's what my friend Israel Roth says. "It's not a contest of whose life is worse. When the Gettys are sad, their misery is as real as mine or yours. Money is a retreat, not a fortress. Maybe I understand your mother, may she rest in peace, a little bit different than you. Life changes a person. Maybe she would regret some of her ways, take some things back. But she's gone and nothing can change the dead. Just say Kaddish and move on."

Mr. Roth, unlike me, has earned the right to be philosophical about death. The Nazi tattoo on his forearm says so.

Still, things had been good. Katy's design business was taking off. Sarah—the smartest, most beautiful child on earth—was being two with a vengeance, but that was as it should be. City on the Vine and Bordeaux in Brooklyn, the wine shops Aaron and I owned, were booming. I had my doubts about Reaganomics, but the money seemed to be trickling down at least as far as our cash registers. What did I know about economics anyway? I voted for Jimmy Carter. Twice!

So, like I said, things had been good, were good. I wasn't even particularly itchy anymore. I'd worked my one case as a private investigator and gotten the notion out of my system. Besides, all I'd got for my trouble was bruised kidneys and a trunk full of other people's secrets. Who needed the grief? I had enough of my own. So I put my license back in the sock drawer with the rest of my dreams. Even the dust bunnies thought my license was a bit of a farce, a frightened man's conceit, a hedge against the ifs in life. Then we had the miscarriage. There are no hedges.

"Come on," I said, tugging on Katy's hand. "Let's go home and see Sarah, okay?"

She smiled in spite of herself. Whatever other tragedies she'd suffered, whatever regrets Katy had, there was always Sarah to go home to. Sometimes that kid of ours could be an amazing source of strength for the both of us.

"Okay, Moe," Katy relented, standing up and smoothing out her dress. "Just give me a minute."

As I waited outside the door, I tried imagining the face of a woman I'd never met before or even heard of until fifteen minutes ago. I wondered if her father was thinking about her at that very moment, if he had hedged against the loss of his daughter. It was a day to think about fathers and daughters.

"Where have you got to, Moira Heaton?" I mumbled under my breath.

"Did you say something?" Katy asked, reappearing at my side.

"It's not important."

The dappled June light smelled of fresh-cut grass and possibility. Hope and potential were easy to believe in on a sunny wedding day in June. Just as we stepped out, Constance and Craig were getting into the limo that would take them to the airport. I hadn't thought to ask where they were headed. On a day like this, they could go anywhere. But anywhere they went, they would not remain untouched for very long. That was always the test, I thought, not how good you were at avoiding the blows, but how you dealt with them after they landed.

CHAPTER TWO

OUR PRECARIOUS EQUILIBRIUM HAD RETURNED. I WAS GRATE-
ful for it. Even in the previous day's incident I could see an end to
the grief in sight. Katy snapped back more quickly each time and
had finally started working on some long-neglected accounts. She
was down in her studio and Sarah was next door with her friend
Mary. I was busy watching the second act of a twin bill slaughter
of the Mets by the Astros. *Macbeth* had been less bloody than this,
certainly more humane.

Still, I could not get Moira Heaton off my mind, nor could I
get my head around Mr. Geary's cryptic lecture about the art of
golf. Considering my history, I understood my fascination with
Moira. Geary was a different story. All my life I'd been told that
rich people were different. Of course, having grown up in the ass
end of Brooklyn, my concept of rich was somewhat skewed. To
me, a kid who had his own room and no hand-me-downs was like
a king. People who owned their own homes and two cars . . . Forget about it! Both college and the job had expanded my horizons
some, but not as much as you'd think.

Until Aaron and I opened our first shop on Columbus Avenue

five years ago, I never really dealt with people of any significant means. Black or white, Jew or gentile, clean or corrupt, almost everyone I had contact with up until then was in the same boat as me. Some sat at the captain's table, some traveled in steerage. Nevertheless, it was the same boat. So I understood them. I was them. I didn't get men like Geary. What allure could some political hack hold for Geary? How rich was rich enough? I couldn't help but remember my father's pitiful mantra: *If I could only put twenty grand together . . .* That was my dad's problem; he dreamed small and failed big.

There wasn't a thing I could do or wanted to do about Geary except wait for his call. Moira Heaton, on the other hand, may have been missing, but not from the public record. Unfortunately, the parts of the public record I wanted to see were behind the beige brick walls and locked doors of the Sheepshead Bay branch of the Brooklyn Public Library. I tried thinking back to Thanksgiving Eve of '81.

I had been a little too preoccupied to have paid much attention to the news of Moira Heaton's disappearance in those weeks. Thanksgiving Eve 1981 was the night Arthur Rosen hanged himself. Rosen had tried to hire me to look into the death of his sister Karen. Fair enough, but there were these two minor sticking points: Arthur was as mad as a March hare, and Karen, a high school classmate of mine, was one of seventeen workers who had perished in a Catskills hotel fire in 1966. I turned him down flat, throwing him unceremoniously out of the shop.

Days later, when I went to apologize, I found Arthur's body, his neck in a belt, and my name scrawled in blood on his bedroom wall. It was just my name, but it felt like an accusation. I changed my mind and took the case. Maybe too late to do Arthur any good, but not too late for me. I spent the next week or so up in the Catskills. Crazy Arthur Rosen had been right in the end; the fire that killed all those kids so many years before had been no accident. Though, as it happened, I doubt he would have clicked his heels up at the truth. The dead had been spoken for, finally. The guilty paid the bill, belatedly, but in full. So it was no wonder to me that Moira Heaton had escaped my notice.

"Katy," I called down, opening the basement door, "I'm going out for a few hours, okay? Sarah's next door. I'll bring back a pizza."

"No problem. I'm almost done anyway. Where ya going?"

"I'm not sure."

In some sense, I wasn't.

* * *

I raced the sun along the Belt Parkway. Less than a mile into the trip, I drove past Coney Island, the neighborhood in which I'd spent most of my life and nearly my entire career as a cop. It was a stretch I drove every day whether I was headed to Bordeaux in Brooklyn or City on the Vine. I made the trip so often that I no longer noticed the landmarks. They were no longer even blurs or random shapes or splashes of color. Familiarity breeds a kind of blindness. Today, I took the time to notice. Katy wasn't the only one coming out of a coma.

Pete Parson was a broken-down old cop like me. These days he was a minority partner in a grimy artists' hangout in TriBeCa called Pooty's. Even if I had come by just to play the juke, he would have been happy to see me. It had been a slow Sunday to begin with, as half the population of Manhattan was out on the southeastern tip of Long Island. Anyway, Pete had a low tolerance threshold for the artsy-fartsy posers who populated his bar arguing over Twyla Tharp and Mapplethorpe instead of the Yankees and the Mets.

"How the fuck did I ever wind up in this place, Moe?" he asked, clapping me on the back. "When I was working the job, all I ever dreamed about was owning my own place, some neighborhood joint with pretzels and a pool table and guys reading the *Racing Form*. Someday I'm gonna move down south and open up a wine shop for you and your brother."

"Yeah, sure, Pete, Merlot in Macon. If you think you got nothing in common with your clientele now . . . Besides, you couldn't tell Ripple from a Cotes du Rhone with a road map."

"Fuck you. What a ya havin'?"

"Dewar's rocks."

"Not that I'm not happy to see ya, but you haven't been in since—you know. How's Katy holding up?"

He put my scotch on the bar and opened a bottle of Bud for himself.

"Better. She's doing better. We all are, I think."

"Cheers!" He tipped his bottle to me. "So what's up?"

"Remember I told you about working that case up in the Catskills?"

"That was like two years ago, right? The thing with the fire, all them kids. Yeah. What about it?"

"Nothing about it. It's just I know you're good at keeping up with the news, and when I was up in the mountains, there was something I guess I missed."

"What was that?"

"A girl disappeared."

"Girls are always disappearing."

"This one was working as an intern for a state senator."

"That Brightman thing?"

"That's the one."

"Jeez, Moe, she was a cop's kid. Other than that, I don't know what I can tell you."

"Whatever you can tell me is more than I know, so . . ."

"So what's this got to do with you, anyways?"

"I don't know yet, probably nothing," I said, only half hoping it was true. "Was there any indication of foul play?"

"Nothin' obvious, no signs of a struggle, no blood or nothin' in the office, as I recall. One minute she was there and the next minute she wasn't. Sort of like . . ." He drifted off. "So, you ever hear anything about him?"

He didn't have to specify which him. I knew his name like I knew my own, better maybe. Patrick Michael Maloney, Katy's younger brother, had walked out of this very bar in December 1977 and into oblivion. It was bizarre how months could go by without anyone mentioning Patrick, and then his name would start rolling off people's tongues like hello. Yesterday it was Geary. Today it was Pete. When Patrick's name started getting bandied about, it was never a good omen. It usually meant people wanted something, specifically, something from me.

"Not a word, Pete. Every once in a while we get some schmuck looking to make a quick buck off the reward money, but the tips never pan out. Between you and me, I think Patrick ran as far away from here as he could get and he's never coming back. Given my asshole father-in-law, I can't say that I blame him."

"Amen to that."

Pete had gotten a bellyful of Francis Maloney Sr. after Patrick vanished. My father-in-law, once a big-time fund-raiser for the state

Democratic Party, pulled strings in order to get Pooty's bar license revoked. That was Francis Maloney for you. His son disappeared, so heads would roll. Whether those heads bore any responsibility for his son going missing was almost beside the point.

The Dewar's was turning to dust in my mouth. Any protracted discussion involving my father-in-law did that to me, but it wasn't all on Francis. There were things I knew and things I knew he knew about his son's disappearance that we kept silently between us. These were dangerous things, these secrets, like time bombs sitting in the hall closet. They would remain dormant as long as Katy stayed out of the loop. One word, one leak, one slip, and we'd both lose her forever. Tick . . . Tick . . . Tick . . .

I decided to get back to the subject at hand before I needed a second scotch to wash down the one that had turned to dust.

"You remember any other details of the Heaton girl's disappearance?"

"Christ, Moe, that was a long time ago. There was some rumblings about hanky-panky between the girl and Brightman. You know, the papers tried playing that up."

"They would."

"Hey, it sells papers."

"Did it have any legs?"

"Nah," Pete said, grabbing the Dewar's bottle. "He denied it, put up reward money, cooperated with the cops. Let 'em search his home, his office, whatever. He was clean."

"Clean, huh?" I waved a second drink off. "Clean is always a matter of degree."

"Clean ain't clear, though. Brightman's political career took a big hit. They were grooming him for the major leagues, the next fair-haired superstar."

"Yeah, they all start out as the next Jack Kennedy and end up fixing parking tickets for the local head of the chamber of commerce."

"Fuckin' politicians!" Pete shook his head in disgust. "You know, if you really wanna find out about the guy, there is someone who would know better than me."

"Who's that?"

Pete suddenly looked as if he'd swallowed a beehive and washed it down with Black Flag. I suppose he hoped I'd figure it out on my own.

"Who, Pete?"

"You know."

"Who, for chrissakes?"

"We were just talkin' about him. Katy's old man."

I decided I wasn't that curious, not by a long shot.

CHAPTER THREE

THAT'S THE THING ABOUT CURIOSITY—LIKE A CRAVING, IT WILL fade if given enough time. Mine had faded into the routine of work and family.

Wednesdays were my days to open the new shop. Located on Montague Street, Bordeaux in Brooklyn had a bit of a different feel than City on the Vine. Some of that was because Brooklyn, no matter how you dressed her up, would never be Manhattan. She would always be the poor relation in last year's dress; pretty enough, but a half a step behind. Another contributing factor to the different atmosphere was the actual physical layout of the place. The Brooklyn shop was in the basement and on the first floor of a converted old brownstone with apartments above. And because we were located in a historic district, we were very limited as to the type of signs we were permitted to use.

BORDEAUX IN BROOKLYN
IRVING PRAGER & SONS, INC.
Purveyors of Finest Wines and Spirits
Established 1978

So read the gilt lettering on the front door and the plate-glass window. Of course my father had died years before we opened either store. The corporation name was a tribute to his memory. Aaron and I were determined that Irving Prager's name should be remembered not for his failures but for his sons' success.

I liked my days in this shop not only because it was less of a schlep back and forth from home. I liked it because I once again got to hang out with Klaus. Klaus, the store manager, had been with us since '79 and was sort of a cross between Calvin Klein and Johnny Rotten. He knew more about the fashion and the music scenes than most people whose business it was to know. Klaus came from out west somewhere, from a family who found the distance now between them a convenient tool for ignoring their son's homosexuality.

Klaus liked Wednesdays as well. He missed working with me as much as I missed working with him. I was a far more receptive audience for his antics than my brother. Popular culture still really interested me, whereas Aaron's interest had come to an end during the early years of LBJ's presidency. "I love your brother," Klaus had once confessed, "but he is more a fugue than a frug kind of guy."

But it was another man, not Klaus, waiting for me on the front steps of the old brownstone. He was a pudgy little man in a cheap brown suit speckled with dandruff and old sweat stains. He had a pasty, humorless face and a fat vinyl briefcase in his paw. His one concession to convention was his unsuccessful attempt at camouflaging his civil service karma with a quarter bottle of Aramis.

"Mr. Prager?" he asked, reaching into his pocket.

"Yes."

"Moses B. or Aaron F.?"

"Moses B. Who wants to know?"

He handed me a card. "Leon Weintraub," he said, not offering me his hand. "I'm an investigator for the New York—"

"—State Liquor Authority. Yeah, that's what the card says."

Now he showed me his official ID. I finished opening up the shop and asked him in before getting to the subject of his visit. As I opened my mouth, Klaus came through the front door.

"Klaus," I said, cutting off any possibility he might start in on our guest's sartorial ineptitude, "this is Mr. Weintraub from the state liquor authority."

Klaus turned on the charm. "Can I get you gentlemen some coffee? Some pastry?"

Weintraub did something with his mouth that was his excuse for a smile. "Black, two sugars. Seeded roll, extra butter." A civil servant was never born who could turn down free anything.

Klaus was shrewd enough to not bother waiting for a please and thank-you. He'd lived in New York long enough to know better. "Usual for you, boss?"

I nodded, but as Klaus retreated he could not help pulling a face behind Weintraub's back. He pinched his nose with the fingers and feigned gagging. I almost bit through my tongue trying to keep my composure.

"Come on into the office, Mr. Weintraub. What can we do for you?" I asked as I showed him downstairs.

"Just a routine spot check."

Routine spot check my ass! I'd been around the block enough to know better. Go ask Pete Parson if you don't believe me. The liquor authority was one of the most politicized institutions in the Empire State. In a state where "Patronage, Nepotism, and Influence" is the unofficial state motto, that's really saying something.

"Fine," I said. "Have a look around. Let me know how I can help you. Here's the office. Klaus will be down with your breakfast in a minute. Now, if you'll excuse me, I have to finish opening up."

Klaus quickly tracked me down once he'd delivered the complimentary continental breakfast to our uninvited guest.

"So what's that grubby little man doing here?"

"A spot check?" I sipped my coffee.

"A spot check indeed. He needs to do one on that hideous suit of his. Oh . . . my . . . God! I thought that color brown was outlawed by the Geneva Convention. I know several homeless men who wouldn't be caught dead in—"

"All right, I get the point."

"But what's he really doing here?"

"Sending a message, Klaus, sending a message."

It didn't take long for the other shoe to drop. About an hour after Weintraub waddled out the front door, the phone rang. I didn't race to pick it up, but I knew it would be for me.

"Boss, pick up!" Klaus called on the intercom.

I pressed the flashing button and put the receiver to my ear. "Prager, Moses B.," I spoke into the mouthpiece. "Message received loud and clear."

There was an almost imperceptible laugh on the other end of the line. "I'd like you to meet me at Spivack and Associates, Suite 1404, 40 Court Street. Are you familiar with the building, Mr. Prager?"

"I am."

"In an hour?" It might have been phrased like a question, but it wasn't.

I didn't bother putting the phone back in its cradle. It was my turn to start making calls.

"Intelligence Division, Detective Steptoe," a woman answered.

"Sorry," I said, going over the number I'd dialed in my head, "I thought this was Detective McDonald's line."

"Who?"

"Larry McDonald, Detective Larry—"

"You mean Captain McDonald?"

"If you say so."

"Let me transfer you."

With the passing years my contacts in the NYPD had withered. Some of the guys had, like me and Pete, gotten hurt on the job and been put out to pasture. Many made their twenty years, trading in their badges for golf bags. To the kids coming up as I was headed out the door, I was a relic, a fossil who didn't understand the job or the day-to-day bullshit they had to put up with. I remembered feeling the same way about the guys who'd come up before me. Whenever they started a sentence with "In my day . . ." I, too, would roll my eyes. But I could always depend on Larry McDonald. We'd worked together for years in Coney Island, and he owed me, big-time.

"*Captain* McDonald. Should I just genuflect or do I have to kiss the ring, too?"

"You gimpy Jew bastard, you couldn't genuflect if your life depended on it. Shit, I haven't heard a peep from you in years. I thought you were dead."

"Wishful thinking."

"Wha'd'ya need, brother?"

"State Senator Steven Brightman."

There was a long silence on the other end of the line.

"I'm the one who's supposed to be dead, Larry, remember? Hello . . ."

"This a fishing expedition, Moe? 'Cause if it is, I can't have any part in this. A politician and the missing daughter of an ex-cop; it's not a winning combination for anyone."

"Calm down. Calm down. I'm not out to fuck the guy. Fact is, I might be working for Brightman. Someone's got his ear that thinks I might have some luck finding the girl."

"Come on, man. You know what happened to her. You were a fucking cop before that piece a carbon paper fucked up your knee. She's a pile of bones somewheres out in Bethpage State Park or in the Gowanus Canal."

"Probably you're right, but I don't think I'm gonna have much of a choice about working the case. I need everything on both Brightman and the girl, Moira Heaton."

Again, there was an uncomfortable silence. The last time Larry helped me out he hadn't yet made rank and the information had come from departments outside the city. Now the landscape had changed. This was Larry Mac's own little fiefdom. Traditionally, each bureau or division within the NYPD jealously defends its turf. It was hard enough getting these various entities to share information with each other, let alone a guy like me.

"Christ, Moe, I don't know," he hemmed and hawed like a man asked to pick his own pocket. "It's not like back in the day. They keep closer track of things than they used to."

"Yeah, yeah, Big Brother and all that, but 1984's still six months away. Why don't you just see what you can do and I'll check back with you, okay?" I knew not to argue with him.

"All right, let me see. Gimme a day or two."

"Thanks, Larry."

"Don't thank me yet and don't send me good champagne either. My wife just makes mimosas with it."

When we were done, I thought about making a second call, a much harder call to make. I put the phone down instead. There's an old baseball adage about some of the best trades being the ones you don't make. I didn't fool myself that it applied here. The call was going to get made, just not yet.

* * *

They didn't call it Court Street for nothing. You could throw a rock across the road from the lobby of number 40 and hit the State Supreme Court Building. If you took to heart Shakespeare's line about killing all the lawyers, blowing up 40 Court Street would have been a good start. With its proximity to the court and the Brooklyn Tombs only a few blocks away on Atlantic Avenue, the dirty brown skyscraper was chock-full of lawyers. Where there are courts and jails and lawyers, there are investigators. Spivack and Associates among them.

When cops are on the job they love lawyers like lions love hyenas, only minus the mutual respect. But the minute a cop puts in his papers and goes into private investigations, he finds as many hyenas as he can and becomes an associate member of the pack. When you beg scraps, it pays to stay close to the pack. That's why Spivack and Associates was such a natural fit in the brown building on Court Street. If I had gone into the business full-time, I too might have rented office space here.

Suite 1404, all glass, stainless steel, and uncomfortable furniture, had a rather antiseptic feel to it. I suppose they could always rent it out to local hospitals for ambulatory surgery. The receptionist barely got "Good day" out of her mouth when a drill sergeant type approached. Easily six foot three, he had a graying brush cut, a square chin and shoulders, rough features, and impatient blue eyes.

"I'm Spivack," he barked, shaking my hand in spite of himself. "This way."

Spivack wore a short-sleeve white shirt, black slacks, black tie, black shoes. He sort of looked like an angry escapee from 1950s middle management. His strides ate up carpet in big chunks.

He stopped. "Here," he said, pushing open his office door.

His office, while not exactly inviting, was less antiseptic than the rest of the place. The chairs looked sat in, the desk was scratched and chipped. There were photos on the wall, certificates and diplomas, and a Lucite display featuring a green beret, an army-issue .45, and handcuffs. I took a more careful look at some of the photos. Several featured a younger Spivack in a U.S. marshal windbreaker escorting prisoners.

Mr. Geary was seated on a black leather sofa and waited for me to finish checking out the office before standing to greet me.

Spivack sat down behind his desk and glared even more contemptuously at Geary than he had at me.

"Hello, Moe," Geary said, the butter melting in his mouth. "Good of you to come."

"I know a command performance when I see one."

Geary didn't waste time disputing the facts. "I see you've met Joe Spivack."

"Sort of, yeah."

He beckoned me to come join him back on the sofa. I was amazed at how in command he acted in someone else's place of business. He treated Spivack as another piece of furniture. I sat.

"Mr. Spivack's firm did the original investigation into Moira Heaton's unfortunate disappearance. I won't bore you with the details. Let's just say it was an expensive and thorough, if not very fruitful, exercise for Mr. Spivack and company."

Geary gestured to Spivack as if he were calling the busboy to refill his water glass. Spivack handed an accordion file to Geary, who handed it to me.

"Don't bother going through it now." It wasn't a suggestion. "This is the salient material. Take it home with you, Moe. I'm told there are several more boxes of ancillary material which we'll have delivered wherever you'd like. Mr. Spivack will lend you all possible assistance and answer any of your questions."

"Wait a second! Wait a second," I barked, my patience wearing razor thin. "Mr. Spivack, is there a room where Mr. Geary and I can talk in private? There's some stuff him and me have to get straight."

"Will right here do?" Spivack asked, happy at the prospect of getting out from under Geary's thumb.

"Works for me," I answered.

If Geary was upset by being left out of the decision-making process, he didn't show it. Spivack got up and left before that changed.

"I'm sorry, Moe," Geary offered as soon as the door clicked shut. "I've behaved badly, I know. I've taken things for granted."

"I don't like threats, Mr. Geary."

"Thomas," he corrected. "Call me Thomas."

Yeah, right, I thought. And we'll go have some buttered scones and tea afterward.

"Like I was saying, I don't like threats, even implied ones. I didn't appreciate that little visit this morning from the New York State Liquor Authority. Not one bit."

"It got your attention, though?"

"I'm here, aren't I?"

"That was my idea, I'm afraid. I would ask you not to hold it against Steven, Senator Brightman. He would disapprove."

"I'm liking him better already."

Geary smiled. "Then you'll do it. You'll look into this matter for us."

"I didn't say that."

"But you will, won't you?"

"I may have been a cop once, Mr. Geary, but that doesn't mean I'm stupid."

"Far from it, I'd say. That's part of the reason you're here at all."

"Pardon me if I don't thank you, but that's been bugging me all weekend long," I confessed. "And now that I'm in this office, it's bothering me even more. Why do you need me? I'm a part-timer with no network. I mean, look around you. This guy is major league. He's a former U.S. marshal. They're like fucking bulldogs. What can I do to find Moira Heaton that Spivack and Associates and their network and friends and informants couldn't?"

"Would it suffice to say you come highly recommended?"

"No."

"I didn't suppose it would. How about this then?" he asked, reaching into his inner jacket pocket.

I knew even before his hand reappeared what it would hold. *"Gotham Magazine,"* I said, "pages seventeen through twenty, continued on page ninety-three, far left column."

When Katy's brother Patrick vanished in '77, an ambitious reporter for *Gotham* had done a piece about the disappearance and subsequent search. The reporter, correctly sensing there was a lot more to the story than what the press had been spoon-fed by the family, thought the story had Pulitzer Prize written all over it. Unfortunately for him, the people who knew the truth, myself included, kept it to themselves. The story turned into more of a puff piece and part of the puff was about me or, more accurately, about me and a little girl named Marina.

On Easter Sunday of 1972, Marina Conseco, the seven-year-old daughter of a city firefighter, went missing in Coney Island. Several days later, while searching the area with some off-duty firemen, I got the idea to check out the wooden rooftop water tanks on some of the older buildings in the neighborhood. We found Marina, battered but alive, in the third or fourth tank we checked. In an undistinguished career as a cop, finding her was my one shining moment. People would forget Patrick, but never Marina. It was this same story that had brought poor Arthur Rosen to me. However, there was nothing remotely poor or needy about the man who stood in front of me at the moment.

"Bravo, bravo." He applauded, his left hand hitting the folded pages in his right. "Bravo."

"That was eleven years ago when I found the girl."

"Don't be modest," he said coolly, the smile running away from his face. "I know much more about you than you'd think."

"What's that supposed to mean?" I asked, beginning to feel light-headed.

He didn't answer, checking his watch instead. "We can discuss your fee at a later date. I assure you you won't suffer financially. As I said previously, you can expect the fullest cooperation from Mr. Spivack. I must be on my way."

"You didn't answer my question. Why me?"

"In a word, luck. You're lucky, Mr. Prager."

"We're not on a first-name basis anymore, huh, Tom?"

He ignored that, too. "Spivack is good, as good as good gets. We've had two unproductive years of good, Mr. Prager. It's time for a little luck." He about-faced, reaching for the doorknob.

"One condition," I said.

"Yes, Mr. Prager," he answered impatiently. "What is it?"

"I interview Brightman, alone."

"I'm afraid that won't be—"

"That's my condition. You won't meet it, forget about my luck. You can threaten me and try to intimidate me till the fucking cows come home and I won't take the case. I need to look into your boy's eyes."

"I'll arrange for it. In the meantime, get to work."

He closed the door behind him without bothering to look back.

*   *   *

When I got back to the shop, Klaus was quick to tell me that Aaron had called in a panic. Apparently, one of Mr. Weintraub's colleagues had paid our Columbus Avenue location an afternoon visit. I doubt if Geary knew it at the time he arranged for it, but he'd done me a big favor. My absence from the business for the foreseeable future would be much easier for my big brother to swallow now that he'd gotten to experience firsthand the depth of Thomas Geary's influence.

The business meant everything to Aaron. Would he sacrifice his family for it? No. My charm and less than encyclopedic knowledge of wines was another matter altogether. Besides, one of the conditions of our partnership was that I had the option to take vacation time to work cases. I'd exercised the option only once in five years, when I went up to the Catskills.

"City on the Vine," Aaron answered the phone.

In those five syllables alone, I could hear the worry in his voice.

28

"New York State Liquor Authority," I taunted.

"Fuck you."

"So I hear you had a visit."

"What's going on, Moe? Klaus said something about it being a—"

"—message. Yeah, it's a message to me. Remember how we couldn't figure out why we got invited to Connie's wedding?"

"Sure, but what the fuck's this got to do—"

"Everything, apparently. Connie's dad wants me to work a case for him, and today's bit of muscle flexing was to help me make up my mind in his favor. At the wedding, when Katy lost it, I was out on the driving range with Mr. Geary. That's when he first suggested it might be in my best interest to consider taking him on as a client."

"And he thought strong-arming you was the way to go?" Aaron was incredulous.

"I guess he doesn't believe in long courtships. He made his point pretty effectively, though. You gotta give him that."

"What about . . ." Aaron hesitated. "Maybe we should—I mean, maybe you should call . . . Why don't you call your father-in-law? He's probably still got political contacts. Maybe he could insulate us from—" Aaron understood I loathed my father-in-law, but not why, exactly.

"Forget it! Just forget it! I can't—*we* can't afford to owe him. I'll work the case hard for a week and we can all move on. You can spare me for a week."

"Do you think he's serious?"

"Geary? Would he really fuck with us if I turned him down? I don't know. I don't think so, but I'm not in the mood to find out. Are you?"

"Consider yourself on vacation, little brother."

"Yeah, okay, I'll get out my Hawaiian shirts."

"Very funny. What's this case, anyway, that Geary's gone to all this trouble for?" Aaron was justifiably curious.

"All you need to know is there's a missing girl at the end of it."

"Oh, I get it," he said, as if I'd explained quantum mechanics in a single sentence.

How nice, I thought. Now maybe he could explain it to me.

The wine business had always been Aaron's dream. Even my taking the test for the cops had been on a drunken dare. A good chunk of my adult life had basically been the product of grafting my energies onto someone else's schemes. Careerwise, the only thing I'd ever wanted for myself, the one thing that was mine alone, was the right to work a case or two here and there. And now that one footnote to my own destiny was getting yanked out of my hands.

"How the fuck did I ever wind up in this place?" I repeated Pete Parson's question. It had been a good question on Sunday and was an even better one today. I opened up the accordion file and found a picture of a woman of whom I knew very little except her name. "I hope you're worth it, Moira Heaton."

God had infinite ways of displaying love and cruelty. Anyone over the age of twelve who hadn't figured that one out was on his way to either beatification or long-term therapy. But it was the way he manipulated imperfection to such disparate ends that fascinated me. Reconciling holocausts and hurricanes was beyond me. I'd let the big questions turn my rabbi's hair gray. I looked for God's handiwork in people's faces. And in Moira Heaton's face I found ample traces of the Almighty's mischief.

I'm uncertain of what I expected, but whatever it was, Moira Heaton wasn't it. Not immune to the whiff of scandal, I suppose I had envisioned her as darkly beautiful or as a red-haired colleen, the kind of prize an older, accomplished man would be unable to resist. She was neither. Moira was plain. In a culture that values attention almost beyond anything else, even money, plainness is a curse.

I wondered what it said by her high school yearbook photo: *Most likely to be forgotten?* Moira's life, over or not, had served some purpose. Maybe I wouldn't be clever enough to figure it out, maybe no one ever would, but I'd taken notice of her and wasn't likely to forget.

CHAPTER
FOUR

HEADING EAST ON THE L.I.E., I PASSED THE HIDEOUS TWIN giants of Queens County: the Elmhurst-Maspeth gas tanks. Rumor was they were going to deconstruct the corrugated steel monsters bit by bit and give the sky back to the moon, the sun, and the stars. Some neighborhood groups were actually protesting the move. No surprise there. When they started tearing down the big blue gas tank in Coney Island, a few idiots threw themselves in front of the demolition equipment. I guess if you stare at something long enough it begins to resemble Stonehenge.

As I left the tanks behind, I couldn't help but wonder what the nineteen flips of the calendar had done to John Heaton since the last of his daughter. Moira had not been removed from his life one piece at a time. She was there, then she wasn't. Over the past five years I'd seen firsthand how Patrick's disappearance, the uncertainty about his fate, had eaten away at my mother-in-law. I looked in the mirror. I looked at my wife. I had seen what the miscarriage had done to us. I didn't like thinking about what would become of me if anything ever happened to Sarah. In the end, it wasn't Geary's threats or the potential size of the retainer that interested me. It was the human cost. It always was.

I pulled off the L.I.E. at Queens Boulevard. Mandrake Towers was a ten-unit apartment-building complex in Rego Park. It was one of countless characterless projects which had sprung up like redbrick weeds during the building boom of the fifties and sixties. I'd lived in places just like it. The facelessness of these buildings did not end at the exterior walls, but rather turned inward, pervading the hallways, elevators, bedrooms, and baths. Each apartment as much a cell as a home. You had your friends in the building, but most of the people on the other side of the wall, the people above your head and beneath your feet, were strangers.

The security office was in the basement of Building 5, between the garbage compactor and the laundry room. It wasn't exactly the war room in the basement of the White House. The door was ajar and through it came the sweet sound of Marvin Gaye's voice rudely interrupted by the static-filled squawking of walkie-talkies. I knocked, didn't wait for an invite, and walked in.

A large, heavyset black man in a khaki uniform that had fit him ten years and thirty pounds ago sat behind a long card table reading the *Daily News*. Before him on the table sat a walkie-talkie, a phone, his trooper-style hat, a full ashtray, and a radio.

"What can I do for y'all?" he asked, not looking up from the paper.

"John Heaton around?"

That got his attention. His relaxed demeanor seemed to run out through the bottom of his shoes. He stiffened, put the paper down, shut off the radio.

"Who wanna know and why?"

I showed him my old badge. As it didn't come stamped with

an expiration date, it usually helped cut through the bullshit. Not
this time.

"That's only half the answer, man."

"It's about his daughter."

"They find her?" He perked up.

"Nah, I've been hired to have a fresh look into it."

The room got very chilly. "Hired? You a cop or ain't you?"

"I'm retired," I confessed, showing him my investigator's license. "I'm working this private."

"He ain't here," the guard stonewalled, standing up in sec-
tions to unfurl all six feet eight inches of himself. I guess he wanted
me to get that he meant business.

"Come on, I'm not here to bust his balls or anything. Look,
Officer . . . Simmons," I read his name tag, which was now just
a little below my eye level. "I know I shouldn't've flashed the
tin, but—"

"He ain't here 'cause he don't work here no more." He shook
his head and pantomimed taking a drink. "They let him go, if you
know what I'm sayin'. He was doin' awright for a while, but jus' in
the last few months, he couldn't handle it no more. He loved that
girl. Moira was a good girl."

"I'm not here to say different."

"Then what you here for? Little late in the game, don't ya
think, to start nosin' around? All you gonna do is hurt the man."

"You know the man and I don't. I'll give you that," I said.
"But don't you think he'd trade a little more pain for a chance to
find his daughter?"

"He ain't got much left to trade, mister. He and his wife split.
She move down to Florida with their boy. I s'pose you could have
his soul, but there ain't much a that left neither."

I said nothing. There was no answer to that, no way to dress it up and take it to the prom. As a cop, I'd seen people kill themselves in all sorts of ways. Some more violent than others, but the saddest suicides were the long marches of self-destruction.

I held my hand out to Officer Simmons. "Moses Prager," I said. "Most people call me Moe. I'm sorry we got off on the wrong foot. I'm really not the asshole I appear to be."

"Preacher," he offered, his hand fairly swallowing mine. "Most people call me Officer Simmons." A mischievous smile flashed across his face. "And I am the tough-ass motherfucker I appear to be."

"Preacher Simmons," I mumbled to myself, something stirring in my memory. "Preacher 'the Creature' Simmons? Boys High, 1964 all-city team, right?"

That knocked about half the smile off his face. He was happy I remembered, but afraid I'd remember more. I did. Preacher "the Creature" Simmons had gone on from Boys High to Georgia Atlantic and gotten mixed up in a point-shaving scandal. Unlike Connie "the Hawk" Hawkins, who had, thanks to the ABA, salvaged at least some part of what might have been one of the brightest futures in basketball history, Preacher had fallen off the radar screen. No wonder. It's hard to spot a man so far below ground level.

"Preacher 'the Creature' been gone since before we landed on the moon, Moe. I been jus' plain Officer Simmons now for near fifteen years. I owe that to John Heaton. He got me this gig."

"Judging people's not my business, Officer Simmons. Finding them is." I handed him a card. "There's plenty of numbers there you can reach me at if you can think of anything that might help me. I don't suppose you'd wanna tell me where I can find John now?"

"Wine stores, huh? You jus' a jack a all kinda trades."

"I've never been great at anything."

"I have," he said, his smile having fully retreated. "It's over-rated."

Ready to leave it at that, I thanked him and turned to go.

"Glitters," he called out to me when I was nearly out the door.

"Glitters?"

"It's a topless joint in Times Square. John workin' there off the books doin' this and that. Down there, they don't judge people neither."

* * *

The things that become of people's lives. That's what I was think-ing about as I pulled my car out of the lot at Mandrake Towers. In his day, Preacher "the Creature" Simmons was as much a legend as Lew Alcindor. It's sad when the mighty fall or when injury dimin-ishes greatness, but I felt sick at the sight of Preacher Simmons, forgotten by the world, living out his days in a cinder-block bunker. I wondered what would kill him first, the cigarettes or the what-ifs.

Anyway, I hadn't the heart to argue with him when he sug-gested too much time had passed to start looking into Moira's dis-appearance. If my investigation into the Catskills fire had taught me anything, it was that the passage of time, even sixteen years, cuts both ways. Sure, cold leads freeze over and witnesses move, forget, die off. But though time tightens some tongues, it greases others. As years pile up, perps can get overconfident, sloppy, and alibis rot away like unbrushed teeth. Guilt can set in and fester. But time's greatest benefit is distance. Distance allows for perspec-tive. All manner of things become visible that were previously impossible to see. The passage of time had helped me get to the truth of the Fir Grove Hotel fire. Whether it would help lead to Moira Heaton, I could not say, but what it had done to her father was clear enough.

Glitters was what the guys on the job so affectionately referred to as a titty bar. Preacher's calling it a topless joint had been unfairly generous. It was more a bucket of blood with tits and ass thrown in. When new, the dump was probably just cheap and ugly. Now cheap and ugly was something to aspire to. And the stink of the place! Between the spilled-beer carpeting, cigarette smoke, sweat, and cheap perfumes, it smelled worse than the Port Authority men's room.

I guess Glitters was no different than a hundred other places in town, maybe no different than a thousand other places in a thousand other towns. We had a bar just like it in my old precinct. It was too everything: too dark, too smelly, the drinks too watery, the women too old and too much the victims of gravity. Everything about the place gave credence to the line about all that glitters not being gold. At that place in Coney Island, a lot of the girls turned tricks for drug money. But none of its myriad faults put a dent in its popularity with my precinct brethren. Maybe that was because head was on the house for the local constabulary. As our precinct philosopher, Ferguson May, was wont to say: "It sure beats the shit out of free coffee."

I couldn't remember the last time I'd been in a topless place. Probably some cop's bachelor party. What a silly concept. I think the last time bachelor parties served a useful purpose was during the second Eisenhower administration. I'm no prude and no one's ever mistaken me for a saint, but I've never been much of a fan of places like Glitters, even the ones that don't smell like the insides of my sneakers. Maybe it's the pretense of it all. I mean, a lot of the performers were gay and were as enthusiastic about being pawed by the patrons as burn victims were eager to receive skin grafts from a leper colony. Maybe it was just the mercenary aspect of it all. Who knows? Some things defy logic.

Even now, standing just inside the front door, as the music blared so loudly I thought my ears would bleed, I could barely bring myself to look at the women onstage. I paid my ten bucks to get in, but that was as far as I wanted to go. I asked the doorman if John Heaton was around. He didn't quite ignore me. He was distracted, having trouble making change for a twenty for the guy behind me. When that was taken care of, I repeated the question. This time he ignored me on purpose.

The doorman was a real musclehead: handsome, with a store-bought tan and perfectly coiffed hair. He looked strong as an ox but tough as tissue paper. He was the window dressing meant to dissuade the casual assholes from getting too drunk or carried away with the girls. Somewhere, lurking in the shadows, would be the real muscle; a smaller man, an ex-boxer or ex-cop. If any serious trouble started, you wouldn't see him coming. Maybe that's what Heaton was doing here, supplying some backup muscle. At this rate, I was never going to find out.

I considered flashing my badge, but thought better of it. Instead, I found myself a seat at a lonely little two-top set back from the stage. As ineffectual as Adonis at the door might be, he couldn't afford to get caught accepting a bribe. Besides, he seemed to have trouble counting past twenty. A cocktail waitress at a table in a dark room was more likely to be accommodating.

"Dewar's rocks," I shouted just to be heard.

The waitress had no trouble filling out her black lace blouse, velveteen hot pants, and nosebleed heels, but she was a little long in the tooth to be up onstage, and the shade of her blonde hair wasn't on God's original color palette.

"Eight bucks," she screamed back, a come-and-get-it smile painted permanently across her face.

"Here." I threw a ten and a twenty on her tray. "The ten's for the drink and a tip. The twenty's for an introduction to John Heaton."

She sucked up the ten like a sleight-of-hand artist, but put the twenty back on the table. "Listen, mister, my job's to get you to buy as many drinks as your wallet can stand. My only concern around this place is me, myself, and me. See on the stage up there? For all I care, Marilyn Monroe could be playing 'Yankee Doodle' on JFK's dick. You catch my meaning?"

She was talking a lot and not saying anything.

"Okay," I said, placing a business card and the twenty back on her tray. "Keep the twenty as a gesture of goodwill. If you should happen to make some room in there between me, myself, and me for John Heaton, give me a call."

"I'll be back with your scotch in a minute." This time, she didn't return the twenty.

A different waitress brought me my scotch. I asked her about Heaton just to be consistent. Though equally unforthcoming, she wasn't quite as chatty about it.

I finished my drink, moved over to the bar, and switched to beer.

"I dated a guy named John Healy once, but he's dead now," one of the barmaids said. "He had to lay down his Harley and wound up under a semi. I don't remember where he's buried. Why you lookin' for him, anyways?"

That was the closest thing I got to an answer at the bar. Luckily, the men's room was downstairs and not too far away from the dancer's dressing room. I wasn't stupid enough to try and worm my way in. In the movies it's all just a lighthearted romp, sneaking into the women's dressing room. In real life you get the shit kicked out of you. I was nearly two years removed from my last asskicking. Call me crazy, but I just wasn't quite up for another.

I waited to catch one of the dancers at the end of her shift. First, I hung out just inside the lavatory door, holding it open far enough to give myself a reasonable view down the hall. Above my head, the ceiling literally moved with the thump thump thumping of the only kind of music that made me rue the evolution of rock and roll. Then I made believe I was on the pay phone for ten minutes. Too bad nobody was on the other end of the line. I was funny as hell.

A woman I recognized from the stage upstairs slipped out of the dressing room and walked past the pay phone. They called her Domino, and she had done this dominatrix shtick to Devo's "Whip It." She'd worn a shiny black latex getup, thigh-high boots, and a leather mask and strutted about with a riding crop. Now she was dressed in a halter, jeans, and sandals.

"You're Domino, right?" I said like some goofy stage-door Johnny. "You were great."

She yawned. "Thanks, buddy, but I'm tired, and it's against house rules to mix with the gentlemen."

House rules! Who was she kidding? This wasn't exactly the Lonesome Piper Country Club. For a fistful of fifties and a nice smile, you could get anything you wanted in a place like this.

While I figured out what to say next, I took a careful look at Domino. She had been pretty once, maybe very pretty. At close quarters, however, the wear and tear showed. She was on the wrong side of thirty-five, and the fluorescent light wasn't doing her any favors. I was on that same side of thirty-five myself, but I wasn't trading on my boyish good looks for room and board and who knows what else. The whites of her eyes weren't. Yellow was more like it. She had a touch of drippy junkie nose, or maybe she'd done a few lines too many. She'd get older faster than I, much faster if she didn't get clean. Women like Domino can have short, violent careers, and when things start to go, they go quickly. There's no safety net to catch you and no ladder back up.

"Look, I need to talk to John Heaton," I admitted, unwilling to spin too much of a tale. "I know he works here and it's pretty obvious he's a hard man to see." I gave her my card. "Just tell him it's about his daughter, all right?"

She didn't answer, but took the card. Her eyes got big as she looked past me. Before I could turn around, a powerful hand clamped down on my left shoulder.

"This asshole bothering you, darlin'?" a gravelly voice wanted to know.

"It's okay, Rocky. He's just a fan," she said to the man standing behind me, then refocused on my face. "Thanks for the compliment, mister. Come back again soon."

I bowed slightly. "You're welcome."

She walked past me, her sandals clickity-clacking on the stairs. The vise loosened its grip on my shoulder, and I turned around to have a look at Rocky. So this was the extra muscle. He was definitely an ex-pug. Gee, a boxer named Rocky, what a concept. Though a light heavyweight now, he'd probably fought as a middleweight. By the look of his face, he'd no doubt been a world-class bleeder. His brow and the bridge of his flattened nose were thick with scar tissue. That and the fleshy reminders of a thousand un-blocked left jabs made him look like he was wearing a pair of skin-tone goggles.

"You're a real fuckin' pest, chief," he growled. "Everybody from the doorman to the girls behind the bar say you been givin' 'em a hard time."

I considered arguing the point, but I wasn't willing to risk even a playful tap from this guy. He may well have been a bleeder, but the thing about bleeders is they're usually big punchers. It's how they survive. I'm sure more than a few of his opponents left the ring in a lot worse shape than he. It's better to stand and bleed than lie glassy-eyed on the mat. I showed him my badge.

"What precinct you from?" he asked.

"Not this one. Listen, I'll get outta your hair in a minute. I just want a word with John Heaton and I'm gone."

Rocky gave it some thought. "He ain't in today."

"Don't bullshit me, Rocky, okay?"

"I swear, he ain't in today."

I pulled a pen out of my pocket and wrote "Moe" plus a seven-digit number on the wall.

"Tell him to call me when he does get in. I want to talk to him about Moira."

"All right," Rocky said, "I'll pass word along."

I shook his hand and left.

After an hour in Glitters, the air on Eighth Avenue seemed al-most fresh. Darkness should have been in full bloom, but all the gaudy neon and street lighting fooled the eye. I headed back to the outdoor lot on Tenth and Forty-fourth where I'd stashed my car. The crowds had thinned by the time I got to Ninth, and here the ar-tificial lighting at least gave the fallen night a fighting chance. As I stepped down off the curb onto the crumbled blacktop of Ninth Avenue, I noticed the footfalls of a man walking right up behind me.

"He won't talk to you, you know."

I turned. "Are you talking to me?"

"I am indeed, Mr. Prager."

His short, slight stature was unimposing if not exactly unthreatening. He was impeccably dressed in a gold-buttoned blue blazer, khaki pants, a white oxford shirt, a superbly knotted red silk tie, and loafers. He was an older man, in his midsixties, but his gray-blue eyes beneath stylish tortoiseshell glasses were still very young and fiery. His head was tan and bald, and his chin was adorned with a rich gray goatee.

"Who won't speak to me? *You* seem perfectly willing to chat."

"I do, don't I? But it's John Heaton to whom I refer. He won't speak to you."

"I won't even get into how you seem to know so much about my business. There seems to be a lot of that going around lately. So, how do you know John Heaton won't talk to me?"

"That's easy, Mr. Prager." My new acquaintance showed me an expensive white smile. "I'm paying him not to."

"That's a switch. Most of the people who don't speak to me do it for free. Maybe I should give them your number. No sense letting their animosity go to waste if they can make a few bucks on the deal."

"Very good. Very good. Can I buy you a scotch?"

"Not back at that dump," I said. "I've had my fill of tawdry for the year."

"Oh my, no, Mr. Prager. I was thinking more along the lines of the Yale Club."

* * *

The Yale Club was just west of Grand Central Station, a block or two north of Forty-second. It was a charming old building that was only slightly less difficult to get into than Skull and Bones. There wasn't a hint of ivy anywhere. No one sang "Boola Boolà," and, much to my chagrin, none of the staff wore plaid golf pants.

My host's name was Yancy Whittle Fenn, but I was to call him Wit. Everyone called him Wit, so I was told. Though I hadn't recognized his tanned and bearded face, I immediately recognized his name when he was finally gracious enough to share it with me on the ride over. Y. W. Fenn was one of the most famous journalists around. He wrote for everyone from *Esquire* to *Playboy*, from *GQ* to the *New Yorker*. His forte was the celebrity exposé. Not just any old celebrity would do, however. No, Wit's subjects, or more accurately, targets, tended to be from among the ranks of the rich and the powerful, particularly those who had landed in the chilly womb of the criminal justice system.

"You know, Wit," I said as the waiter slid my chair under me, "I don't see John Heaton as the typical subject of one of your pieces."

"How very perceptive," he mocked.

"How are you this evening, Mr. Wit, sir?" asked the nimble, gray-haired black man who had attended to my chair.

"Very good, Willie. Good. And yourself?"

"Same as always, sir. Same as always. What can I get for you and your guest this fine evening?"

"The usual for me, Willie. My guest will have . . ."

"Dewar's rocks."

"Very good, gentlemen. One Dewar's rocks and one Wild Turkey heavy on the wild."

Wit and Willie had a good laugh at that. Man, they really got wacky at the Yale Club. Wit waited for Willie to leave before speaking to me.

"Of course I'm not interested in John Heaton as anything more than a source. Actually, he's a bit of a drunken bore."

"He's got his reasons."

"So have we all, Mr. Prager. My grandson was himself kidnapped and murdered several years ago in New Mexico."

"I'm sorry."

"Yes, well, 'sorry' is a particularly empty word to me these days. But I digress. I suspect you have a good idea of whom my piece will focus on. He's your client, if I may be so bold."

"I can't dis—"

"—cuss my clients. Blah, blah, blah. Please, Mr. Prager. Next thing you know, you'll be telling me you can't drink whilst on duty."

"Nah, I'm pretty confident the word 'whilst' doesn't appear once in the ethics code."

Willie brought the drinks, placing them atop blue-and-white napkins embossed with a block Y.

"Enjoy your drinks, gentlemen."

Wit and I clinked glasses. He took all of his in a gulp, got Willie's attention, and pointed at his urgently empty glass. When Willie looked my way, I shook my head no.

"Well then, for argument's sake, let us say your client happens to be a certain New York state senator whose biggest backer is a rather wealthy man from that part of Long Island once known as the Gold Coast. Let us further say that said senator had quite a bright—excuse me—a *promising* future until one of his interns went poof!"

"You're buying." I took another sip of my scotch. "It's only fair that I play along."

"And now I hear that this certain senator feels he's spent

enough time in the doghouse for circumstances completely out of his control and that the moment has come to begin resurrecting that once promising career."

Willie brought Fenn's second drink. Both men dispensed with the pretense and chatter this time. Wit guzzled the bourbon right in front of the waiter and held up three fingers to indicate a third round would be in order. Willie gave me a glance, saw my drink was still half full, and left.

"As I was saying, resurrection is upon us, praise the Lord. But I'm as yet unwilling to let go of Moira Heaton's disappearance. No resurrection without resolution."

"So you're paying off John Heaton for his exclusive story. At least that's what you're telling him, right?" I said. "What you're really doing is trying to stall until you can dig up some dirt on this hypothetical client of mine."

"Maybe. You know what fascinates me, Mr. Prager?"

"Other than bourbon, no."

"Good. That was good. I'm curious why you went to Heaton first. It's not the logical place to start an investigation into the girl's disappearance."

"You're right. It isn't," I conceded. "But all the logic got squeezed out of this case a long time ago by the cops and by the private investigators. I wanted to get a feel for who Moira Heaton was. That's important to me. It's the way I work."

"You're a pretty sharp fellow."

"For an ex-cop, you mean."

He ignored that, and Willie's reemergence couldn't have been better timed.

"Bring me the chit, Willie," Y. W. Fenn ordered, the false chumminess completely gone from his voice.

"Very good, sir."

"So I'm a little slow on the uptake, but I get you didn't bring me here to buy me a drink. You want something, Wit, something from me."

"Everybody wants something from somebody. It's Newton's unwritten law of thermodynamics. It's really what makes the world spin about. I think we might be able to do one another some good and get to the truth while we're at it. It's that simple, Mr. Prager."

"I didn't know horse trading was a course offered up at New Haven."

"Oh, indeed it is, or it was, once," he said, this time sipping on his bourbon. "I majored in it. I'll let you review all my notes and research and, if it's that crucial to you, talk to John Heaton."

"And in return . . ."

"Whisper in my ear so that no one else can hear. That's all."

I got the odd sense that our setting impressed Wit far more than it impressed me, and the liquor wasn't helping his perspective any. Did he think I was just going to roll over on my client because he had Ivy League connections? Or maybe, just maybe, he was playing me. I didn't like either scenario.

I stood to go. As I did, I leaned over and whispered in his ear: "Thanks for the drink and go fuck yourself."

But if I thought this was going to get some angry rise out of him, I was dead wrong.

"We're going to do quite well together, you and I. Quite well."

I didn't hang around for an explanation.

CHAPTER FIVE

I WAS USUALLY FAIRLY FORTHCOMING WITH KATY ABOUT MY work, but not this go-round. She knew I was on a case, and this time that seemed to be enough for her. Neither one of us, it seemed, was willing to risk another setback. I think her falling apart at Connie's wedding had pissed her off. That Sunday, the day after the wedding when I went to talk to Pete Parson, Katy's demeanor had changed. Enough was enough. So I was a bit surprised to find her up and pacing the living-room floor when I got back from the city. I was even more surprised at the smell of cigarette smoke and to see the half-empty bottle of Bushmills out on the coffee table.

"What's the matter? Is Sarah—"

"She's fine. She's fine," Katy reassured me. "I just wanted to talk to you, Moe."

"You never needed a drink or a cigarette to talk to me before."

"I never needed any courage to talk to you before."

I moved to hold her, but she turned away.

"No, no, I need to get through this. I need to say the words."

I couldn't believe this was happening. Nausea rolled over me

49

in waves and I literally lost my balance so that I had to prop myself up against the back of the couch. You hear stories about it, but you never think it's going to happen to you. Your doctor's never going to utter the words "inoperable tumor," and the wife you love more than your own soul is never going to say "I'm leaving." But the moment was here. Never was now.

"Say it, Katy." I forced the words out of my mouth.

"Okay, here goes." She drew a deep breath and turned back to face me, silent tears streaming down her cheeks. "I just wanted to say I can't go through this again, Moe. I know you wanted more kids, but . . . I just can't . . ."

I was filled with such a profound sense of relief that I was struck dumb.

Katy misinterpreted my silence. "You hate me now, don't you?"

"Hate you! Are you nuts? I couldn't hate you. Maybe I could dislike you a little bit," I teased, "get a little annoyed with you every so often, but I could never hate you."

She folded herself into me in that way she had so that I knew our world was right again. Suddenly, without warning, my thoughts drifted to John Heaton, alone and drunk somewhere. And in that same moment I knew I wouldn't need to make deals with self-impressed little lizards like Y. W. Fenn. No, if John Heaton thought there was a chance of locating his plain-faced girl, he'd find a way to talk to me, payoffs be damned.

"So it's okay with you?" she whispered, her wet cheek pressed against my chest.

"When I'm done with this case, I'll make sure we won't have to go through this again."

"But—"

"But nothing. I've got everything I ever wanted, right now. As long as Sarah and I are enough for—"

"Shhh," she said, pressing her finger across my lips. "Let's go to bed."

"Are you sure?"

"The only thing I've ever been more sure of is when I said 'I do.' "

Who was I to argue?

* * *

The phone rang, but it wasn't John Heaton. That would have been too much to ask. It was Thomas Geary's increasingly familiar if unwelcome voice that greeted me. He did have the good form to keep it short and sweet. The meeting with Senator Brightman had been arranged for later in the day out at Geary's house in Crocus Valley. Before I could protest, Geary assured me that I could have all the time alone with Brightman I wanted.

Katy was gone, her side of the bed still creased and warm from where she'd slept. I stayed behind for a little while to enjoy the scent of her that still lingered in the air. I felt light enough to float. They say you never really miss things until they're taken away. We would continue to wonder about what could have been and to quietly mourn our lost child. They also say you don't know how much you miss something until you get it back. I put my hand in Katy's vacant space, running a finger across the creases in the sheet. I knew I had missed her, but not quite how much until now.

* * *

I didn't see it until I got behind the wheel. There was something stuck between my windshield and wiper blade: a business card.

That's what you get, I thought, for being too lazy to pull into the garage. As I got back out of the car, I tried to guess what life-altering product or program this card was promoting. Was I going to make extra money working out of my home? Was I going to lose forty pounds safely and naturally, or was I going to learn how to buy real estate with no money down? I plucked the card. It was, oddly enough, one of mine. There was something written on the back.

There once was a man named Moses
Who didn't know his ass from where his toes is
He took a case that was a total disgrace
So that a killer could come out smelling like roses

It was unsigned. A pity, considering Shakespeare, Blake, and Eliot were now all shaking in their shoes at the prospect of being dethroned. I crumpled up the card and flicked it at the sewer grate. My aim had been better when I was a kid. I hesitated and went to pick the card back up. Unballing it, I smoothed the card out as best I could and slipped it into my wallet.

The ride to the Brooklyn store went by in a flash, the words of the limerick repeating over and over again in my head. I ran through the list of possible candidates for its authorship. Whoever was responsible had gone to a lot of trouble to leave it for me to see. I hope he took the time to see the sights of scenic Sheepshead Bay. Maybe take in the late show at Pips Comedy Club or guzzle down a dozen littlenecks at Joe's Clam Bar.

Klaus seemed surprised to see me, but I let him know I was there only to pick up messages and do some work in the office. As far as the wine business went, he was to either handle it himself or refer it to Aaron.

"There's one message on your desk from a Larry McDonald, E-I-E-I-O, and one from someone who called himself Wit," Klaus remarked with a smirk. "You know Wittgenstein? My boss, the closet philosopher."

"Yancy Whittle Fenn," I said in my defense. "All his best friends call him Wit."

"Y. W. Fenn! Now I *am* impressed."

"Good thing one of us is."

I'd picked the Brooklyn store because it had an empty room next to the office. It was the perfect space to lay out the contents of the Spivack and Associates file. While what I'd told Wit was true, that I didn't always work in a conventional manner, I wasn't exactly a psychic reader, either. Straightforward police work had its moments. I skimmed through the thick file, copying down certain facts and data that I might be able to put to use between now and my appointment with Brightman. I wrote down the street address of Brightman's community office, the place where Moira Heaton was last seen, and the name and number of the NYPD detective who'd handled the case. That done, I retreated to the office to make some calls.

"Hey, Larry, it's Moe."

"Like I don't know your voice, schmuck."

"So?"

"Remember the Hound's Tooth?"

"Now who's being a schmuck?" I chided. "I'm retired, not senile."

"Nine o'clock?"

"Ten's better."

"We'll split the difference. Okay, Moe?"

"See you there."

Actually, I felt kind of stupid now for having had Larry go through the trouble of getting me the files. What I hadn't known at the time I asked the favor was that I'd be the recipient of Joe Spivack's largesse. It was too late now. I doubted there was anything in the official police record that wouldn't be in the Spivack file. In fact, I wouldn't be at all surprised if the police record was substantially less comprehensive. Cops can afford to follow up on only so many leads. They're limited by time, caseload, and funding. On the other hand, private investigations are limited only by the depth of the client's pockets.

I dialed another seven-digit number.

"Who the hell is this? It's . . . The sun is still out, for heaven sakes." Wit was sounding a wee bit hungover.

"You like limericks, Wit?"

"My head's killing me. Who is—"

"It's Moe Prager, your potential horse-trading partner. So, do you like limericks?"

"There once was a man from Nantucket . . . You mean that sort of tripe?"

"Exactly. You wanna hear one?"

He didn't answer. I took that as a yes. I read off the back of my card.

"Such atrocious grammar," he critiqued, sounding more like himself. "Is that supposed to have some significance to me?"

"I don't know, I just thought I'd run it by you. Basically, I'm returning your call."

"Have you given my proposition any further consideration?"

"I gave you my answer last night."

"That," he sniggered, "was *an* answer. You still have time to go back and change it."

"Nah, I always heard it was better to go with your first answer when you're being tested. Besides, too much erasing makes it hard to score."

"Don't lose my number, Mr. Prager. We're still only in the first hour of the exam."

I had to give the guy credit. He didn't back down easy. I'd have to watch him closely. His type could sneak right up and bite you in the ass.

*   *   *

Detective Rob Gloria was only too happy to meet me at what had once been State Senator Steven Brightman's community affairs office. Fortyish, bright-eyed and barrel-chested, he looked a little sharper than what I'd expected. Well deserved or not, Missing Persons had the rep of being a dumping ground for the barely adequate and downright inept. And my one close encounter with Missing Persons during the search for Patrick had only served to reinforce its bad reputation. But there were studs and stinkers in every bureau of the NYPD.

The now vacant storefront was on a busy street squeezed between a Chinese takeout and a real estate office. It was not unfamiliar to me. I'd seen pictures of the place in the Spivack file. The only hints of its former tenant were a sun-bleached campaign poster Scotch-taped to the inside of the plate-glass window and, just beneath it, a sign listing the new office address and phone numbers for reaching Brightman.

"You wanna have a look-see?" Detective Gloria asked, jingling a ring of keys.

"Sure."

He opened the door with the ease of a man who'd done this

several times before. He hadn't had to struggle, figuring out which keys went where. I liked that. He'd spent a lot of time here. This case meant something to him.

"Did you know John Heaton when he was on the job?" I wondered as Gloria pushed the door back for me.

"Nope." He strode a few feet to his left. "This is approximately where Moira Heaton's desk was. There were generally three or four other people working here, answering phones and such. She was the last one to leave that night, supposed to lock the doors at eight."

"Supposed to?"

"No one was here to see her do it, and we only have an iffy witness or two who might or might not have been driving by that say they saw her leaving."

"But the front door was locked?" I said, my eyes drifting to the gray steel back door.

He followed my gaze. "I'm way ahead of you. You're figuring someone locked the front door from inside and dragged her out through the back. Didn't happen that way. Produce delivery to the Chinks next door. There were people in and out of the alleyway for fifteen, twenty minutes."

"A delivery at night?"

"Because of the holiday the next day. They didn't wanna get caught short. It's kosher. We checked 'em out and the driver, too. Clean all around. Besides, both doors were locked, and the Heaton girl didn't have keys to the back door. Nope, we figure whatever happened to her didn't happen here."

"What makes you think something happened to her and she didn't just split?"

Detective Gloria looked at me like I had three heads. "Come on, you were on the job. You know."

"I had to ask."

"I guess."

"Why'd this case get to you?"

There was an attempt at denial in his eyes, but it was a weak one. "I used to think it was because she was a cop's kid, you know? Now I'm not so sure. It's too fuckin' clean. Even if she split on her own, it's too clean. Nothing's missing from her apartment. Her bank account and credit cards are untouched. There's zero physical evidence, no witnesses. Look, you get conflicting evidence all the time so's it can make you crazy. But here, there's like negative evidence. You work cases long enough, you get a sense about these things. It's like when you're riding your patrol sector, you just know when something don't feel right."

I knew exactly how that was.

The siren scents of frying ginger and garlic came calling through walls. I asked Rob Gloria if he wanted to heed their call.

"Order me a number five with extra duck sauce on the side," is what he said.

So we sat and ate, silently at first.

I broke the ice. "There's something you're not saying."

"There's a lot of things I'm not saying. You're workin' for Brightman, right? How come?"

"I guess I could say because he hired me, but the truth is I sort of got forced into taking the job. It's a long story not worth repeating. Why he hired me is easy. I think he wants to run for higher office and needs to get any stink off him before he tries. I can't tell you for sure, because I never met the man. What's John Heaton like?"

"Typical hotheaded donkey. Why?"

"Just curious."

"Somebody else's been sniffin' around, you know?" he said, shoveling a forkful of pork lo mein into his mouth.

"Y. W. Fenn?"

"You met the little prick, huh? Yeah, he's a queer duck, that Wit. Just being in the same room as him makes me want to shower."

"You think Brightman did the girl, don't you?"

"What I think's my business. What I can prove is something else."

"Then maybe it's a good thing Wit and I are around. Maybe we can shake a little dust out of your clean case."

"I doubt it," he said, throwing a five on the counter to cover his end. "I doubt it."

I sat with my mostly untouched food in front of me, watching Detective Gloria's unmarked Chrysler retreat. Of course, it's what he didn't say that intrigued me. His silent accusal of Brightman didn't shock me, per se. That was the point of this whole exercise. It's why Brightman needed someone like me. Brightman could jump through hoops of fire and have Jesus himself testify to his innocence, but without concrete evidence that he didn't do it he was screwed. The public outside his district would treat him with the same silent suspicions as Rob Gloria.

Klaus was just being flippant before when he mentioned my closet philosophy. As it happened, however, his casual remark was quite prescient. Trouble was, I couldn't prove a negative in Philosophy 1, and I didn't think my chances had improved with age.

* * *

Crocus Valley was a quaint hamlet to the northeast of Glen Cove on the North Shore of Long Island. It proudly displayed its rustic trappings to strangers passing through, but only in an effort to cloak the smell of money. You weren't apt to see Jags and BMWs out on the street like you might in Sands Point or Great Neck. That's not to say residents of this little piece of heaven didn't drive luxury automobiles. Quite the opposite was true. The people of Crocus Valley had that Waspy humility and false sense of good taste to park them around back.

Thomas Geary's digs weren't hard to find, as his property line was only a chip and a putt away from the twelfth hole of the Lonesome Piper Country Club. If I got the chance I'd have to sneak a peek to see if the out-of-bounds stakes were made of solid gold. The Gearys' was a white country manor surrounded by corral-type fencing. I could see stables in the distance, and I recalled Constance talking about her love of riding. A semicircular drive-way led up to the front portico. The minimum lots in this neck of the woods were five acres. My guess was the Gearys' property more than doubled that.

I parked in front. Although the wine business afforded me the luxury of no longer driving a rolling advertisement for AAA membership, there was little danger of the good-taste police citing my host. By the time I made it onto the porch, Geary was standing in the front-door jamb. The sight of him dressed in jeans and riding boots and holding a Manhattan was priceless.

"Come in," he said, dispensing with his put-on manners.

I followed him into a big study. Here there was a grand piano, naturally, a harp in one corner, a wet bar, and expensive but muted furniture. There was a trophy cabinet filled to the max with medals, ribbons, cups, statuettes, etc. All bore Connie's name and were for excellence in music or riding. There was a rustic fireplace with a maw bigger than my garage door. Since I hadn't seen another car outside, I figured maybe Brightman had parked in the fireplace.

"Jesus, Constance won all these," I said, just to say something.

Geary frowned. He seemed not in the mood for small talk. "Ah, a man with the flare for the self-evident."

"Feel free to fire my ass anytime you want."

His expression said he liked that better. He still didn't offer me a drink or further conversation.

"I thought you might want to know there's somebody else poking around about Brightman and Moira Heaton's disappearance. He's already been to the cops and he's paid off Moira's father not to talk to anyone else. I also kinda get the impression he's no fan of your boy Brightman."

"Wit is being rather a pain in the ass. Will you join me?" he asked, holding up his drink.

"A beer, if you've got any. So you know Wit?"

"Bass Ale or Michelob?"

"Mick."

"Yes, Moe," Geary said, handing me a bottle, "everyone of breeding and means knows Wit. He's a bit of a hanger-on. He has the right pedigree, but the wrong banker. If you understand my meaning. He used to be fun back in the day, a life-of-the-party sort; funny, biting, and bitchy. Amusing to have around, but ever since . . . Well, he's become tiresome."

"Since his grandson was—"

"Yes, since then. But try not to alienate him. He could actually be quite useful. When you get to the bottom of Miss Heaton's unfortunate disappearance, Fenn's name could add credibility. And speaking of that, how is the investigation going?"

"It's too early to tell, but someone left this for me." I showed him the limerick. "The cops think Brightman's guilty, you know."

"Yes," he agreed, "but guilty of what?"

"Whatever."

He handed the card back to me. "Atrocious writing."

"You and Wit agree on something."

A car pulled up the bluestone driveway. "That would be Steven," Geary said. "Let us greet him and get this interview of yours over with. After you."

Ooh, the code-enforcement people weren't going to like this. Brightman had parked his Mercedes right behind me.

He was about five years my senior, my brother Aaron's age, slender and four or five inches short of six feet. He wore a yellow golf shirt, loose black slacks, deck shoes, and a rich tan. A real man of the people. He was classically handsome, with an angular jaw, a straight nose, hazel eyes, brownish red hair, and an easy smile. Strangely enough, he did have that kind of young Jack Kennedy mojo.

He ambled up to me and extended his hand, looking me straight in the eyes. "You must be Moe. I'm Steven Brightman. Tom, could you give us a few minutes?"

Okay, now I got it. Brightman had the gift. Without doing much of anything, he had made me feel like I was the most important person in the metropolitan area. It was like that inexplicable movie-star thing. Some of the greatest actors in the world came off flat on film. Whereas people on the set could never understand Marilyn Monroe's magic. The camera, they say, either loves you or it doesn't. With politicians it was the ability to connect with the crowd itself and individuals in the crowd at the same time.

"Let's walk," he said, and guided me around the back of the

house in the direction of the stables. "So, I hear you want to talk to me."

"Did you kill Moira Heaton?"

"No."

Right answer. No prevarication. No *I'm glad you asked that.*

"Were you having an affair with her?"

He hesitated. "Technically, no, I wasn't."

I tried rattling his cage a little. "But you had slept with her?"

"Twice, yes."

Right answer. Again, there was no *oh, God, forgive me* bullshit, no mea culpas about how he wasn't proud of what he'd done.

"She wasn't much to look at," he went on, "but she was still a very attractive young woman."

"I hope I get a chance to find out for myself," I said, not really believing it. "Where?"

"Once in the office. Once at a motel under assumed names, obviously. It was good between us, but we both understood that it couldn't go anywhere. It had ended months before she vanished."

"When?"

"That August."

"But you weren't married then."

"Not then, no," he admitted. "A condition I have happily since rectified."

"So why end it?"

"Actually, it was Moira who put an end to things. Politics were her passion, not politicians. I suspect once she got over the thrill of it, she wanted to get back to the real world. In the end, I think I was more attracted to her than she to me. Have you ever been curious or fantasized about sleeping with a black woman or a Chinese girl or any sort of specific type of woman? When you finally fulfill your fantasy, you get beyond it. It was like that for Moira with me."

"Do the cops know?"

"They don't. I'm afraid that I did lie about that one aspect of our relationship."

I laughed. "Don't worry about it. They probably didn't believe you. I wouldn't've believed you either. We cops can be such distrustful pricks. But just because you slept with her doesn't mean you killed her."

"Is that your opinion or theirs?"

"It's not theirs. You're a politician. They're not fond of you on general principal. And me, I'm still making up my mind."

"That's fair. Do you think she's—"

"—dead?" I finished the question. "Yeah, I think she's dead."

"I've always thought so as well. Moira was such a responsible person, so dedicated. She wouldn't just run off. When she didn't turn up after the first several days, I . . ."

"I guess that's something else you neglected to share with the cops."

He smiled that smile at me. "I can see why you came so highly recommended, Moe. No, I kept that to myself. I played out the string by offering a reward and being so public. Did I think it would help? In the end, no. I guess there was some measure of faint hope."

"Hey, Senator Brightman, you wanna save me the trouble and just tell me about anything else you might have conveniently forgotten to tell the police? To my mother's eternal regret, I never wanted to be a dentist. I don't enjoy pulling teeth."

He laughed, but not too loudly or long. That was part of his gift. He knew just how to modulate his responses.

"You'd make a shitty politician, Moe. You know that?"

"That's the nicest thing anyone's ever said to me. Thanks, Senator. But you haven't answered the question."

"No, there's nothing else."

We were now standing just outside the stables. Thomas Geary was there waiting for our arrival.

"Satisfied, Moe?" Geary asked.

"Gentlemen," Brightman interrupted before I could answer. "You'll have to excuse me. I've got an appointment back in the city, and the rest of this conversation would be best carried on in my absence. Moe," he said, offering me his hand, "I hope you can find out what happened to Moira. I owe at least that to her family."

"It wouldn't hurt your career either," I added.

He smiled. "Not at all. Like I said before, don't go into politics. Bluntness is not considered an attribute. So long. Thomas, we'll speak tomorrow. My best to Elizabeth."

Both Geary and I waited until Brightman's slender frame faded against the vibrant orange of the late afternoon sun.

"He's a natural," I said.

Thomas Geary smiled like a proud father. "He'll do great things for this state."

"Yeah, maybe. You know, Mr. Geary, I'm a little bit confused. I can see what Brightman gets from his relationship with you. Who knows, maybe you two even really like each other. But what do you get out of it? It can't be more money."

"Come with me, Moe."

Geary led me to the stable door and slid it back. He gestured for me to enter, and when I did, he followed. I didn't much like horses. Maybe it was their imposing size, their smell, or the inscrutability of their eyes. I was a city boy. Geary took me by the elbow and we walked.

"That's Ajax, there," my host said, pointing at a beautiful palomino.

Ajax's regal head and long neck stuck over the stall door. For reasons beyond my understanding, I felt compelled to rub his snout. My face smiled involuntarily.

"Here, feed him this." Geary handed me an apple.

Ajax chomped it right out of my hand.

"You don't like horses."

"That obvious, huh?" I asked, now patting the horse's muscular neck.

"But look at you, Moe. Look at you and Ajax. He has that effect on people."

"It's a shame he can't run for office," I said. "Next time I meet with Brightman, I'll have to remember to bring an apple along."

He looked at me with utter disdain. "You can find your own way back to your car."

As I climbed into the driver's seat, I found I felt better, if not exactly wonderful, about my involvement with Brightman and worse about working for Geary. Geary was a manipulator, a puppeteer. I never much liked puppet shows as a kid, and age hadn't changed my opinion. Brightman, on the other hand, had been straightforward even when the truth worked against him. He'd given me the right answers, not the best or easiest ones. Still, I'd have to watch out for him. In spite my parting byplay with Geary, neither of us was foolish enough to see Brightman as a show horse.

*   *   *

The Hound's Tooth was a cop bar near the Fulton Fish Market in lower Manhattan. Its walls were coated in a sticky resin of dust and old cooking grease. Mounted on the sticky walls were pictures of every crooked New York politician since Boss Tweed. Needless to say, there wasn't much free wall space. You didn't see young cops in the Hound's Tooth. It was the kind of place you tended to gravitate to after several years on the job. They checked you for gray hair and crankiness at the door.

It had become an even less popular hangout for low men on the totem poll since the nearby construction of One Police Plaza. "Too much brass and not enough ass," as the late Ferguson May was fond of saying. And these days, Larry McDonald was definitely brass. I wondered why Larry had chosen the Hound's Tooth for our meeting, whether it was about his ambition or, given the crooked politicians on the wall, he had wanted to make a point about Brightman. But seeing him here in his element, I decided it was the former. He was three quarters of the way up the totem pole and climbing. The altitude agreed with him.

"Hey, gimpy, get over here," Larry called to me from a close-by booth. When I approached, he stood and held my face between his palms. "Oy, such a *punim!*" he exclaimed in perfect Yiddish.

"I don't care what the birth certificate says, your milkman musta been a guinea. You're the least Irish-looking Irishman I've ever seen."

"Fuck you, Moe. And what were you, switched at birth and raised a Jew?"

We went through some version of this routine whenever we saw each other, which, since my retirement, wasn't very often. Friendship is frequently a product of proximity and shared experience. Well, we no longer shared physical proximity, and our most recent shared experiences dated back over five years.

"Gimme a Johnny Red and one Cutty Sark rocks," Larry Mac shouted at the barman as if to prove my point. I'd stopped drinking Cutty Sark a few years back. I let the order stand. When the bartender put them up, Larry threw some money at him and brought the drinks to the table.

I thanked my old friend, we clinked glasses and made small talk. He loved his new house in Massapequa Park out on the South Shore of the island. It was a different life out there. The schools were great. The air was fresh. There was no crime to speak of. He made it sound wonderful. What I purposefully neglected to mention was his choice of adjectives. He said it was a different life, not a better one. It had been my experience that cops who made the move out to the Burger King landscape of the suburbs never stopped pining for the city. The suburbs were everything Larry described and more, but they were also less, often much less.

"So, you ever hear from Rico?" Larry asked the inevitable.

"It's been a few years."

"He made detective. You know that, right?"

"Yeah, and Robert Johnson mastered the blues. I wonder if it was worth the price."

Larry looked perplexed, but didn't ask for an explanation. Good thing, because he wouldn't have gotten one. At one time Larry, Rico, and I were so close we were called the Three Stooges by our precinct mates. For a long time I considered Rico a second brother. Then, during the hunt for Patrick, Rico crossed a line that could never be uncrossed, erased, or forgotten. He'd tried to play me, to use me to further his own career.

"Whatever that means," Larry said, waving his hand dismissively. "He's making a name for himself in Narcotics."

"Next subject, Larry."

"Whatever you say, Moe."

"Were you able to get your hands on the—"

"They're in my car. We'll head out in a few minutes." He took a sip of his scotch, waved at a few of the faces as they came in, and headed out of the place. "I took a look at 'em, Moe. There's a lot of paper and not much in it."

"You don't mind if I take a—"

"Hey, hey, don't get touchy with me. I was just making conversation."

"Sorry. It's been a long, weird day. So, you looked at the files. You got any ideas?"

"None that the files would back up," he said. "According to everything in there, your politician's as pure as the driven fucking snow. The Blessed Virgin's got nothing on him."

"In other words, you think Brightman did the girl?"

"Yop."

"Why?"

He touched his nose. "Because this says so."

One myth every cop, myself included, buys into is that he can smell a rat. What civilians get wrong is that crap about reasonable doubt. Reasonable doubt is for juries, not cops. Cops don't doubt. Cops make up their minds early. Whenever you hear that nonsense about the cops having no suspects, it's pure bullshit. Cops always have suspects. It's getting the evidence to fit that's the hard part.

"It is a lovely nose, Larry, to be sure," I complimented. "I didn't notice Brightman's picture on the wall. Is it up?"

"Give him some time. Come on, finish your drink and let's go."

So many people shook Larry's hand or slapped his back or grabbed his forearm on the way out, you'd think he was a walking rabbit's foot. He was definitely working his way up the food chain, and his fellow brass knew it.

We walked around the corner to his car in silence, neither one of us willing to put the jinx on his rising star by talking about it. He popped the trunk and handed me a cardboard box of photocopied documents.

"Thanks."

"Don't thank me. I owe you, Moe, and we both know it. Just mark this against my account, okay? And listen," he said gravely, taking hold of my arm, "don't come back to me on this case. What you got in your arms is all the help you're gonna get from me this time around."

"Not an issue," I said. "Thanks again."

I didn't wait for him to drive away. I just turned and headed back to my car. On the way, I looked over my shoulder in the direction of the World Trade Center, but rows of Wall Street office buildings obscured the view. It was strange how on a clear day like today had been, you could see those two ugly shoe boxes from all five boroughs and Jersey, but not from just a few blocks away. Although they'd been up for only a little more than ten years, I couldn't remember the skyline without them.

CHAPTER
SIX

WIT ACTUALLY DID ME A FAVOR BY CALLING. I WAS IN THE
Brooklyn store about to take on the task of checking the police files
Larry Mac had grudgingly handed over against the Spivack file. It
would probably have been a tremendous waste of time, and I'd already gathered a list of people I wanted to speak with. Though I'd
been at it for only a few days, the truth was I hadn't gotten anywhere. The only thing I knew about Moira Heaton today that I
hadn't known twenty-four hours before was that she'd slept with
her boss. While that didn't make her a harlot, it didn't exactly inspire me either. I had to get a better idea of who she was. Once I
got a sense of her, I might get a handle on how to look for her.

"Yeah, Wit, it's a little too early for drinks at the Yale Club."

"Do you think?" he asked, followed by a pause. I imagined
him checking his Piaget. "I suppose so." He was unconvinced.

"What is it?"

"A body. Well, more accurately, badly decomposed human female remains."

"Where?"

"That depends?"

x

71

"What the fuck is that supposed to mean, Wit?"

"It means I need a lift."

"Where are you?"

"The Pierre."

Now it was my turn to check my watch. "Be in front in twenty minutes."

The first hour of the trip out to Suffolk County was pretty quiet. I think Wit old boy was nursing a hangover. After witnessing him handle his Wild Turkey or, more factually, watching the Wild Turkey handle him, I understood that this was probably a regular event in Y. W. Fenn's life. I took the time to enjoy the rarity of a nearly traffic-free Long Island Expressway. I would have enjoyed the sights if there had been any sights to see, but the L.I.E. is not renowned for its scenic beauty.

To the rest of New York, Suffolk County was the netherworld of potato and sod farms sandwiched between the Nassau County line and the civilized outposts of Sag Harbor and East Hampton. Only twenty or thirty miles beyond the city line, it might as well have been a penal colony or another planet for all the notice it got. Some places exist to be visited. Others exist to be passed through. Today, at least, Wit and I were going to stop and look.

"Where is this we're going again?"

He pulled a piece of Pierre stationery out of his jacket pocket, blinking desperately to focus. "Someplace called Lake Ronkonkoma. What is that, an Indian name?"

"No, Wit, it's Yiddish! Of course it's an Indian name."

"You take Exit 59, Ocean Avenue. Turn left onto Ocean, which turns into Rosevale Avenue. We take that to Smithtown Boulevard, turn right, and it'll be a mile or two farther on. The lake is on the right, but we're to look left."

Such was the extent of our conversation.

The lake itself was rather bigger than I had expected, quite pretty, really. The same could not be said of the trailers and shacks bordering one side of the lake. Though it was a hot, lazy day, there didn't seem to be much activity on the far shore beaches. Again, the same could not be said of the blond-reeded marsh to our left. There were blue-and-white units, an ambulance, a car from the county coroner's office, and a crime scene van parked along the guardrail. Two bored-looking cops were stationed on either side of the official vehicles, directing traffic and discouraging the curious. I drove past and pulled into the parking lot of some big old German restaurant.

Wit and I walked back to the marsh. I showed one of the cops my badge and license. He began to hem and haw. Wit shook his head at me.

"Captain Millet said you'd let us pass. My name's Y. W. Fenn. This is—"

"Go right ahead, guys. The captain's back there. Watch your step. It's kinda muddy."

The cop wasn't lying. Wit's loafers stuck in the mud three times before we got to the assembled crowd. This was just the kind of place abandoned cars, bald tires, broken bottles, and bodies got dumped in all the time. There were places like it all along the coast in Brooklyn near Plum Beach, Sheepshead Bay, and Jamaica Bay. The reeds formed a curtain blocking roadside views, and the mud and brackish water kept foot traffic to a minimum.

"Where do you know this Captain Millet from?" I asked Wit as he stopped to retrieve his left shoe.

"I did a story on the Chartoff murders a year or two back. You remember them, don't—"

"I remember."

"Well, I met Millet when I was doing that story. When this Brightman assignment came up, I gave all my New York police contacts a call and told them what I might be interested in."

"So why bring me?"

"As I said, I needed a ride."

"Don't be an asshole, Wit. There's a hundred ways you coulda gotten out here that didn't include me."

"Let's call it a show of good faith on my part."

I left it at that. Captain Millet stepped out of the crowd to greet Wit. He was a tall man, red-faced, with a nose full of gin blossoms. I guess he and Wit got to be such good friends over drinks. Wit introduced us, adding that I'd once been a cop. Millet liked that.

"Some drug addict from the treatment center on the other side of the lake found her," the captain explained. "He had half a bag on and was hiding until he sobered up. Tripped right over her. She's been here a long time. Come on, let's have a look."

The cops parted like a blue sea as Millet approached. Only the crime scene guys and the coroner's man didn't move.

"How long she been there, Klein?" Millet asked the coroner.

"Hard to say. From what I can see she's skeletal. A year, two, maybe longer. Some of the clothes are still intact. When we have a look at them, it might help us with a time frame."

"Thanks."

A grain of sand blew into my eyes and I reflexively turned away. When I could see again, I noticed silent tears streaming down Wit's cheeks. He noticed me notice and quickly wiped them away. It didn't mean I no longer thought of him as a pretentious, condescending drunkard, just a more human one.

"Why don't you boys go have a drink across the way there.

Reggie's has a lunchtime happy hour that can't be beat," Millet proffered with great authority. "It's right next to the German place."

As Wit and I began the muddy walk back to the road, something struck me.

"Captain Millet," I said, "where's the guy who found her?"

"The junkie? He's . . . he's over there with Detective Daniels. Why?"

"Do you mind if I have a word with him, alone?"

Both Millet and Wit raised suspicious eyebrows at that, but the captain nodded his approval. "Daniels," he called out, "let this fella have a word with . . . with *him*. Whatever the fuck his name is."

I told Wit to stay put and I plodded over to where Daniels was hand-holding the junkie. Detective Daniels seemed happy to get a few minutes' break. What I was about to do could land my ass in jail, so I had to put on the best show I could for the curious eyes that might be watching.

"Hey," I said, offering my right hand to my new best friend, "I'm Moe."

He took my hand out of confusion. I squeezed it hard and reeled him in with it, throwing my left arm over his shoulder.

"You're fuckin' hurtin' me, man," he whined.

"Not anything like I'm gonna hurt you if you don't tell me where the fuck you dumped it, asshole," I growled, but quietly.

"What the fuck you talkin' a—"

"I'm not a cop anymore, shithead, so your crying don't mean shit to me. So where the fuck did you dump her bag?" I squeezed his shoulder a little tighter. "And don't even fuckin' lie to me. If you tell me now, there's a fifty in it for you and I'll fix it with the cops not to bust your balls about robbing the corpse. If you don't . . . I think we understand each other."

He swallowed hard, looking over to where the cops were. "A fifty?" he asked. "And no shit about—"

"You heard me." I turned him around so that we faced the cops directly. "The clock's running."

He tilted his head. "Over there, by the road near the gas station."

"Very good." I stuffed two twenties and a ten in my friend's pocket. "If the cops ask, tell them I gave you a few bucks to get some food in you. They won't bug you about it and they'll think I'm a fucking saint."

"What was that all about?" Wit wanted to know when I got back.

"Let's go get that drink," I said.

I led Wit in the direction of the bar, but through the marsh. I spotted a mud-caked handbag and a woman's wallet right about where my buddy said they would be, at the place where the marsh, the road, and the gas station lot began to converge.

"Wit! Gimme a pen."

He handed me a black Montblanc without missing a beat. I knelt down and flipped the wallet over.

"Fuck! It's not her," I said to myself, but loudly enough for Wit to hear.

"But it's somebody," he reminded me.

I hated when people did that, when they refused to conform to first impressions.

"Yes, she is. You better get Millet over here."

*　*　*

Her name was Susan Leigh Posner, a graduate student in psychol-
ogy at the nearby State University of New York at Stony Brook.
She'd been missing for nearly fourteen months. That's what Millet
told us. Susan had been having trouble with her boyfriend and was
falling behind in her work. "Something about not turning in her
Ph.D. data or some shit like that," as the captain so articulately explained. He was sorry it wasn't our girl.

"That's okay," Wit comforted him. "At least one set of parents
can finally start grieving."

We got that drink, Wit and I. I think I needed it even more
than my hungover companion. I had beer. Wit stuck with his
usual, but had it in a tall glass with a lot of water. The bartender
asked us about all the police activity. And when we told him the
cops had found a body, he told us about the curse of Lake
Ronkonkoma. An Indian princess had drowned in the lake hun-
dreds of years ago while trying to save her lover, so the story went.
Every year, when the warm weather came, her ghost would pull
swimmers and boaters down to the depths of the lake in the hope
that one might be her lost love.

"Yes, sir," the barman said, "at least one or two people get
pulled to the bottom every year."

Somehow, seeing the bones of Susan Posner had, for the day at
least, taken all the romance out of myth or death. Undoubtedly,
however, her death, at her own hand or someone else's, would be
woven into the fabric of local lore. This writer, a regular customer
of mine at City on the Vine, said he never let the facts get in the
way of a good story. So it would be here. Wit and I moved to a
table.

"How did you know?" he asked, finally acting the part of the
journalist.

"I was a street cop in Coney Island for ten years before the wine shops. Junkies are junkies, drugs make them a little less human. They see some bum, a stiff, they're not thinking about CPR or calling 911. They're wondering if they can steal something they can sell from the bum or if it's a stiff. You get the picture. I guess maybe I didn't feel like waiting around all day. And you," I said, "with tears in your eyes. What, were you thinking about your grandson?"

"Always. I'm always thinking about him."

For the next half hour, one bloody detail at a time, Wit outlined the events surrounding the kidnapping, torture, and death of his only grandchild. He had identified the body, refusing to let his daughter or his son-in-law suffer any further trauma. I wanted him to stop, to not have to relive this part again, but it seemed as if stopping him would have hurt more. I felt sick. Me, who'd found Marina Conseco left to die alone at the bottom of a filthy water tank. Me, who'd seen what knives and shotguns and maggots could do to the human body. I was sick. My second beer glass remained utterly untouched.

I broke the painful trance. "You know, Wit, Geary and Brightman think they can use you."

"I know, Mr. Prager. They all think they can use me. It's a rare talent I have." He mocked himself. "Somehow they never do manage to use me quite in the manner they expect."

"And you thought you could use me."

"We can use each other," he said, but didn't explain.

The car ride back into the city began as quietly as the trip out. Again, there was very sparse traffic. I decided I wanted to see something other than blacktop and concrete barriers, and switched over to the Northern State Parkway. Here there were trees, bushes, lush green shoulders, tiger lilies, and pretty stone overpasses.

"So, Thomas Geary tells me you two know each other."

"We do."

Okay, the cordiality thing was short-lived. If he was going to give me one- or two-word answers, it wasn't worth trying. But I figured I'd give it one more shot.

"What's Brightman's story?"

"I'm here to write it," Wit answered smartly. "What do you want to know about him?"

That caught me off guard. "I don't know. . . . What part of the city is he from?"

"He isn't."

"He isn't what?"

"From the city. Brightman was born in a very lovely little town in New Jersey."

"Is there such a thing as a lovely little town in New Jersey?"

"This question asked by a man from Brooklyn . . . Please!"

"Was he rich?"

"To you, I imagine his family would have seemed quite wealthy, yes," Wit said without a hint of guile. "To someone like Thomas Geary, he would seem almost poor. The Brightmans were well off, I would say. His father was a senior partner in the biggest real estate law firm in the country, but he did have to earn his keep. The mother came from old money, but there was more old than money by the time it trickled down her way."

"When'd the Brightmans move into the city?"

"In '57, when he turned fourteen."

I stopped asking questions. This was all very interesting, much like the rest of the case, but it got me no closer to Moira Heaton. I knew more about Susan Leigh Posner, for chrissakes! Wit might've been able to detail every aspect of the lives and times of Thomas Geary and Steven Brightman and it probably wouldn't do me a damn bit of good. I was now more determined than ever to get some insight into Moira Heaton.

* * *

I dropped Wit back at the Pierre around three. That still left me plenty of time to get over to Brightman's relocated community affairs office. Not wanting to give anyone time to concoct a story or edit his responses, I didn't call ahead.

This office was pretty much like the storefront I'd been at with Detective Gloria, only it was flanked by a pizza place and a unisex hair salon. It must've been difficult for Brightman's staffers to keep their weight down. I got lucky. At least that's what I thought when I first walked in. Everyone on my list was still in the office. Unfortunately, Brightman had earlier alerted them that I might be dropping by someday soon. So much for the element of surprise.

"Could you sign in, please?" a round-faced woman asked, pointing at a clipboard. "It's a rule."

"No problem."

The place was nicely appointed with gray carpeting, wood veneer desks, leather furniture. There was a water cooler, a coffee machine, a little fridge. The walls were covered with informational placards, a few in Spanish, ranging in subject from how to reach a suicide hotline to how to apply for food stamps. The main feature on each wall was a poster featuring Moira Heaton's face. It was much like any such poster. MISSING—$25,000 REWARD was printed boldly above her picture. Her physical description, the date she disappeared, what she was thought to be wearing at the time, and a phone number were listed below.

It was sort of a wasted trip. All five members of the office staff seemed to try their best to cooperate, some clearly distraught and frustrated over their inability to contribute anything to the search for Moira. To a person, they treated me with complete respect, even when I asked the ugly but necessary questions about their boss and Moira. It wasn't quite a total waste of time, because certain themes became clear to me during the course of the interviews.

The staff were categorically behind Brightman, certain he would never sleep with an employee, let alone murder one. They were at least half wrong about that. He was a caring, compassionate warrior for the causes in which he, and by extension they, believed. Generous to a fault, he inspired loyalty not only from his staff, but from the voters in his district. Even after Moira's disappearance, he won reelection with over a 70 percent majority. A wise man once said that all politics are local. Like most adages, it was only partly true. Because he got the streets plowed in the snow, he could probably get reelected for the next hundred years in his own district, but he wouldn't be elected to any higher office until the nagging suspicions about Moira Heaton's disappearance were cleared up.

Something else was becoming painfully clear to me. Moira Heaton had been almost as difficult to know before she disappeared as she was after. Though the office staff were all quick to point out that she had been head and shoulders the best intern they'd ever been associated with, a woman willing to overcome her lack of political savvy with hard work and tenacity, Moira apparently didn't inspire much affection. They all used the same phrase: "She was a very private person."

"Not shy, exactly," said Sandra Sotomayor, Brightman's most experienced staffer. "Very good with the people who come in off the street. She don't take no bullshit from city agencies or nobody when people need help, but with us, she keep her distance."

I thanked them all very much for their cooperation and left numbers I could be reached at in case they remembered anything, even if it seemed stupid, that might help. What the visit did more than anything else was convince me that my first instinct had been the right one. I had to talk to John Heaton, whether Wit liked it or not.

* * *

Glitters was far more sedate than during my first visit. In fact, everyone from the doorman to the cocktail waitresses seemed to be in a bit of a stupor. The thump of the drumbeat sounded a bit less insistent. The dancers were nearly sleepwalking, the expressions on their faces devoid of either passion or pain. Maybe the heat and humidity of the first oppressive day of the year had infected the place, seeping in through cracks in the windows and beneath the doors. The air-conditioning was rendered helpless against the drowsy atmosphere.

In spite of the general malaise, my reappearance seemed to inject a bit of a spark back into things. Adonis at the door scowled at me even as he took my ten bucks. I was potential trouble, that's all he cared about. I waved hello to one of the bartenders I recognized from my last visit, the one who had wondered why I was looking for her old dead boyfriend. She smiled back before quickly retreating to the far end of the bar. It's nice to be popular. I found that lonesome little two-top I had sat at previously and bided my time until the stupor set back in.

Luckily, the waitress from my first visit, the woman with the otherworldly blonde hair, had my station. It took her a second, but the flash of recognition rippled across her face. I'd seen happier expressions on morticians.

"You again," she hissed.

"Yeah, but you can call me Typhoid Mary."

"Huh?"

"Never mind."

"Dewar's rocks, right?"

"Right. You didn't call. I'm hurt."

"Only a cop would think twenty bucks would buy him anything but a smile around here. You guys are the cheapest motherfuckers on the planet."

I smiled, doffed an invisible hat. "And a pleasant day to you, too, ma'am."

"I'll be right back with your scotch."

So, word *had* spread after I flashed my badge. Though it clearly hurt my chances of being elected homecoming queen, it was too early to tell whether it had improved my chances of talking to John Heaton.

The waitress dropped my drink, sticking around just long enough to get paid. The first chords of "Whip It" blasted over the PA. It was time for Domino's black rubber romp across the stage, and the club, which only minutes before had seemed empty and tomblike, was abuzz. She was good, so good I found I was watching her in spite of myself. She was so good that when she got around to removing her mask, she almost appeared to be enjoying herself. In a dive like this that was no mean feat.

After Domino left the stage, Glitters quieted back down some, but not all the way back. No, she had revved things up considerably. The stupor would not return this evening. I sat, drank my Dewar's at a leisurely pace, and rehearsed the words I thought I might use. My plan was to try and see Domino again. During my last trip in I thought I had spotted a drop of sympathy in her yellowy eyes. Of course, I might have wanted to see it.

It hadn't been my intention to ask directly about John Heaton. I was thoroughly aware how little that approach had brought me. No, this time someone else would do the pleading for me. If I had to spend several hundred dollars of Thomas Geary's money to convince Domino it was in her best interest to act on my behalf, so be it. I couldn't afford to count on her phantom sympathies. I had a second scotch before heading downstairs.

I didn't have to wait very long for her to pop out of the dressing room, and she saved herself the embarrassment of fending me off with that lame bullshit about the house rules. Today she was wearing denim shorts and a tube top.

"Whaddya want?"

"To buy you a drink and talk some business."

She laughed. "Shit, I never heard that line before, especially not from a cop."

"We must not know the same cops," I said.

"Oh, yeah, that must be it, 'cause the cops I know never use the words 'buy' and 'business.' Their vocabulary only includes words like 'free' and 'on the house.'"

"I was wrong. I guess we do know the same cops, but that's not the kinda business I'm interested in."

"You're a man, right?"

"The last time I checked, yeah."

"Then you're interested in that kinda business."

She wasn't wrong. She was a commodity. That's what Glitters was, a kind of commodities exchange. Only here, no one traded on their futures, just their yesterdays and todays. Though I wasn't interested in using her body, I guess I was hoping that John Heaton might be. Wit had it right: using people was what made the world go round.

"Yeah, okay, maybe I am," I confessed. "Can I buy you that drink?"

"Sure, stud, why not?" She shrugged her shoulders. I turned to go up the stairs, but she stopped me, slipping her arm through mine. "Screw the stairs, we'll go out the side door."

She led me the opposite way down the hall, through a door marked PRIVATE, through a storage room, and out a steel door that fed us into an alley that stank of cat piss and garbage. In other words, it smelled like any other alleyway in the city. As soon as the door clicked shut behind us, Domino pressed herself against me, but I ducked out of the way. If she was offended by my reluctance, she didn't show it. Once again, she looped her arm through mine and started us toward the street. We didn't quite make it.

As we passed several steel Dumpsters, Domino unhitched herself from me. A strong hand reached out of the shadows, yanking hard on my left wrist. I was thrown completely off balance. Domino was running down the alley toward the street, her sandals clickity-clacking against the grimy cobblestones. A steel fist drove itself so hard into my gut that you could have seen the knuckles on the skin of my back.

"Oh, fuck!" I gasped with the breath the punch forced out of my lungs, the words tasting like regurgitated scotch.

When I tried to recover, a bat struck me across the backs of my knees and I collapsed into a bag of bruised flesh and bone. Knowing, experienced hands patted me down. My .38 was pulled out of the holster I kept clipped to my belt. Its cylinder was opened. The falling bullets pinged off my forehead and face. The cylinder was snapped shut. Metal creaked as the lid to a Dumpster was lifted. Something clanged against the metal. My gun, most likely. A shoe pressed down on my cheek, squeezing my jaw against the paving stones.

"Next time, asshole, take the hint. Come around here again and it'll be your teeth, not bullets, bouncin' off the floor. Get it?"

When I didn't answer immediately, the foot pressed down even harder on my face.

"I get it," I gurgled.

"What?"

"I get it. I get it."

The shoe was off my face, but the pain stayed behind. I was in no shape to do anything but listen to two sets of feet retreating unhurriedly back down the alley toward the club. After about five minutes, the pain eased enough for me to sit up and get my bearings. I rubbed my jaw, wiping the grit off both sides of my face. I tried standing to test out my knees. They both burned with pain. The surgical one wasn't any less stable than usual. Actually, the doctors hadn't left enough tissue in there to damage. My good knee was of more concern. It responded pretty well, and I went about collecting my bullets and searching the myriad Dumpsters for my .38.

I didn't need to be a rocket scientist or even an ex-cop to figure out what had just taken place. It was to laugh. Domino, in her way, *had* introduced me to John Heaton or, rather, had smoothed the way for him to introduce himself to me. All that and it hadn't cost Thomas Geary a penny. But it had cost me. I'd be back to collect, and when I came back, I'd have my head up instead of up my ass.

CHAPTER
SEVEN

IT HAD BEEN MY EXPERIENCE THAT PAIN SELDOM EVOKED PLEAS- ant memories. This morning did nothing to dissuade me from that view. Sure, my gut ached, my jaw, too, but that pain didn't come with any baggage, not even a carry-on. My knee, however, was quite another story. It usually ached in damp weather. You can't have all that I'd had done to it and expect a free ride. Today was different. Today it hurt like a bastard, like it hadn't hurt since right after the second surgery. I stood there in the bathroom watching my hands shake as much from remembering those days as from the freshness of the pain.

It was August of 1977. Copwise, it had been a good few weeks. Word was out that the department was reconsidering the freeze on promotions. Something that was owed me as far back as Marina Conseco's rescue. I'd also been making a shitload of overtime since the July blackout. And now that Son of Sam had extended his franchise to Brooklyn, that overtime was only likely to increase. By snuffing out the life of Stacy Moskowitz and putting a bullet into Robert Violante's eye, Sam had unknowingly set in motion the end to both our careers.

When they captured him and brought him in for arraignment, they bused a bunch of us in from precincts all around the city to work security and crowd control. Today, it's hard to recall just how huge Sam's capture was. This pudgy little bar mitzvah boy from the Bronx had held the city in his murderous grasp for months. He had set off the biggest manhunt in New York's long history, perhaps the biggest manhunt in the history of the United States. Unless you lived through those days, it would be easy to forget the other factors which had so frayed our collective nerves.

The city was teetering on the edge of fiscal collapse. We had just endured one of the coldest, snowiest winters on record, and in mid July the city was plunged into a blackout. In '65, during the first big blackout, there was no looting to speak of, but in '77 the town went nuts. The looting and rioting went on for days. In some ways, it almost felt disconnected from the blackout itself. It was as if years of resentment over Vietnam and the failed promises of the sixties boiled up to the surface in one crazy, angry moment. And casting a shadow over it all was the Son of Sam.

So after Sam's arraignment and the press conferences, after the handshakes and backslapping, they shipped us back to our precincts. In my absence, the maintenance crew had waxed the precinct floors for the first time in months. I never did find out why they had chosen that particular day. Anyway, on my way to the locker room, one of the precinct detectives called out to me, busting my chops about how I had looked on TV, standing there behind Sam and Detective Ed Zigo. When I turned to answer back, I slipped on a piece of carbon paper some careless schmuck had thrown on the newly waxed floor.

They tell me my knee got so twisted up that some of the guys got nauseated just looking at me. Luckily, I guess, I was knocked silly when my head hit the floor. But by the time I got to the ER at Coney Island Hospital, the pain had made itself intimately familiar. I had known that pain to differing degrees every day since. That day in August of '77 was the last time I ever wore my police blues.

The phone rang and I was transported back to the present, to the pain my knees felt now. I waited for Katy to pick up, but she must have been in her studio. Phones were strictly verboten down there. Katy thought telephones were the bane of creative thought. I'm not sure I would have gone quite that far, but I was no artist. I hobbled over to the nightstand and picked up.

"Hello."

"He wants to talk to you." It was Domino. I didn't have to ask who *he* was.

"Put him on. I don't think they make a baseball bat that stretches this far."

She ignored that. "He wants me to talk to you first."

"This is bullshit! If he wants to talk to—"

"He says it's this way or no way."

"All right. Where?"

"As far away from Glitters as—"

"You know Coney Island?"

"I've heard of it, but I don't get out much."

"Think you can find it?"

"Yeah, I'm a big girl. I pick out my own G-strings and everything."

"Very funny. Meet me on the boardwalk at West Fifth Street in two hours."

"But—"

I hung up before she could finish her objecting. All I knew was that I'd be there. The rest was up to her. Besides, I had to stop at the bank. Somehow I got the feeling this little talk wasn't being arranged out of the goodness of anyone's heart.

* * *

My car seemed to know the way, easing down Ocean Parkway, slipping beneath the el at Brighton Beach Avenue, and sliding finally around the smooth neck of Surf Avenue. I was plenty early, giving myself time enough to make sure I wasn't being set up for John Heaton's second at bat. First, I drove past my old precinct house across from Luna Park.

Sixty or seventy years ago, Luna Park, like the Steeplechase, had been its own amusement park. There were four or five separate parks back then, each with distinct character and attractions. Luna Park, for instance, was world famous for the thousands upon thousands of incandescent bulbs strung across every inch of the place. Scientists have speculated that it was so bright, it might have been visible from space. Luna Park burned to the ground three or four times. Now a collection of hideous apartment buildings stand disrespectfully on its ashes. You can't see them from space, and the rest of the neighborhood wishes you couldn't see them from across the street.

I thought about driving farther into the throat of Coney Island, past the abandoned factory building where the firemen and I had found Marina Conseco. The city had long since removed the water tank from its roof, and I hadn't been there since I'd showed it to Katy five years ago. No, I decided, it was best to leave my past behind, even if the rest of the world wouldn't let me. Instead, I parked in the shadow of the ugly apartment houses and walked back to the boardwalk.

It was another scorcher and sun was warm on my face, but in Coney Island there's always more to the equation than just the sun. The breeze was blowing hard in off the Atlantic so that you could almost be fooled into believing the remainder of the day would be pleasant, even cool. The beach was still more crowded with gulls than people, and the boardwalk was quiet if not quite deserted. This would all change in a week or two, when schools let out for the summer. The handball courts were busy, as they always were.

From where I positioned myself I had a clear view of the boardwalk in either direction, of the steps leading up to it from the street, and of the steps leading from it down to the beach. To sneak up on me, someone would have had to parachute in or materialize out of thin air.

Domino took a more conventional route, strolling alone from the Brighton Beach end of the boardwalk. She wore denim cutoffs, a black bikini top, and those now famous sandals. They clacked against the wooden planks as they had against the cobblestones the night before. As she walked, the taut muscles in her legs and abdomen flexed and relaxed, flexed and relaxed. Just as she had at Glitters, she had injected a spark into things. The old Russian men stopped playing chess, stopped talking, to watch her approach and then pass. Even the gulls seemed to take notice.

What I noticed as she got close was the abject paleness of her skin and the faint red marks on her forearms. She wasn't lying; she didn't get out much. Not while the sun was up, anyway. It was an awkward moment. Neither of us knew quite how to greet one another. Maybe if I had been sure of what the hell it was we were really doing here, I might have been able to work out the proper protocol. In the end, we both sort of shrugged our shoulders and leaned over the guardrail.

"That's a stupid game," she said, pointing at the crowded hand-ball courts below. "Men slapping a ball against a concrete wall."

"Stupider than some, less stupid than others."

"It must hurt their hands."

"It's like anything else, Domino. You get used to it."

"Yeah," she snickered, "tell me about it. Men and their fuck-ing games. Look at them clowns down there." Domino nodded at two men exchanging money. "They actually gamble on this shit?"

"Men gamble on anything, especially when women are watch-ing. A lot of money has changed hands on West Fifth Street."

"That old prick over there must be eighty. He's gonna drop dead."

"It's been known to happen," I said. "Anything worth gam-bling on is worth dying for. It's an old Brooklyn rule."

"Fuck the rules and Brooklyn, too."

I didn't argue the point, getting instead to the matter at hand. "You have a message for me?"

"John wanted me to say he was sorry."

"Apology's not accepted. Move on."

"He was drunk." Domino was going to plead his case even if court wasn't in session. "He gets a little, you know, outta control when he's had a few."

"That's too fucking bad for him." I walked a few steps to show her how I was limping. "See this knee? I've had two major surger-ies on it. That asshole coulda crippled me. So you'll forgive me if I don't cry in my beer for his drinking problem. All the fuck he had to do was talk to me."

"But he can't," she said.

"Why, because Wit's money says so?"

That confused her some. She didn't say it with her mouth, but her eyes asked: *How did you know about Wit?* And suddenly I got the funny feeling Domino was trying to play me too. I began to wonder if Heaton had sent her here at all or if she'd gotten the bright idea to use her knowledge of the situation to her advantage. Maybe she thought she could squeeze me for a few hundred bucks in order to set up a meeting between Heaton and me that might or might not happen. You had to admire her entrepreneurial spirit.

I started walking away without saying a word.

"Where the fuck you going?" she called after me in a trembly voice.

"Cut the shit with the shaky voice, all right? You teed me up like a golf ball last night and I'm not gonna let you do it to me again. If John Heaton's interested in me finding his daughter, he can find a way to talk to me."

"He don't trust you," she said.

"He doesn't trust *me*! He doesn't know me. Look, Domino, I'm not in the mood for games. I'm gonna tell you some truth. Then maybe you can tell me some back. We both know your boy John's being paid by some big-shot journalist not to speak to me or anybody else about his daughter. It's got nothing to do with him trusting me or not."

"Whaddya want from the man? He's got no money."

"He gets a cop pension just like me."

"It all goes to that bitch wife of his and their son down in Florida."

I was getting tired and impatient. "So how much does he want?"

She liked that a lot. Domino reached into a little bag she had slung over her shoulder, pulling out a pack of Marlboros and a lighter. If it was a victory cigarette, she was getting a little ahead of herself. First off, the hard ocean breeze kept blowing out her lighter. Second, asking about price doesn't mean you're buying.

"Depends," Domino said, giving up on the cigarette.

I started walking away again, more quickly this time.

"A grand," she blurted out.

I kept walking.

"Eight."

I was almost to the stairs down to the street.

"Seven."

I stopped and limped back to her. "Five hundred, take it or leave it."

She frowned, her once pretty face looking old and mean.

"You can divide it up any way you want to," I added, slipping a hundred-dollar bill into her bag. "That's a goodwill gesture between the two of us."

"Does that come out of the—"

"A finder's fee." I smiled.

I could tell she was pleased when she reached for her cigarettes again. This time I helped her light up. She screwed up her lips to blow the smoke away from my face.

"You know," she said, "I think maybe John and me can trust you a little bit. You get good at sorting out men after working long enough in the shitholes I worked in."

"Yeah, how long is long enough?"

"About five minutes. Most of the men in my world are complete scum. A few are just scummy. Then there's guys like you and John who are a step above."

"I'm honored."

"Don't be. It's a small step." She crushed the cigarette out between her sandal and the boardwalk. "I'll call you when every-thing's arranged."

I watched her for a little while as she retreated back toward Brighton Beach. Then I turned my attention to the action on the handball courts. A young Puerto Rican kid was cursing as he handed money over to the old geezer Domino had suspected of being on the verge of cardiac arrest. The level of play on the other courts was pretty weak. Most of the players were young and inex-perienced, not as good as I had been before I hurt the knee. Now, however, the worst of them could run me off the court. That con-cept hurt worse than my knee. Time to go.

*　*　*

Waiting for me at the Brooklyn store was a message from on high. Brightman had called, inviting Katy and me to a black-tie Demo-cratic fund-raiser at the Waldorf-Astoria. Klaus let me know that it was more of a demand than a request. Brightman said that Geary had purchased a whole table's worth of tickets and Katy and I were expected to fill two of the seats. I called Katy to ask if she was up to it. She was up to it, all right, but didn't stay on the phone very long. She had to run to the cleaners to get the dress she'd worn to Constance's wedding, and she had to call Cindy to see if she and Aaron could take Sarah for the night.

Katy, unlike me, had been to several of these types of affairs before. It was easy for me to forget—maybe because I wanted to forget—that Katy's dad, Francis Maloney Sr., had once been a major fund-raising force within the New York State Democratic Party. But his was not the black-tie type of fund-raising. No, my father-in-law was the old-school, nuts-and-bolts type. Everybody who got a state, county, or village job within the confines of

Dutchess County unofficially tithed a part of his or her salary to the local Democratic Party. If you wanted a contract to pick up garbage, supply food to the schools, do office cleaning, your firm kicked back a percentage to the local Democratic Party.

There was nothing particularly unique about this sort of thing. It's the way both parties had operated for the last century. Just try getting a civil service job in Nassau County without listing your party affiliation as Republican and/or tithing a chunk of your income to that same party.

What set Francis Sr. apart from the rest of the political hacks was his ability to broker his results into power that extended beyond his county. He was a man to be feared and reckoned with. Even the sharpies in the city and Albany listened when Francis Sr. spoke. In the end, however, that influence led to his demise. He had gotten a little too powerful, a little too influential, to suit the party bigwigs. So in keeping with the time-honored tradition of state politics, they cut him off at the knees. What only my father-in-law, my ex-friend Rico Tripoli, and I knew was that they had used me to do it.

I had a few hours to kill before going home and retrieving my tuxedo from the back of the closet, so I went to the room next to the office and set about mixing and matching the Spivack and police files. As I had anticipated, the Spivack file was far more exhaustive. They had run complete background checks on nearly everyone they interviewed in connection with the case. There were even surveillance reports on some of Moira Heaton's former professors from Fordham University. The cops had spoken to many of these same people, but hadn't been nearly as thorough.

As I had twice before, I copied down some names, numbers, and addresses. To what end, I was unsure. I would be the third, fourth, or fifth person to talk to these people about the same five seconds in each of their lives. By now they would no longer be discussing what they had seen or thought they might have seen, but would simply be repeating lines as an actor might in a play he or she had performed several times. Maybe the problem was that not enough time had elapsed between Moira's disappearance and now.

I treated myself to a beer out of the office fridge and turned on the radio. I could tell Aaron had been around, because the radio was tuned to an AM news-only station. When I did paperwork, I wanted to relax, listen to music. Aaron relaxed by getting tense about something other than work. You had to love my big brother. Lately, I'd been listening to this new wave station that featured anorexic Englishmen with strange haircuts and synthesizers. Welcome to the eighties!

Klaus called me on the intercom as I was getting up to change channels. Things were slow out front and he wanted to bullshit about what I was going to wear to the Waldorf.

"I was thinking of borrowing your Dead Kennedys shirt," I said.

"Unfortunately, I've gotten rid of that old thing. Too bad really, considering how incredibly inappropriate it would have been at a Democratic fund-raiser."

"Good point."

"That's what you have me for."

"No. I have you to manage the store. Good-bye, Klaus."

I finished my beer without bothering to turn the dial. It wouldn't kill me, I decided, to listen to the news. Depress me, yes, but not kill me. Recently, I had stopped listening to the news, stopped reading the papers. The papers were once a great passion in my life, but the miscarriage had changed all that. It was selfish of me, I know, to turn my back on the rest of the world because of a small tragedy in my life. I had just found it too hard to be constantly reminded.

So now I sat back and listened to the litany of carnage that we New Yorkers had come to accept as news. A street cop had been killed in Brownsville last night when an undercover drug bust went sour. The suspect had been killed too. The trial of a vicious rapist—Ivan the Terrible, the newsman called him—had gotten off to smooth start at Queens Criminal Court. Ivan the Terrible; very cute. I wondered how the victims felt about the snazzy nickname. But given that four hundred people had been drowned in Bangladesh when their ferry sank and that another mass grave had been discovered in Cambodia, New York was having a relatively good news day.

* * *

I was not so foolish as to suppose that my sudden invitation to the Waldorf was the result of my good looks or boyish charms. It was partially a payoff, one of the perks I was to receive for taking the case. Access, casual or otherwise, to the people Katy and I would share drinks with this evening was worth its weight in gold. A quiet word dropped in the proper ear by Geary or Brightman could mean that Irving Prager & Sons, Purveyors of Finest Wines and Spirits, would receive a favorable hearing when bidding to supply all fund-raising events within the five boroughs. Or if, for some odd reason, one of the party elite needed a private matter looked into by a discreet ex-cop . . . It was the classic carrot-and-stick scenario. By having Weintraub and his buddy show up at our stores, Geary had shown me the stick. This evening was all about a close-up view of the carrot.

A smaller, but no less significant, part of the evening's agenda was to showcase Steven Brightman. I think Geary was anxious to see me see the state senator in action. Maybe the both of them wanted that. I got the sense that Geary and Brightman preferred having true believers on board. Lord knows Brightman's office workers were fiercely dedicated to him and would, I imagine, have forgiven him his foibles if he dared admit to any. Beyond loyalty and love of family, I wasn't the true-believer type. They couldn't've known that, so I couldn't really blame them for trying.

Thomas and Elizabeth Geary and six of our table-mates were already seated when we arrived. One glance at Mrs. Geary revealed much about her daughter. Constance had inherited her mother's calm demeanor, indigo eyes, and handsome, if not quite beautiful, looks. At sixty, she might have passed for forty-five. I found myself thinking of Domino and of how soon she might pass for sixty.

"What is it?" Katy prodded, catching me drifting off.

"Nothing important."

We did the expected round of polite introductions. Everyone was pleased to meet everyone else. Everyone looked lovely. Everyone would forget everyone else's name in five seconds. Thomas Geary tried to ensure that some names would not drift aimlessly out of people's ears and into space. He took Katy by the arm, bringing her near his seat. He tapped his water glass with his fork.

"Ladies and gentlemen, ladies and gentlemen." He waited until he had the table's full attention. "This beautiful young woman is indeed the wife of Mr. Moses Prager, but years before she held that honor, Katy here was the daughter of Francis Maloney Sr."

No one stood. There were no *Bravos!* from the table. They did, however, applaud as if she'd sunk a tricky thirty-foot putt on the eighteenth green of the club championship. Even five years after his "retirement" the mere mention of Francis Maloney still elicited grudging respect and appreciation.

Katy beamed. She loved her dad and, I think, was enjoying the spotlight after so long grieving the baby.

"Yes, how is Francis these days?" Elizabeth Geary asked out of respect more than curiosity.

"He had a small stroke a few years back," Katy said, "but he's fine now. You know how stubborn a man he can be."

Everyone at the table, myself included, nodded their heads in agreement, but the Francis Maloney Sr. lovefest was at its end. Good thing, for it was time for the Brightmans' grand entrance. No man in a powdered wig banged a baton against the floor to formally announce their appearance. Peter Nero did not stop playing the piano. The brass section did not trumpet the couple's arrival. No one quite applauded, yet it seemed to me all heads turned as the couple came toward our table. Much handshaking and backslapping occurred between the door and our table. The star had arrived, and everyone in the room knew it.

"Will you look at her," the gentleman sitting next to me whispered in my ear. "She makes Jackie Kennedy look like one of Cinderella's sisters. Fucking guy's already banged all the best society pussy in the tristate area and now he's married to a goddess."

I had to check to make sure I wasn't sitting at the bar at Glitters, but at a table in the grand ballroom of the Waldorf-Astoria. In any case, his point was well taken. Brightman's wife was stunningly, breathtakingly gorgeous, and not only in the long view. During the second round of introductions, I had a chance to get a closer look. Katerina, that was her name, stood a good six feet tall in heels and moved like a swan. She had perfect brown skin, and lustrous black hair worn in a bob, not teased up and sprayed to death as was the current fashion. Her cheekbones were high, her jaw and nose were clean and angular, and her green eyes were flecked with gold.

By the time everyone's blood pressure returned to normal, the evening's festivities had begun. Some party functionary gave a welcoming speech followed by twenty minutes of Rodney Dangerfield doing his no-respect shtick. He was great, adapting his material to the audience. President Reagan's name was bandied about in concert with the names of myriad Democratic pols from Jimmy Carter to Mario Cuomo. In the world according to Rodney, the Democrats got no respect. Who says comedians don't know anything?

After Rodney came a few more speeches, a little dancing, the appetizer and salad courses. During dinner, some southern politico, the attorney general or governor of Arkansas, gave a rather windy and overearnest speech about holding on to the Democratic Party's ideals in the face of stiff Republican opposition.

My buddy leaned over to me again. "This joker's gotta be kidding me with this speech. What's he trying to do, bore us into contributing money? Jesus!"

"What's his name?" I asked.

"Who, Jethro up there? Clinton, I think. Bob Clinton, maybe. He better stay in Arkansas, because he has about as much chance for national office as the Mets have of winning a second World Series."

"Amen."

After the main course, Carly Simon, a notoriously stage-shy performer, did a few Gershwin standards. Katy and I held hands under the table during "Someone to Watch Over Me." It was corny, but sometimes corny is okay. Shortly before dessert, Brightman slipped away from the table, only to reappear at the head of the dais.

He gave a brief but rousing speech about the eventual end of the cold war and his belief that the time for mapping out a post–cold war world was upon us, that once the end came, planning would be moot. He touched on many subjects: AIDS, the growing power of the religious right, and the burgeoning national debt. His most impassioned words, however, were about overcoming tragedies and roadblocks to achieve one's goals.

"For nearly two years now," he said in a hushed voice, "I have struggled, letting an unjust and undeserved stain on my reputation keep me from accomplishing the great things for this state and this nation I know I was put on this earth to do. But great things are never done in isolation, so please help me help you. With that help, your help, I know I will clear my name and reputation. Join me. Will you join me in this mission to unite our party, to unite our state and country so that our grasp will no longer exceed our reach? Will you?"

The applause was thunderous, deafening. That Clinton guy, I thought, should have taken notes. The room was on its feet, stomping. "Brightman. Brightman. Brightman," they chanted. The atmosphere was more Baptist church revival than fund-raiser. Intentionally or not, State Senator Steven Brightman had just hung an albatross firmly around my neck. High-minded speeches were all well and good. But unless I found out what had really happened to Moira Heaton, and soon, Brightman was going nowhere but the political scrap heap. His bold words would be nothing more than wasted rhetoric.

It was no coincidence that Geary nodded at me just as Bright-man delivered his line about the unjust stain on his reputation. I guess what Geary didn't comprehend was that I already had all the incentive I needed to get to the bottom of things. All the carrots and sticks in the world weren't going to create leads where there were none, nor would they produce physical evidence that didn't exist.

People seemed to simply drift away after the coffee was served. No one felt the need to make a show of polite good-byes. The only thing I can compare it to is the end of a big fight card. After the main event, the crowd go their separate ways. And if I had been expecting one of Geary's little lectures on golf, horses, and politics, I was going to be disappointed. He and his wife simply waved at us as they exited the ballroom. Brightman, like a fighter coming off an injury to announce his return to the ring, was too busy accepting the accolades of an adoring crowd to even remember I existed.

* * *

Katy was still buzzing halfway back home to Sheepshead Bay. For her the night had been a coming-out party, and not only because it helped put the miscarriage behind her. Politics, though not particularly her calling, were definitely in her blood. She had watched her father work it so well for so long that the thrill of events like this evening's were inescapable. That scared me a little. Any similarities between Katy and her dad scared me.

"Brightman's a natural," Katy said as we passed under the Verrazano Bridge. "I can see why Mr. Geary is so anxious to back him. He's worth the gamble."

"You liked him? Brightman, I mean?"

"As a candidate, of course. What's not to like? His wife alone is worth a bump in the vote. She's unearthly."

"I hadn't noticed."

Katy punched me playfully. "Liar. She was the talk of the powder room."

"Was she? I thought she'd more likely be the talk of the boys' locker room."

"God knows I love you, Moses Prager, but what you don't know about women . . . Besides, I thought you hadn't noticed."

"Oops! So what were they saying?"

"That while he was single, Brightman had bedded half the models in the city. Apparently, he had a sweet tooth for all things beautiful, especially women."

"The fat guy sitting next to me said the same thing. Good thing you hadn't met Brightman until this evening."

"Thank you." Katy leaned over and softly kissed my neck. "By the way, that fat guy sitting next to you was Scott Schare, the CEO of Schare, Light, Cohen, and Halter."

"The big ad agency?"

"The very big ad agency. Him I knew before. Remember the company I was working for when we met?"

"I remember everything about when we met."

"We did some of the subcontract design work for their less significant clients. We were always invited to their holiday parties."

"You think he was there by accident?"

"My dad always said nothing in politics happens by accident."

I was inclined to believe that.

Katy faded, drifting quickly off into silence and light sleep. The colored lights of Coney Island, even without the dazzling incandescence of Luna Park, were clearly visible out the right side of the car. I usually found comfort in the sights and sounds of my old precinct, but not tonight. I felt oddly uneasy. I thought back to earlier in the day, to my meeting with Domino and the deal we had made. Maybe John Heaton would call. Maybe not. I don't know, maybe I was finally feeling the pressure of the case. Brightman and Geary had certainly gone out of their way to pile it on me. But there was something else eating at me, something like a dull ache I couldn't quite pinpoint or describe.

As the lights of Coney Island disappeared behind the tall buildings of Trump Village, I looked over at my sleeping wife and decided tonight was not a night to dwell on aches and pains.

CHAPTER EIGHT

I DID WHAT ANY SANE MAN WOULD HAVE DONE GIVEN THE PRES-sure I was under. I took my daughter to her first Mets game. The Astros had finished pounding them, as had the Dodgers. Today's game, an afternoon affair, was the last of the series against the Padres and of the homestand. The teams had split the first two games. The heat and humidity were a bit less oppressive than they'd been in recent days, but the cloudlessness of the sky gave the sun license to roast the two of us and the 27,322 other knuckleheads who thought an afternoon getaway game at Shea was a good way to spend their time.

Sarah, less than two months away from her third birthday, was beside herself with excitement. I think she loved the subway ride and the crush of people and that first rush you get from stepping out of the tunnel into a gigantic stadium. The Mets cap, hot dog, and cotton candy didn't hurt either.

"Look, Daddy!" she shrieked. "The men are watering the lawn like you."

"That's right, kiddo, just like me."

She asked me a million whys and I answered them all as if I really knew what the hell I was talking about. Soon enough she would be able to see through that ploy, to see that there were many more things in the world that Daddy didn't understand than he did. It hurt a little just to think about her seeing any bits of clay, no matter how small, falling from my feet. But it would be good for her in the end, I rationalized, to see the faults in people. She would see her parents' faults first of all.

Sarah stayed with the game for the first two and a half innings, during which time the Mets built a 3–0 lead. Then her concentration faded, giving way to a fit of antsiness and a chorus of "I'm bored." By the top of the fourth, she was conked out.

"That's a beautiful little girl you got there, mister," the man in the seat behind me said as the Padre pitcher grounded to first for the last out of the top half of the inning.

I tilted my head to see his face, but the blinding sun forced me to turn away. "Thanks."

"Such pretty red hair," he kept the conversation going. "Irish?"

"On her mother's side, yeah."

The cop in me was wary of these unsolicited comments about my daughter, but there was nothing remotely threatening or inappropriate in his tone.

"I had a daughter once too," he kept on.

His use of the past tense was not lost on me, nor was the smell of alcohol on his breath. More than a few beers, I guessed, with a scotch mixed in there somewhere.

"Girls are great," I said, now a bit more concerned than I had been only a moment ago.

"They sure are."

Curious, I asked: "What's your daughter's name?"

"Moira."

I turned back to look at him again, this time using my right hand as a visor against the sun. John Heaton was a sloppy, red-faced man, his cheeks covered in peppery gray stubble. Though he was potbellied, he had big, round shoulders and the kind of thickness of limb which no amount of weight lifting could replicate. His face was not unfamiliar. I recognized him from the 7 train, and he had stood directly behind us on the ticket line. So, Domino had kept her end of the deal.

"How's the knee? I'm sorry about that. I was . . . You know."

"Keep your apologies for someone who might be interested."

"So what are you so anxious to talk to me about?"

"Don't be dense, Heaton," I groused. "I wanna talk to you about Moira."

"Why? If I had anything worthwhile to say, the cops and that dick Spivack would have already used it."

"It's the way I work. I need to get a feel for her, what Moira liked and didn't like, stuff like that."

He tilted himself forward and whispered cruelly in my ear: "My daughter's dead, Prager, and you know it."

I wasn't hypocrite enough to debate the point. "More than likely."

He was skeptical. "What you gonna find that the cops and Spivack couldn't?"

"Maybe nothing. I've been lucky in cases like this before." There, I'd said it. I was lucky. I wondered if Geary's ears were burning.

The Mets were up at bat now, the people around us paying even less attention to my conversation with Heaton than before. Sarah was fast fast asleep.

"I'm risking a lot by—"

"Save it, Heaton. I know all about Wit paying you to keep quiet. I bet you didn't tell him you had nothing worthwhile to say. What kinda bullshit you been feeding him to keep the paychecks rolling in?"

"Nothin'. I swear. He hasn't even interviewed me yet. He just don't want me to talk to nobody is all."

"But you're taking his money."

"And yours, too, boyo. I need it. My son's starting college in the fall and my wife's milking my tits dry."

"We're here about Moira," I reminded him.

He held his hand out to me. I slapped it away, not hard, not playfully either. "You'll get your money, but not here and not now."

"How do I know I can trus—"

"Because I say so. Because I was a cop like you." I found I was looking at Sarah, wondering if I could ever sink quite as low as John Heaton had. I hoped never to find out.

"Then go ahead and ask," he said.

I did. Most of his answers were as enlightening as a fortune cookie and as deep as a sun-shower puddle. I thought Moira plain. He thought her homely. She wasn't a dim bulb, but it was hard work and determination that got her her good grades. She had graduated with a bachelor's degree in political science from Fordham, had been accepted to several area law schools and the police academy. She surprised everyone by choosing politics instead.

"She woulda made a helluva cop," Heaton said, flagging down the beer vendor. He ordered two, and though neither was for me, I paid for both.

I wondered. "What makes you say she'd've been a good cop?"

"She was a pit bull, Prager. When she got a bug up her ass . . .

watch out! She never let go of anything until she got what she wanted."

I recalled the staff at Brightman's office offering a similar assessment.

John Heaton said he loved his girl, but that she was always to herself. Most of her friends growing up had been family, her cousins, and she had been a mystery even to them. From the time she was a little girl, she kept her own counsel. She wasn't dour, exactly, though her father couldn't recall a time when she'd danced without being forced to or telling a joke worth a damn. She'd dated a little, but there'd never been a serious boyfriend that Heaton could remember. He suggested I fly down to Florida and talk with her mother. Moira loved her little brother.

"John Jr. and Moira, the two of them were close," he admitted.

I was discouraged now not only because the Mets had relinquished two-thirds of their advantage, but because I was no closer to connecting with Moira Heaton than I had been yesterday or the day before that. She seemed to be an unknowable quantity. I was, at least, getting a consistent image of her if not an in-depth one. Brightman, of all the people, appeared to have the best handle on who she had been. That was sad, I thought, very sad indeed.

"Do you think Brightman had anything to do with it?"

"Nah," John answered without hesitation. "What could she have done to hurt him? She was an intern, for chrissakes! He's loaded, so he wasn't on the take. Even if she . . . If they had an affair, she was no threat. He wasn't married at the time. No, she walked out of the office that night and—" His voice cracking, he stopped. "Should the two of us ex-cops sit here and go over old cases? Can you even count the homicide scenes you were at?" He pointed at Sarah. "Look at her sleeping there. Bad things happen to lots of people's little boys and girls. Most of the time, they're strangers to you. Sometimes you might know the family. Sometimes, God help us, it's your own kid."

He shifted in his seat, preparing to leave. My mind was racing. This might be the last chance I would have to talk to the man, and not only hadn't I learned much, but I'd already run out of questions.

"John," I blurted out, "what was the last thing you talked about? When did you talk to her last?"

He hesitated, thinking back. "We talked that Monday," he answered in a rough, distracted whisper. "The Monday before Thanksgiving. She called me."

"What about?"

"She wanted to know what to bring to her aunt Millie's for Thanksgiving."

"Was there something else, another question maybe? What did you guys talk about after you talked about Aunt Millie's?"

"Yeah, Moira asked me something. She wanted to know about the statute of limitations."

"What?"

"Don't get excited, Prager. It was no big deal," Heaton assured me. "Moira did that sometimes, asked me law shit when she couldn't get hold of a legal aid lawyer. She probably had some woman at her desk wondering if her kid stole a car ten years ago, could he go to the slammer for it now. It was always about some poor woman or some homeless guy who needed help."

I perked up anyway. "What exactly did she ask you? Try to remember."

"She asked if the statute of limitations was different from state to state and if there were any crimes that it didn't apply to."

"And what'd you tell her?"

"That as far as I knew, it was different from state to state and that I didn't think there was a time limit in any state on homicide, but that I couldn't be sure. I told her she should check with a lawyer."

"Did she?"

He was suddenly agitated. "Did she what?"

"See a lawyer?"

"How the fuck should I know? I told you, it was the last time we talked," he barked, the two beers fueling his anger. "You fuckin' stupid or what? Waste a my fuckin' time, this crap. I don't even like the damned Mets."

He was gone before I could explain about my enthusiasm getting ahead of me. Not that he was in any mood to understand. Of course he couldn't have known if Moira consulted a lawyer. Finally, I had something to hang my hat on. It wasn't much. And like Heaton had said, probably nothing more than an innocent question. It was, however, a place to start.

Shit! I could have kicked myself. There *was* something I'd neglected to ask him: Had he shared the details of this last conversation with the cops? I looked after Heaton, but he was long gone. I made a mental note to call Detective Gloria as soon as Sarah and I got back home. And the Mets were trying their level best to ensure that Sarah and I got an early start to the exits. They had batted around, tacking four runs onto their lead, and there were still runners on second and third with only one out.

I scooped Sarah up, cradling her in my arms, her sleepy head on my shoulder. Damp wisps of red hair spilled out from beneath her cockeyed Mets cap. She barely stirred as I carried her along the sloping ramps that led down from the mezzanine and out to the subway. Several roars erupted as we made our way. No doubt more runs for the boys in white, royal blue, and orange. Sarah's first game would be a win, but she wouldn't remember the victory. That would be my job, to remember it for her.

On the subway ride from Flushing, I found myself staring across at the front page of the *Post*. There was a big picture of a man in his late twenties or early thirties. He had shoulder-length, scraggly hair, a cruel smile, and dead black eyes. The kind of face nightmares are made of. I was glad Sarah was still sleeping. Whenever I looked away, I found my gaze drifting back. There was something about those eyes gazing back at me, beyond me, through me, all the way to hell. Above his photo, the headline read:

IVAN THE TERRIBLE SAYS:
"CATHERINE WAS GREAT"

So this was the animal I'd heard about on the radio yesterday. I could only imagine what the headline was referring to. I didn't have to imagine for long. A few stops along the line, the gentleman who'd been reading the paper stood up to exit the number 7, leaving the paper in his seat.

"Do you mind if I have a look?" I asked.

Seeing that Sarah had her head resting against my leg, the man retrieved his *Post* and handed it to me. "To be a kid again, huh?" he said wistfully. "Here you go."

"Thanks."

He gave me the thumbs-up. "Let's go Mets."

There was another picture of Ivan the Terrible on page 3. His hair was shorter. He was dressed in a suit. His eyes were still dead.

The story went on to explain the front-page headline. Ivan Alfonseca was alleged to have stalked, raped, beaten, and robbed at least twelve women in Manhattan, Queens, and the Bronx over the past two and a half years. While at Rikers awaiting trial, Ivan, already having been convicted of three counts in the Bronx, had shared the gory details of his alleged escapades with cellmates. It hadn't taken long for some of these to filter into the press.

Catherine Thigpen, one of his last victims, had been courageous in fighting him off and in identifying herself in the press. She had already been victimized by him once, she said, and wasn't about to let him force her into a life of silent shame. Hearing that she had come forward and was anxious to testify against him at trial, Alfonseca had bragged to his fellow Rikers inmates. Hence the headline. Cops are seldom ambivalent about the death penalty, and the Ivan Alfonsecas of the world are why.

I could feel my grip getting tight on the edges of the paper. He had gotten to me. The little piece of crap was a natural victimizer. I'd run into his type before. They were like human tornadoes, incapable of doing anything except leaving damage and destruction in their wake. I folded the paper up and slid it down the long plastic bench as far away from Sarah as I could.

I felt that dull ache again, that queasiness from the night before, but I couldn't hang it on Ivan the Terrible. No, I had to focus. I had to call Detective Gloria about Moira's last conversation with her father. I had to stay on point.

"What's wrong, Daddy?" Sarah mumbled, her eyes fighting to stay open.

"Nothing, kiddo," I lied. "How'd you like the game?"

"It was hot."

"It was too hot. I'm sorry about that. Next time we'll go to a night game when the sun isn't out, okay?"

"Okay." She sat up and straightened her cap. "Did we win?"

"We did." I was guessing, but she didn't have to know that.

"I'm firsty."

"Me, too, kiddo. When we change trains in Manhattan, we'll get vanilla egg creams."

She squeezed the life out of my arm and kissed me on the cheek. Her love was almost enough to make me forget the evil in the world. Almost.

* * *

Detective Gloria was gone for the day. Though I left a detailed message, I wasn't going to rely on his receiving it. I was determined to call him every hour on the hour from the start of his next shift until we spoke. I tried not to get too excited about the statute-of-limitations conversation between Moira and her father. I wasn't succeeding. It just seemed like such an odd question. There had to be an extraordinary reason why it'd come up. I knew I was blowing this way out of proportion, but a man lost in the desert celebrates even a thimbleful of water.

My edginess hadn't escaped Katy's notice. I'd hardly eaten any dinner, and now, having put Sarah to bed, I couldn't sit still. Katy poured me a few fingers of scotch without my asking.

"Moses Prager!" she shouted at me. "If you don't calm down, *I'm* going to need a drink."

"Well, I could think of something that always calms me down."

"Men are such pigs!"

"Oink."

It was wonderful to be playful again. Rediscovery has unexpected fringe benefits. There was a new depth, a desperation and determination in our embrace that surprised the both of us. But as I lay there, Katy folded into the hollow of my left arm, that edginess rushed back in. This wasn't a dull ache. No, Ivan the Terrible had crept back into my head under cover of darkness. That piece of shit had gotten to me again. No other man had a place in my bed, especially not him. I needed to act, to get out of there, to do something. Sleep wasn't an option.

"Katy . . . Katy," I whispered. "I'm going to work."

She picked her head up and looked over my body at the clock. "Now?"

"I've gotta get this case behind me and I can't sleep."

"Okay. Be careful. I love you, Moses."

I kissed her forehead and pulled the sheet back over her.

*   *   *

My hair was still wet when I pushed back the door to Bordeaux in Brooklyn and hurried to cut off the alarm. Sheepshead Bay to Brooklyn Heights, a drive that during rush hour could take over an hour, had taken me about twenty minutes. It's amazing how several hundred thousand fewer cars on the road can cut down on your commute.

I liked the store when it was empty and quiet. Of course, there's no quiet in Brooklyn, ever, not really. Even at this time of night you could hear the buzz of car tires against the roadway grates of the Brooklyn Bridge and the rumble of the subway just up the street. I suppose I mean I liked it when it was peaceful. Tonight, however, there would be no peace, not for me. I locked the door behind me and retreated to the room next to the office.

It was all well and good that I was motivated to do something, but I hadn't figured out what. I was kind of hoping it would come to me during the drive over. When it didn't, I hoped staring at the files spread out on the floor might do the trick. I was fresh out of inspiration when I got down on my hands and knees and began wading through the files for the third time. Finally, something—out of desperation, I think—occurred to me to try. Previously, I'd spent my time matching the police file to the work Spivack had done. In other words, I was looking at overlap, looking for names and faces that appeared in both files. If a piece of information turned up in both, I figured it carried more weight.

Maybe because I'd been a member of the NYPD and, in spite of its numerous shortcomings, believed it was the best police department in the world, I had pretty much dismissed the more esoteric pieces of information gathered by Spivack and Associates. Sure, I'd glanced at the surveillance reports on Moira's professors and the interviews with her sophomore roommates. But I had assumed that Spivack's own people had gone over all this material several hundred times trying to comb out leads. Now it was my turn. Instead of looking for overlap, I did the polar opposite. I separated out everything—name, photo, document, etc.—that was unique to either set of files. Not unexpectedly, I culled a small mountain of unique information out of Spivack's files.

I guess it was around four in the morning when I got to the sign-in logs of the community affairs office. Everybody signed in and out of that office or the staff wouldn't help them. I'd had to do it. I think it had something to do with getting administrative funding from the legislature. The more people you serve, the bigger next year's allocation. The cops had had some of these logs as well, but the Spivack file had copies of the logs that went as far back as the day Moira Heaton was first interviewed for her intern position. There were thousands of entries.

For example:

SIGN-IN (Please Print)	DATE	TIME IN	TIME OUT	STAFF MEMBER
Maria Chianese	3/29/80	9:30	10:45	Sotomayor
George Matsoukis	3/29/80	9:40	9:55	Abramson

Unless I worked backward from the day she disappeared, I figured to be in that room until the new millennium. Call me selfish, but I wanted to catch at least the last couple of years of the twentieth century. By five I was nearly out of my mind, and I'd only gotten as far back as six weeks before the disappearance. Staring at the same page for a minute or more without seeing anything, my head would drop and I'd startle awake. Punchy as I might be, I sensed that there was something to see, a name maybe, but that I was just too tired to grasp it. It had to be around six when I drifted off.

I don't think I dreamed. If I did, I didn't remember. My neck was stiff and my drool had blurred some of the copier toner on the logbook photostats. The chirping phone cared not at all for my neck or lack of sleep or dreamlessness. I trudged into the office to answer it.

"Hello," I rasped, "what time is it?"

"You sound like shit, Prager." It was Detective Gloria.

I peeked at one of the promotional mirrors hanging on an office wall. "I look worse than I sound. What time is it?"

"Eight fifteen. I called your house first and your wife told me I might find you at this number."

"Who says the guys at Missing Persons can't find their own shoes without a road map?"

"Very funny. You left a message, right?"

"Yeah, yeah, I did."

"About the statute-of-limitations thing."

"Right, right." Remembering, my heart began to race.

"We knew about that," Gloria explained, sounding slightly defensive.

"And . . ."

"And nothing. Dead end. As far as we can tell it was an innocent question. We got no record of her going to a lawyer or anyone else about it. Apparently, the only one she ever mentioned it to was her father. Like her old man says, she was probably just asking on behalf of someone else or maybe she was just curious."

So much for that lead, I thought, then said: "But it's weird."

"What is?"

"I don't have a record of that interview in the official files."

"You don't, huh?" he asked, his tone changing from collegial to adversarial. "And how the fuck did some swinging-dick private investigator get ahold of police files?"

That was careless of me, mentioning the files to him. If Larry McDonald had been privy to this conversation, he would have been on his way across the bridge to shoot me. Never mind that he'd failed to get me the complete file.

"Look, Detective Gloria, you know the people I'm working for are pretty powerful."

"You fucking threatenin' me now, you piece a—"

"No, no, no. Calm down, for chrissakes! All I'm saying is that there isn't much these guys can't get me access to if I need it. That's all, nothing more complicated than that."

"Okay, all right, 'cause if you got those files through someone in the department, I'll sic fuckin' IA on your inside source."

My heart rate picked up again. "What did you say?"

There was a brief, confused silence on his end of the line. "I said I'd get Internal Affairs on—"

"No, you said IA, you'd sic IA on them. Hold on, just hold on a second."

I dropped the phone and ran into the adjoining room. I rummaged through the sign-in sheets I'd been checking over before I passed out. There it was, a name I'd come across four or five times in the weeks leading up to Moira Heaton's disappearance.

I picked the phone back up. "Gloria, you still there?"

"What the fuck's this all about?"

"Humor me, okay, just for a minute? Try thinking along."

"Christ, Prager, you sound like you're gonna have a freakin' canary. But go ahead, I'm listening."

"If crooks had half a brain—"

"—cops would be in trouble," he finished without my needing to prompt. "So what? I learned that one even before I got on the job."

"Me, too. In Missing Persons you must see a million aliases, huh?"

"That estimate's on the low end. Again, so what?"

"You ever go to a motel?"

"Prager, you *are* outta your mind, you know that? What's aliases got to do with motels?"

"You fill out a card when you go to a motel, right? You always put down some bullshit name and address, but it's not so easy to think of that stuff off the top of your head. You're nervous about getting caught. So if you don't think it through beforehand and you don't use John Smith, what name do you use?"

"I think I get you," he said, relieved he wasn't going to have to have me committed. "You would use a name that sounds like your name or that has the same initials. You'd think they'd learn, but these clowns do it all the time."

"Right. If they had half a brain . . ."

"Okay, Prager, I follow your reasoning, but what's it got to do with Moira Heaton or anything else?"

"Maybe nothing, Detective, but maybe everything. You know 40 Court Street in Brooklyn Heights?"

"I can find it."

"Do that. I'll meet you in the lobby in two hours."

"Two hours."

"And Gloria . . ."

"Yeah?"

"Start praying."

I ran out to talk to Joey the Gimp at the newsstand and to get a fifty-five-gallon drum of coffee. I had a lot of ground to cover in the next two hours.

* * *

It was a motley crew assembled in the lobby of 40 Court Street, and none of them was particularly happy to see the others. I almost wished I had a video camera to tape the introduction of Y.W. Fenn to Captain Larry McDonald to Detective Robert Gloria to Pete Parson. One thing I can say without qualification is that the elevator ride up to Spivack's was the quietest, most uncomfortable elevator ride I'd ever taken.

As on my first visit, Joe Spivack hung back just long enough for the receptionist to greet us. And in keeping with everybody else's rotten moods, he seemed particularly miserable this morning.

"This way," he growled, his eyes burning holes in my forehead.

I understood the reason for his dissatisfaction. Not more than an hour before, I had had the unpleasant task of informing him that he was going to host a gathering of people he probably had no interest in meeting. I'd also demanded that he not inform his employer and mine, Thomas Geary, of this get-together.

"Who the hell do you think you are?" he'd screamed over the phone. "I don't work for you, you small-time little shit. I can lose this account if he finds out I didn't—"

"As I recall," I said calmly, "Geary promised me your full cooperation, so cooperate and maybe I can spin this so you don't come out looking bad."

He couldn't have liked hearing that, and if I was correct, there were things he was likely to hear that he would like far less. What Spivack didn't know, what he couldn't have known, was that I had extracted individual promises from everyone else involved to keep this meeting, the things discussed during it, and the events leading up to it confidential. If things broke right, confidentiality wouldn't be an issue. If they didn't, confidentiality would be in everyone's best interest.

Spivack walked us past his office to a large conference room. We all found places around a black oval table that shone like a freshly waxed car. I did a second series of introductions.

"What the fuck is this, Moe?" Larry Mac asked the inevitable.

"I think I know what happened to Moira Heaton."

Detective Gloria gave voice to what he'd thought all along: "Brightman?"

"Sorry to disappoint you, Detective, but the only thing Brightman did wrong here was hire Moira Heaton. It was wrong because it gave the real perp access to her."

"She dead?" Pete Parson asked.

"I'm pretty sure, but I think we all assumed that all along anyway."

Silently, they nodded their heads in agreement. Although he'd known the reality of the situation from the day he'd taken the assignment, Wit seemed distressed at the unanimity of opinion. The death of hope is never a pleasant experience.

Now it was Spivack's turn. "So . . ."

I pulled out the sign-in sheets from Brightman's office, selecting five sheets in particular. I passed them around, letting everyone get a good look.

"The name Ishmail Almonte appears on these sheets five times in the six weeks leading up to Moira Heaton's disappearance. As far as I can tell, his is the only name that appears that frequently."

"That's kinda thin, ain't it?" Pete wondered.

I didn't answer directly. "You got the sheets in front of you. Anyone wanna tell Pete something else about Ishmail Almonte's visits to the community affairs office?"

Wit spoke up. "He saw Moira Heaton on all five visits."

"That's still thin," Larry Mac said. "Can't build a case on that."

"You're right," I agreed. "Now, I know the answer to this already, but I'm going to ask anyway. Mr. Spivack, how many people on these sign-in sheets have you or your employees interviewed over the last nineteen months?"

"Every one of them," he boasted, "with the exception of the deceased, the infirm, and people who've dropped off the face of the earth."

"Holy shit!" Detective Gloria was amazed. "Your client got some deep-ass pockets."

"And who interviewed Ishmail Almonte?" I continued.

Spivack squirmed. "I did."

"Why you?" I asked.

"Because I'm not blind. I was a U.S. fucking marshal for twenty-two years. It didn't escape me that his name appeared so frequently."

"And . . . ?" Detective Gloria prodded.

"And nothing," Spivack said smugly. "The guy's story checked out. He said he was an illegal and wanted to find out how to get a green card. He said Moira Heaton was helping him. I ran the guy's sheet. He was clean."

"Oh, please!" Larry Mac was skeptical. "He was clean 'cause he gave you a bullshit name."

Spivack turned an angry shade of red. "Listen, you second-guessing prick, ask your buddy over there from Missing Persons how many of these people *he* interviewed. Ten? Five? One? None? He had access to the same records I had. If the fucking NYPD did their job in the first place—"

Gloria jumped up. "Watch your mouth, asshole. I never met a fed worth his weight in piss."

"Okay, okay, this shit's gonna stop right here and now," I bellowed, pounding my fist on the table. "Right here and right now! Not one person in this room could've done anything to prevent what happened to Moira Heaton. Not one. If who I think did what I think, she was long dead by the time anyone even knew she was missing. So let's stop the name-calling and recriminations. To me, the only thing that matters now is that we find the guilty party and bring a little peace to the family so they can grieve. Agreed?"

They all nodded sullenly.

"Agreed, Mr. Prager," Wit repeated. "But evidently, you think this Ishmail Almonte is responsible."

"Sort of," I said.

"What's that supposed to mean?" Pete was curious.

I turned to Spivack. "I think we all realize you interviewed a ton of people in the course of the investigation, so no one's gonna get bent outta shape if you don't remember what Ishmail Almonte looked like."

"Twenty-five to thirty years of age. Light skinned, Spanish speaker with a Cubano accent. Some English. Five foot six or seven inches tall, one hundred forty pounds, muscular build. Shoulder-length black hair, full beard and thick mustache. Dark eyebrows, dark brown eyes, broken nose. No visible tattoos or scars, as I can recall. But you know all this. There's a copy of my interview notes in the file, Prager."

Wit was fascinated by a single detail. "How did you know it was a Cuban accent?"

"Seven years working in Miami-Dade'll make you an expert," Spivack said. "I can also smell a phony Cohiba from a mile away, for what it's worth."

Strangely, the tension in the room seemed to evaporate. Spivack finally relaxed. Wit lit a cigarette. Larry Mac loosened his tie. Pete Parson took off his jacket.

I pushed ahead. "What Spivack said before about my having a copy of his interview notes on Almonte is true. It's also the case that I looked them over before we came here. That's beside the point. It's not whether I looked the notes over that's important, but whether Spivack looked them over."

"I didn't."

"Come on, Joe." I was incredulous. "Out of all the people you interviewed over the last nineteen months, you remember some little Cuban guy you spoke to a year ago for no more than fifteen minutes."

"I remember a lot of them. You get good at remembering. I was a U.S.—"

"—fucking marshal for twenty-two years," Pete and Larry Mac recited in unison.

"Yeah," Pete chided, "we heard that one."

Everyone laughed, even Spivack.

"Fair enough," I said. "I still remember the faces of people I wrote up for spitting on the boardwalk, of all things. But *why* do you remember Almonte? Was there something about—"

"His eyes," Spivack mumbled almost to himself. "He had those chilly black eyes. You know, the kind that make it difficult to distinguish the pupils from the irises, wet and opaque like the ocean at night."

I reached into my pocket and unfolded the front page of yesterday's *Post*.

"Dead eyes. Eyes like these?"

"Fuck!"

Looking at Spivack's face, I knew. He knew. We all of us knew.

God slammed on the brakes and the world slowed down. My hearing changed too. I wasn't deaf, exactly. At first, it was quite the opposite. I became acutely aware of isolated sounds: the shuffling of paper, the chittering of office machines, individual rings of the phone, my own breathing. Then it blended together. It was like dipping your head beneath the surface of a pool at a party. All the music, the laughter, the chatter, melds into a muted, indistinct drone.

"Moe! Moe!" Larry McDonald screamed. "Are you all right? You look pale as a ghost."

I picked my head out of the pool. Now God hit the gas, the world spinning so fast I held on to the table for fear of falling off.

I heard Wit say: "Get him a drink." He would say that.

"I'm okay. I'm okay." I let go of the table. "It's one thing for me to have a theory, another thing for Spivack to recognize Ivan Alfonseca as Ishmail Almonte, but it's light-years from proving he abducted and murdered Moira Heaton. Until we do that, we got nothing, not even smoke and mirrors."

* * *

We took an hour-long coffee break, Spivack having assorted sand-wiches and pastries sent up from a local luncheonette. No one talked about the case itself. Although he was the only one of us without a law enforcement background, Wit spent enough time around cops to know this was not the moment to ask questions. Instead, we used the hour to bullshit, to trade war stories, to let off some steam. There was a small sense of relief, but not so the walls themselves sighed. The real hurdles were still ahead of us.

Just prior to starting up again, Spivack pulled me over to one corner.

"I feel like shit, Prager. I should have seen this months ago, but I've been preoccupied with the business. Maybe if I'd been paying more attention, I would have recognized him and—"

"Woulda, coulda, shoulda . . . Come on, Spivack, you know better. Your man had a full beard and long hair. If I didn't listen to the radio two days ago or see that front page on the subway yester-day, I'd still be tripping over my own dick. Anyway, like I said be-fore, it wouldn't have mattered if you put two and two together sooner. To Moira Heaton, it would've had no meaning. Her fate had already been decided."

"I'll see if that helps me sleep tonight. One more thing. I know it's your case now, but what's the reporter doing here? He could walk out of this room and blow any chance we got to nail that psycho motherfucker."

"First off, it's *our* case, all of ours. That includes Wit. Geary wanted him around, and wisely so. If and when we do get Alfonseca to cop to this, Wit's word will go a long way in giving credence to the process and reestablishing Brightman's good name and reputation. Besides, he has his own reasons for keeping quiet. He has no love for Ivan the Terrible, believe me."

Spivack was curious, but didn't push.

We spent the next few hours dividing up tasks. The first step was gathering some substantive evidence establishing that Ishmail Almonte was in fact Ivan Alfonseca. As Detective Gloria and Pete Parson had earlier pointed out, what we had to go on was thin. It was so thin, it would have been invisible if you turned it sideways. My conjecture about matching initials, the sign-in sheets, even Spivack's identifying Alfonseca, wasn't enough to get the most ambitious rookie ADA to do more than yawn. Spivack said he had a way to establish Almonte's identity and cement the connection between him and Moira.

Wit raised his hand like a third grader asking for a hall pass. "Someone has to say this, but, I suspect, none of you will appreciate it."

"Go ahead." Larry Mac, so comfortable with authority, gave him permission.

"While Moira does roughly fit the profile of the suspect's other victims—single, white, professional between twenty and thirty years of age, living alone, etc.—she does not fit the crime."

Actually, Wit was wrong. We'd all thought the same thing. At least I had. That very notion had made me hesitate after my initial enthusiasm. Wit was also right. Someone had to say it.

"He's right," Detective Gloria seconded.

Pete kept on. "He never killed any of his victims, Moe."

"Yeah, I was thinking that," said Spivack.

"He didn't kill any of the victims we know about," I corrected. "We know about these twelve women, but that doesn't mean there weren't others, others he killed. Look, no one's found Moira's body. Maybe he killed and disposed of some of his victims."

"That's a fine theory," Larry Mac damned with faint praise. "You're just chock-full of theories today."

"Okay, here's another," I said. "Alfonseca fucked up. I showed you Catherine Thigpen's account of the assault. He pressed his forearm across her trachea during the attack. She said she nearly lost consciousness because she couldn't breathe. You press a little too hard and . . . So now he's killed Moira, probably not his intention, but he has. He's not the panicky type, this guy. So he—"

Wit wept quietly. He cradled his face in his hands. His shoulders shook. None of us said anything, because none of us knew what to say. Men are useless in the presence of tears, their own or anyone else's.

"The son of a bitch who murdered my grandson claimed he hadn't meant to kill him." Wit forced the words out in fits and starts. "As if torturing him with pliers and electric shocks would have been fair sport had he not had the bad manners to die."

Spivack made a silent drinking motion at me.

"Bourbon," I mouthed.

He slipped out of the room, and quickly back in with a bottle of Maker's Mark. He poured Wit a stiff one. We watched him drink it. No one begrudged him his grief or the flimsy hedge against it he quickly emptied down his throat.

"What Mr. Prager has suggested sounds reasonable and likely to me," Wit said. "I just thought the inconsistency needed to be pointed out. He's explained it to my satisfaction. I'm now prepared to do my part in this."

That was good, because a lot of things had to break right for us to get anywhere near connecting Ivan Alfonseca to Moira's disappearance. The scary part was that even if we all did our share and got all the breaks to go our way, a great deal of what we needed was completely out of our hands. Ironically, we were as dependent on Ivan the Terrible's own ego and vanity as on anything else.

CHAPTER NINE

AN ENTIRE DAY AND ANOTHER NIGHT HAD PASSED WHEN I received the call. Katy said there was a Joe Spivack on the phone.

"Good news, Prager. I got it!"

"What?"

"The proof, the original sign-in sheets. I had one of the five dusted just to make sure we weren't wasting our time."

"And . . . ?"

"It's a match. And I don't mean a partial. He must have had something oily on his hands."

"Okay, so we *can* prove Almonte was really Alfonseca and we can tie him to Moira."

"Looks that way."

"Did you call Larry McDonald yet?"

"He knows. Called him the minute I got the results. You can exhale now, Prager. It's not just a theory anymore."

Although the theory was mine, I hadn't wanted to believe in it so much that I might be blinded to the chance I could be wrong. It seemed I needn't have worried. Beyond what Spivack had come up with, there was mounting evidence of Alfonseca's involvement.

Just yesterday, the doorman at Moira's building had identified a picture of Alfonseca. He said he thought he remembered a delivery guy who looked a lot like the picture. Posing as a delivery boy was a ploy Ivan had used to stalk many of his victims.

"Funny," the doorman said, "this guy looks like that guy in the papers." I agreed, not wanting to make too much out of it. And Sandra Sotomayor, Brightman's longtime aid at the community affairs office, thought she recognized Alfonseca as someone she'd seen around, but not for a while. "His face is very familiar." I asked if she might not be confusing this man with someone she might have seen recently in the papers. She said she didn't think so. While we couldn't exactly go to the bank with either the doorman's testimony or Sotomayor's, they would help if we had to go to a prosecutor. Hopefully, that wouldn't be necessary.

"You see the paper yet?" Spivack continued.

"No, not yet. Why, is it in there?"

"Is it in there? Are you kidding? That Wit guy came through in a big way. Wait'll you see the stories. Alfonseca's gonna go apeshit."

"Let's hope so. I'll speak to you later."

I showered and dressed, kissed Katy and Sarah, and headed to the newsstand under the subway station on Sheepshead Bay Road. Spivack was right. Wit had done more than we'd asked for. The *Post* headline said it all:

MYSTERY VICTIM SAYS IVAN WAS TERRIBLE

The story on page 3 detailed the saga of a woman, a thinly veiled Moira Heaton, who had been an intended victim of Ivan Alfonseca. The woman, abducted outside her office in late 1981, claimed to have been driven to an unknown location, where her abductor attempted to sexually assault her. Her would-be attacker, however, proved to be "woefully" inept. Frustrated and embarrassed, Alfonseca had strangled her, leaving her for dead. That was all she remembered, she said, having only recently awoken from a coma in an upstate hospital.

Of course the story was utter bullshit. The reporter credited several unnamed sources for the story and quotes contained within. Those quotes were full of particularly insulting and inflammatory adjectives. The alleged victim seemed very fond of the words "limp," "tiny," and "impotent." She said her attacker had "cried like a little girl when his laughable attempts at penetration failed." The story in the *Daily News* was equally damning. Wit hadn't bothered trying to plant the story in the *Times*.

I crossed the street to the bagel store and got a coffee. When the pay phone came free, I dialed Pete Parson's home number.

"Parson," he answered.

"See the papers today?"

"About old limp dick? Yeah."

"Your son's on today, right?"

"Don't worry, Moe, Captain Peter Parson Jr. of the Department of Corrections, City of New York, will make sure Mr. Alfonseca gets complimentary copies of today's papers and all the translation help he needs. Anyways, you know what Rikers is like. That story got back to him before the papers ever made the island. His *compadres* are probably whistling at him already, calling him *pato* and *maricón*. He'll go fuckin' nuts."

"Yeah," I agreed, "let's hear him brag his way outta this. Thanks, Pete, and thank your son for all of us."

"He's glad to do it."

Now there was nothing we could do but wait. I went to the Brooklyn store to do it.

* * *

I was wrong—waiting wasn't the only thing I would have to do. Klaus rolled his eyeballs as I strode through the doors of Bordeaux in Brooklyn.

"If I were you," he warned, waving several pink message slips at me, "I'd start digging myself a foxhole in the basement. If things get bad enough, I'll just shovel the dirt back over you."

"That bad, huh?"

"Worse. I don't know what you did to get these people so upset, but you did a very commendable job of it."

I snatched the slips out of his hand and walked back to the office, which, I had forgotten, was still in disarray. My life had been so consumed by the case that I had neglected to clean up after my all-nighter. The files were everywhere, spread all over the desk, the floor, and the adjoining room. I picked up enough to allow safe passage. I'd already suffered enough in my life from a careless piece of paper thrown on the floor. What I was actually doing was avoiding.

I turned on the radio, still tuned to the news channel which had first alerted me to Ivan the Terrible's existence. The papers, apparently, weren't the only branch of the media to run with the story Wit had so carefully planted. Someday, if I worked up the courage, I'd have to ask Wit how much personal capital this had cost him. I suspect he had called in more than a few favors.

I called John Heaton first because his pain and confusion would be worst of all, and lying to him would be most difficult.

"Where the fuck's my money?" he screamed in my ear. "It's been two days since you spoke to me."

Oddly, I was quite relieved. Either he hadn't yet seen the papers or he hadn't made the connection or he was too drunk to care. I wasn't about to ask which.

"How much do I owe you again?"

"Five."

"Okay, will you be at the club today?"

"After four."

"I'll be in later," I said.

"When?"

"Later."

"Cash." It was a demand, not a polite request.

"Cash."

I thought about calling Brightman back, but decided against it. Politicians can never be trusted to keep their traps shut, even when it's in their best interest. No, he'd have to stay in the dark. Thomas Geary, on the other hand, was technically my employer. If he hadn't called me first, he'd have stayed in the dark too. But he'd probably already called Spivack, who would have, as agreed, referred him to me. Unlike John Heaton, Geary would not be so easily placated.

Geary's wife, Elizabeth, picked up the phone. We chatted for a moment. She said the expected things about Katy. I thanked her on my wife's behalf and lied about what fun the fund-raiser at the Waldorf had been.

"Hold on, will you, please, while I fetch Thomas."

She placed the phone down softly. I could hear her retreating footsteps. Within seconds I heard another set of footsteps, these louder, much more rapid.

"How dare you tell Spivack not to talk to me? What are you playing at, Moe?" Geary demanded.

I decided not to pretend, but not to tell him the truth either. "Spivack's just following your orders. He's giving me his fullest cooperation. As far as playing goes, I'm not playing at anything."

"Then what's this nonsense in the papers. Obviously, this mystery woman is meant to—"

"Look, you told me to find out what happened to Moira Heaton. That's what I'm trying to do."

"But this, really!"

"If my work offends your delicate sensibilities, fire me. Otherwise, leave me alone and let me do my job."

"I hope this doesn't blow up in your face."

"Don't you mean *your* face. I'm working for you, remember?"

"Are you? That's odd, I must have missed something. I don't recall signing a contract with you or handing you a retainer or taking any sort of action one might reasonably construe as enlisting your services."

"Now who's playing?"

"I don't play."

"That makes two of us." I hung up the phone, hard.

I was several things, but not a fool. It hadn't escaped my notice that Geary had taken pains to make certain no paper trail existed tying him to me. No money had changed hands. My retainer would be discussed later, he had said. In politics it's called deniability. In Brooklyn it's called covering your ass. At worst, Geary could be accused of unwisely helping out a man who had once kindly employed his daughter. One thing was for sure, if the planted stories pissed Ivan off half as much as they'd pissed off Geary, the scheme would work like a charm.

Speaking of charms, I had to see if Larry McDonald's were working on the Queens district attorney. The plain truth was that no matter how outraged Ivan Alfonseca might be at the moment, he probably was neither crazy nor stupid enough to confess to kidnapping and homicide without some incentive to do so. Larry's assignment was perhaps the most difficult of all. He had to convince the DA's office not only to keep our plan a secret, but to offer something to Alfonseca in exchange for an admission of guilt.

In the topsy-turvy world of criminal justice, this was quite a dilemma. On the strength of his Bronx convictions alone, Ivan the Terrible was unlikely ever to see the light of day again. It was the inverse of buying a gift for the man who has everything. What could you offer a man who already knew he was going to prison for the rest of his miserable life? Never mind that the Queens DA was even more unlikely to complicate a high-profile, slam-dunk case with hypotheticals. It would have been different if Moira Heaton had been a confirmed homicide. Then the DA would have been happy to clear the case. But for now, maybe forever, Moira's would remain just one of tens of thousands of unresolved missing-persons cases.

Before I could dial Larry's number, the store phone rang. Klaus picked up.

"It's Ronald McDonald on the phone," Klaus snickered over the intercom. "Don't forget to order me two Big Macs and a large fries. Ask him if Hamburglar is dating anyone. I love masked men."

"Get off the phone, Klaus."

"Okay, boss."

"Larry, what's going—"

"Get your ass over to the Queens DA's office."

"Why? What's—"

"Shut up and get here."

*　　*　　*

It took less than forty-five minutes to get to the DA's office, but I wouldn't have been able to tell you anything about the ride. Although the sky was cloudless, I'd driven in a fog, unable to string memories from one minute to the next. I remembered getting into my car, and then, suddenly, I was there. Larry was waiting for me out front.

"What's going on?" I asked as I had earlier on the phone.

"Come on, the judge recessed today's court session for this. Alfonseca, his lawyer, and the DA are waiting for us upstairs."

"Waiting for us?"

"For you, really," Larry, said leading me to the elevators by the elbow. "Ivan won't talk unless you're there."

"He doesn't even know who the fuck I am."

A court officer was holding an elevator especially for us. We climbed in, the doors closing silently at out backs.

"Just like you figured," Larry continued, "Ivan went totally berserk this morning when word leaked back to him about the stories in the paper. He refused to leave his cell and demanded his lawyer come to Rikers to speak to him. Good thing Parson's son was on duty to smooth the way or this could've gotten nasty."

The elevator jerked to a stop. The court officer pointed out the way. Inside a conference room adjoining his office was Robert Hiram Fishbein, the district attorney for Queens County; Marissa Reyes of the public defender's office; and her client, Ivan Alfonseca. Fishbein, who bore an unfortunate resemblance to Groucho Marx, greeted our entrance with smiles. Reyes, a petite Hispanic woman of thirty, played it close to the vest, barely acknowledging our arrival. Alfonseca, however, looking small and ridiculous in a too-big polyester suit, fairly bristled with excitement at the sight of me. If he hadn't been cuffed to the table, I don't know what he would've done.

To his lawyer's shock and horror, he blurted something out in Spanish. Reyes tried not to show her dismay, but her eyes betrayed her. It didn't help her composure any when, at the conclusion of her client's brief tirade, he spat at me. He missed, catching Fishbein's pants leg instead. I recognized several of the words that had come out of Ivan's mouth: curses, mostly.

"Word for word, please," I said to his lawyer.

"Yes, Counselor," Fishbein barked angrily, wiping the saliva off his pants, "word for word."

She did not hesitate. "My client wanted to know if this was the lying faggot who had the bullshit printed in the papers about him."

I looked Alfonseca right in his dead black eyes, pointed at my chest, and said: "*Sí.*"

"Why?" he asked in English, looking almost wounded, before slipping back into his native tongue.

Reyes didn't wait to be asked. "He wants to know why you did that. He says it wasn't necessary. He says—"

Before she could continue, Alfonseca repeated: "*No fue necesario! No fue necesario!*"

She waited for him to finish. "My client wonders why you didn't come to him like a man and ask him if he did this thing?"

I bowed at him slightly. "*Lo siento.* I'm sorry. You're right, I should have come to you like a man."

"Okay," he said, smiling that cruel, superior smile.

"Now I'm asking, man to man, did you abduct Moira Heaton?"

Normally, this approach would have ruffled a lot of feathers, but this was way far away from normally. Fishbein understood he would never get this hard guy to talk to him. He had nothing to lose and an easy, high-profile conviction to gain. Visions of a press conference with himself standing between the mayor and the newly redeemed Steven Brightman danced in his head. Marissa Reyes, however, was not so quick to abandon procedure.

She put her finger to her lips. "Say nothing!" she admonished her client.

"*Puta!*" Ivan cursed at her. He hadn't enjoyed being ordered around by a woman in a room full of other men.

Reyes ignored him. "Before my client answers another question, we have to know what's on the table."

The DA wagged his finger at her. "Counselor, Counselor, what am I going to do with you? Come, let us talk in my office."

Reyes agreed.

Fishbein turned to Larry. "Captain McDonald, could you ask the court officer to please step in here and keep an eye on the prisoner? And why don't you gentlemen go grab a cup of coffee. This should take about fifteen minutes."

We took the hint. As soon as the court officer stepped inside the conference room, we retreated to the elevators. While we waited, Larry put out his right hand. Reflexively, I grabbed it with my right.

"You did it, Moe," he said. "You fucking did it. Maybe they should've given you that gold shield when you found that little girl. What was her name again?"

"Marina Conseco."

"Right. I gotta admit, it killed me to give you those damned files, but you pulled it off. Congratulations."

"Let's give it fifteen minutes and see, but thanks."

Before we could get on the elevator, Fishbein stuck his head out his office door. "Gentlemen, if you please, the conference room."

It had been a quick negotiation. Reyes had done the best she could for her client, something about a sentencing recommendation that would allow, if the judge agreed, a few of Alfonseca's sentences to run concurrently as opposed to consecutively. As hollow victories went, this ranked in the top five. Instead of getting out a week or two before the sun went dark, Alfonseca might get out of Attica in time to enjoy a scenic vacation on a star cruiser to Alpha Centauri. Basically, he was going to die in prison.

"Mr. Prager"—Fishbein addressed me directly for the first time, waving several folded sheets of paper at me—"Ms. Reyes has informed me that this is a full confession as dictated by her client, Mr. Alfonseca, this morning at Rikers. It is alleged to detail the abduction, assault, and homicide of one Moira Heaton by Mr. Alfonseca. He will not sign it, however, unless he can describe to you the contents of these pages. I cannot by law compel you to—"

"Let's get it over with."

For the next half hour I had to sit and listen to Marissa Reyes recite in English the intimate details of Moira Heaton's last hours on earth. As I did so, Ivan Alfonseca never removed his gaze from my eyes, nor did his cold expression much change. Only when he described actions which refuted the fabrications in the planted news stories did he smile that smile. He was a man who thrived on the distress and discomfort of others.

"Get this piece of shit out of here," Fishbein ordered after Alfonseca had signed the confession, initialing each page and any minor changes.

Reyes looked sick, but no more so than the rest of us felt. As they began to lead Ivan away, he pushed toward me. "Man to man," he said. "Man to man. No tricks."

I ignored him because I was distracted. Something was wrong. A detail was missing, a very important detail that everyone in the room seemed to have forgotten.

"He kept souvenirs from all his victims, right?" I reminded Fishbein. "That's why the cases against him are such slam dunks. Well, where's the souvenir from this crime?"

The DA looked as if my breath stank of raw sewage. How dare I throw a monkey wrench into his plans for higher office? Reyes had already translated my questions to her client. Ivan laughed, bowing to me as if to say thanks for the reminder. He responded quickly, giving what sounded like a street address to his lawyer.

"He says her jewelry is hidden in a bandanna behind the boiler of the building he was living in when you arrested him."

"Anything else, Mr. Prager?" the DA asked.

"No."

The court officer didn't need to be told twice, and Ivan the Terrible was gone. Reyes, still a little shaken, left shortly thereafter. Fishbein was on the phone to one of his investigators, giving the person on the other end of the line the alleged location of Moira's jewelry. When I started to head out, Larry shook his head no. We were to stay until the DA was done with us.

"So, Mr. Prager, Captain McDonald tells me you're the one who worked this little scam," Fishbein said as he put down the phone.

"I had help."

"So I hear." The DA frowned at Larry. "So I hear. And if we find the jewelry where that miscreant has indicated, this will be a very good day for all of us. Captain McDonald also tells me you're Francis Maloney's son-in-law."

"I have that dubious pleasure, yes."

"With all due respect, how is that nasty old prick?"

"The same, only more so."

Fishbein understood completely. He then turned his attention to Larry, speaking in vaguely threatening generalities. A police officer, especially one in the Intelligence Division, could get in a lot of trouble for sharing files and information with unauthorized civilians. At worst, he might lose his job and pension or do time. Even the sweetest prosecutor in town would have to ensure that such an officer would have no possibility of future advancement. On the other hand, such an officer might find it very helpful to his career to have a borough district attorney as a booster and ally. I interrupted Fishbein's rambling.

"Can I use your phone?"

The DA eyed me suspiciously. "It might be unwise to prematurely—"

"An up-and-coming prosecutor would be smart to stay and listen to my conversation," I said, parroting Fishbein's tone.

"Dial nine for an outside line."

Thomas Geary answered the phone. He had regained his composure from this morning and managed not to chew my head off before asking the purpose of my call.

"I'm sitting in a conference room adjoining the office of Robert Fishbein, the district attorney for Queens County."

Geary was unenthusiastic. "I'm well acquainted with Groucho Marx's stunt double, Mr. Fishbein."

"I believe he has some news for you," I said, and handed the DA the phone.

When I did, Larry McDonald gave me the thumbs-up.

"Yes, Thomas," Fishbein said, all the threat gone from his voice, "it's good to speak to you again as well."

For the next several minutes, Larry and I were treated to a somewhat skewed, if not completely inaccurate, description of the day's events. Though the DA was quick to highlight, even exaggerate, his role, he was savvy enough not to go too far over the top. After all, he had no way of knowing how much Geary or Brightman knew. Having concluded his chat with my employer and looking rather too pleased with himself, Fishbein handed the phone back to me.

"You did well, Moe," Geary complimented, sounding justifiably somber. "Though I am, for obvious reasons, relieved and happy at the results you have produced, I am at the same time sad for Miss Heaton's family."

"Watch it, Mr. Geary, you wouldn't want me to get the impression you actually have a heart."

"We can't have that, can we? I must confess to having had my doubts about you, but I could not be more pleased. You and the men who helped you will be well rewarded for their efforts. I would ask only that you not share this information with anyone until I've had an opportunity to—"

"I understand, but there are a few people who deserve to know. They'll keep it quiet if I ask them."

"To this point, your judgment has proved correct. I see no reason to distrust it now. On behalf of Steven and myself, please convey my appreciation. And, Moe, please ask them to make themselves available for the next several days. There's likely to be a lot of publicity connected to the resolution of—"

"I understand."

"I thought you might. Thank you again."

Larry and I waited with the DA until the call came in from the field. Though the detectives on the other end of the line could not be sure the jewelry they found was Moira Heaton's, it was, as Ivan had said, wrapped in a bandanna and hidden behind the old boiler. I half expected Fishbein to break into song or tap-dance on the conference table. I asked Larry to make the calls to the others.

"Where *you* going?" Larry asked.

"To tell a man his daughter's really dead."

* * *

Glitters was doing brisk business when I walked in. Rocky was working the door. I guess maybe Adonis was out getting his body bronzed or something. With his face so distorted by scar tissue, it was difficult to tell if the ex-pug recognized me or not. I didn't leave it to chance.

"Hey, remember me? You tried putting your right hand through my rib cage a few nights ago before your boy took batting practice on my knees."

"About that, John, he—"

"I don't really give a shit, Rocky. Let's just say you owe me one. Get John. I'll be waiting at the bar."

"Here." He gave me my ten dollars back.

I didn't have long to wait. People are usually prompt on pay-day, and John Heaton was no exception. Unfortunately for him, he was going to get a bonus he hadn't counted on. When he sat down next to me, I said nothing, but continued nursing my beer. I removed two white envelopes from my jacket pocket and slid them along the bar to Heaton.

"One's for you, the other's for Domino."

He had the good taste and good sense not to count it out in the open. Apparently, he still hadn't picked up today's papers. I ordered him a drink.

"Can't drink while I'm on," he said, but not in time to stop the barmaid from fixing his whiskey.

"Ever stop you while you were on the job?"

"No, but this ain't the job. Here they're fuckin' serious about it."

"Don't worry about it, Heaton," I said as the barmaid placed his scotch down in front of him. "They'll make an exception today."

He didn't touch it. "Oh yeah, and why is that?"

"Because the guy who murdered Moira just signed a full confession."

He froze in place. Only his face moved, and involuntarily, streams of emotions washing over his bloated red countenance so quickly I couldn't keep up. Finally, it was just a blank mask. "What?"

"You read the papers?"

"Not since—no, not in a long time."

"Drink your drink, John."

He did, in a gulp. I tapped the bar in front of him. The barmaid poured another. He drank. After the third, he was primed.

"It's ugly, huh?"

"Very."

"Tell me."

I didn't argue with him. He'd find out anyway. He was pretty stoic about it until I described how Alfonseca had disposed of Moira's body in pieces off City Island. That he couldn't bear and slammed his forehead down full force onto the bar. It split open like the skin of an overripe fruit, blood pouring down into his eyes, over his cheeks, swallowing up his tears. I told the barmaid to get Rocky. There was little doubt in my mind he'd know how to stem the flow of blood. As for the rest of it, there was nothing anyone could do to help.

CHAPTER
TEN

I'D BEEN TO METS GAMES LESS WELL ATTENDED THAN THIS
press conference. It seemed every media outlet in the free world
had sent at least one reporter and cameraman. Some of the local
TV stations sent both their police beat reporter and their political
analyst. Pete Hamill and Jimmy Breslin were there too. To say
there was a bit of a carnival atmosphere in the crowd would have
been an understatement. On its face, this was about Moira Heaton
and Ivan Alfonseca. Believing that was like believing Christ's last
supper was about the matzo.

This was many things, a sort of political smorgasbord with
something for everyone. Even with all the elected officials in the
room, there was enough free press and publicity to go around.
Mostly, however, this was about Steven Brightman, and everyone
understood as much. About five minutes after the jewelry was confirmed as having belonged to Moira, word began leaking out about
Steven Brightman's innocence. This so-called press conference
was to be a coming-out party, a resurrection of sorts, the kickoff of
his campaign for higher office, whatever office that might be.
Maybe it wasn't right, but I couldn't blame Brightman.

There weren't quite as many people onstage as in the audience. Fishbein stood at the podium, nearly buried behind a sea of microphones. Directly behind him were the mayor, the police commissioner, and Brightman and his wife. I stood in the next row between Larry McDonald, Robert Gloria, both resplendent in full-dress blues, Wit, Pete Parson, and a sad-faced Joe Spivack. Geary, as you might expect, stood in the wings. Also in the wings were John Heaton, forehead stitched and bandaged, his estranged wife, and his son. The wife and son had been flown up overnight on Geary's private jet. Domino was nowhere in sight.

"Ladies and gentlemen," the DA said, tapping the mikes, "good morning. I'm going to make a brief statement to be followed by a few words from some of the people who share the platform with me today. Then we'll take your questions.

"This is a day of mixed feelings. On a personal level, it is a profoundly sad day, while professionally, it is a uniquely satisfying one," Fishbein continued. "As many of your organizations have today reported, this office, in league with the NYPD, the Department of Corrections, and a team of private investigators, has finally determined the whereabouts of Moira Heaton, the young woman who, at the time of her disappearance nineteen months ago, was working as an intern for State Senator Brightman.

"Unfortunately, it is my somber duty to inform you that Miss Heaton is deceased. Our hearts and deepest sympathies go out to her family and friends. And to spare her family any further grief, I shall, at this time, refrain from discussing the details surrounding her untimely death. A written statement will be released later today. What I can say beyond a shadow of a doubt is that State Senator Steven Brightman has been completely and utterly exonerated in this matter. I can state this with such confidence because the man who abducted and subsequently murdered Miss Heaton, Ivan Alfonseca, popularly known as Ivan the Terrible, is in our custody and has signed a full confession which he himself dictated to his lawyer."

The mayor and police commissioner followed the DA. They said much the same thing as Fishbein, blowing their own horns in the process. It was just amazing. As I recall, neither man was at that meeting in Joe Spivack's office. I guess I must've missed something. But now it was time for the main event as Steven Brightman, his wife standing just over his shoulder, stepped to the podium. First a buzz rippled through the press corps, and then an expectant silence. He was not smiling, nor was he morose, again displaying his talent for understanding the moment.

"There is nothing for me to rejoice in today," he began. "As is often the case in life, when one dark cloud moves on, it is replaced by another, more sinister cloud. I would gladly take back the whispers and suspicions, the backbiting and silent accusations, which have plagued me over the last nineteen months in exchange for better news for the Heaton family. Alas, no such deal can be struck, and the Heaton family is left only to grieve.

"The rest of us, however, can take this opportunity, *should*, *must* take this opportunity not to grieve Moira Heaton, but to celebrate her and the thousands of selfless, dedicated young men and women like her across this great country. Moira could have gone to any number of fine law schools or to graduate school. She could have followed in her father's footsteps and become a member of the NYPD. But Moira took the road less traveled. She chose to commit herself to the democratic process and public service. And so, as her family grieves, let us applaud her. Let us not dwell on how her life came to an end, but rather on how she lived it. Let her life stand as an example to the rest of us." He bowed his head and took a long pause. There were dry eyes in the place, but not many.

"I have one brief thing to say in conclusion," Brightman continued. "Many people have already taken credit for getting to the bottom of this matter. Some rightly so." He smiled, turning and nodding at the mayor, the police commissioner, and the DA. That got a laugh from the press. "But there is one man sharing this platform with the rest of us who truly deserves the credit. He is the man who assembled the team, the man who put together the facts that led ultimately to Mr. Alfonseca's admission of guilt. He is a former member of the NYPD and a licensed private investigator." He turned fully around. "Moe, will you come up here please? Moses Prager, ladies and gentlemen."

I could not move. How, I wondered, could he do this to me? Why? Pete nudged me forward so that I was going to either walk or fall. Brightman shook my hand and shoved me onto a very isolated little island.

"This was a case to me, a case I was not anxious to accept," I said. "I am pleased to have successfully fulfilled my professional obligations, but the results are not the results I would have hoped for. I have two—no, three things to say. First, I could not have done this without the help of Y. W. Fenn, Captain Lawrence McDonald of the NYPD, Detective Robert Gloria of the NYPD, Peter Parson, NYPD retired, and Joe Spivack of Spivack and Associates. Second, on behalf of these men and myself, I wish to extend our condolences to the Heaton family. Finally, I would ask that any reward monies due me go to establishing a scholarship fund in Moira Heaton's name at her alma mater, Fordham University. Thank you."

The press started firing questions before I was six inches away from the podium. Thankfully, none of them were for me. A hand reached out of the crush of bodies on the platform and grabbed my forearm. It was Brightman's. Now he was shaking my hand.

"I think maybe I was wrong about you and politics, Mr. Prager," he said, beaming at me. "That scholarship thing was brilliant, just brilliant." That struck me as an odd thing to say. Once a politician, always a politician, I suppose. "Well," he went on, "I just wanted to thank you again. We'll be seeing you and your friends this evening, correct?"

"Tonight, yes," I said.

"Senator Brightman! Senator Brightman!" someone from the press corps called out, and he was gone.

* * *

10-9-8, located in an old meatpacking warehouse on the Lower West Side, was the most chic, coolest restaurant in town, which, in Manhattan, meant hardly anyone knew the place existed. Once its name appeared in the papers or in *New York* magazine, it would sizzle, making money hand over fist, but it would fall precipitately from grace. Popularity is a kind of a curse in the city, the great New York paradox.

Geary had sent a limo to pick us all up. Unlike this morning's press conference, there would be no somber pretense this evening. Tonight was about celebration, about showing gratitude for a job well done. I wasn't going to argue the point. In spite of my past successes, circumstance had conspired to prevent me from sharing them. At last, I had completed a case with no dark secrets to keep, no personal price to pay. The tragedies were someone else's.

We were shown into a private dining room inside what had once been a meat locker, the main design feature being stainless steel. Given Moira's fate, it seemed an odd choice, but even that wasn't going to upset me, not tonight. It was the usual cast of characters: Wit, Pete, Larry, Gloria, Spivack, Geary, Brightman, and me. Geary had promised a dinner at some later date, when things had settled down, that would include our families and friends.

The champagne was flowing and everyone seemed to be in good spirits. Everyone, that is, except the still rather dour-looking Joe Spivack. He had taken his failure to make the connection between Ishmail Almonte, Ivan Alfonseca, and Moira very hard and very much to heart. Not a man in the room blamed him for what had happened. Like I said before, sometimes it takes time and distance to see the things that are there to be seen. Though I wasn't particularly fond of the ex–U.S. marshal, I couldn't help but feel for him. I knew only too well what a case of the ifs could do to a man.

Dinner was okay, if you were fond of starvation. 10-9-8's chef's favorite ingredient seemed to be big, mostly empty plates. Clearly, he had read too much French existentialism and wanted to make a statement about the importance and isolation of the individual in a starkly judgmental world. Who knows, maybe Camus wasn't dead, but cooking in Manhattan.

I whispered to Pete, who passed it down, that I'd treat them all to their choice of a roast beef sandwich at Brennan & Carr's or hot dogs at Nathan's. The world knew Nathan's Famous in Coney Island, but only Brooklynites knew about Brennan & Carr's. It was situated at the strategic crossroads of Avenue U and Nostrand Avenue, and you could smell the roasting meat for blocks around. They'd slice you a hefty mound of buttery soft beef and then dip the bun in the rotisserie drippings. The sandwich fairly melted in your mouth. You just sort of chewed out of habit.

Following dessert—smaller portions on bigger plates—we all

split into groups of twos and threes, chatting, smoking contra-
band cigars, drinking port or cognac. The taste of the earthy,
sweet cigar made Joe Spivack smile in spite of himself. It seemed
to me he was transported back to his time in South Florida when
he was a part of the big agency and the spotlight shone a little less
brightly on an individual's mistakes. I didn't approach him for
fear of breaking the spell. All the alcohol was getting to me, and I
excused myself in an attempt to find a bathroom among the meat
lockers.

When I got back from the bathroom, they'd all returned to
their seats and Geary was giving a little thank-you speech to the
boys. He wasn't quite the speaker his protégé was, but few were.
He was just full of compliments for everyone and asked that each
of us speak with him privately before leaving. That was the Crocus
Valley in him. We were going to get our Christmas bonuses, but
not in a gauche, public display.

Then Brightman stepped up to speak. He hesitated, allowing
enough time for the waiter to fill our fresh champagne flutes with
Dom Pérignon. When the waiter left, Brightman did not launch
into one of his inspirational talks. He asked simply that we raise
our glasses.

"Gentlemen. To Moe Prager. A man who will go a long way
for an expensive meal."

"Here. Here," Larry seconded.

"Expensive, yes," I said, raising my glass, "but hardly a meal."

Even Geary laughed. The champagne, wonderfully cool and
yeasty, went down easily.

"I've done enough public speaking today for several life-
times," I said. "Good luck to Thomas Geary and Steven Brightman. Again, thank you all."

When I sat back down I noticed one of my business cards where the flute had sat before I raised it. I flipped it over.

There once was a man who with magic
Turned to good use events that were tragic
He was cleared of a murder with delicate aplomb
Because his men were blind, deaf, and dumb
And now he's free to run without static.

The handwriting was, as near as I could tell, the same as on the first card. Though the syntax had improved, the general theme remained consistent. Someone, a man most probably in this room, was not so fond of Steven Brightman as he pretended. I slid the card into my wallet to keep the first limerick company. Maybe someday I'd look into the authorship, but not tonight.

Geary called an end to the evening's proceedings. He and his boy thanked us again, individually, as was the plan. Brightman, of course, disappeared when the envelopes were passed out. I went last of all.

" 'Thank you' loses all meaning after a while, don't you agree?" Geary offered, shaking my hand with a genuine firmness I had not expected. "One day you may be able to say that you had a large part in turning this state, maybe the country, around."

"Please, I'm already a little nauseous. Don't make it worse. I just did a job and I got lucky and had a lot of help."

"You see," he said, smiling smugly, "never underestimate luck."

"Never."

He handed me an envelope. "Open it at home, please. As you requested, Steven has made arrangements for the reward money to be placed in a scholarship fund in Moira's name. I have added a matching check to that amount, and Steven has promised to set up a charity to continue adding to the scholarship. Strangely, Moe, it has been a pleasure knowing you. You're not at all what I'd been led to believe."

"Talk about a Jewish compliment."

"Yes, well, things don't always come out quite how you mean them. Please, if you ever need a favor . . ."

I left it at that.

None of us spoke much in the limo. To a man we were pretty well beat and several times drunk by any legal standard. Though we all kept our envelopes unopened, I noticed we all patted our jacket pockets with regularity to make sure they hadn't disappeared. No one seemed inclined to take me up on my offer of free food, and the limo emptied out one man at a time, until only Larry and I were left.

I asked the driver to pass by Brennan & Carr's before dropping me at home. I didn't get out. The place was closed, the spits had long since stopped spinning, but the aroma of the roasting meat had so thoroughly basted the air that my mouth still watered. It seemed every stray dog in the neighborhood had the same reaction. We must have been quite a sight, a long black limo stuffed into the tiny parking lot surrounded by a pack of hopeful strays. The back door opened and someone tossed out scraps to the dogs. Just then, Larry patted his envelope. It was time to move on, I told the driver. My appetite was gone.

CHAPTER ELEVEN

WITH THE FOURTH OF JULY TWO WEEKS GONE, SUMMER WAS IN
full bloom. I have always disliked characterizing my life as having
returned to normal, but it had, at least, returned to a familiar, comfortable rhythm. Even the pain of the miscarriage had ceased
hanging over the front door to our house like Passover blood, and
the hoopla surrounding the events of June had thankfully faded.

The funeral mass and memorial services for Moira were long
complete. Her mother and brother had returned to Florida, and
John was back to the business of drinking himself to death. Ivan
the Terrible had been replaced on the front pages by some other
psycho killer whose name lent itself to witty headlines. And the
men with whom I had shared a very intense few weeks had gotten back to the business of their own lives, all, of course, with a
bit more cash in their pockets and some with more brass on their
collars.

Captain Larry McDonald was now Deputy Chief McDonald.
Detective Gloria had gotten the bump up to first grade and been
moved out of Missing Persons and inside One Police Plaza. Pete's
kid had fulfilled a lifelong dream by exchanging his corrections

uniform for the blue of the NYPD. With the money he received, Pete Sr. finally felt comfortable enough to let his partners buy him out of his share in the bar. Apparently, he and his wife were seriously considering moving down south. Wit's piece on the resolution of Moira's death and Brightman's public absolution was to be the featured story in the August edition of *Esquire*, Aaron and I had received an amazing number of contracts from big catering companies, and our phone-order business was up 50 percent in a month. Coincidence had nothing to do with any of it.

The only person who'd dropped out of sight was Joe Spivack. Soon after the last of the memorial services and dedications, which we were all sort of required to attend, Spivack closed down his office in Brooklyn Heights and moved out of the city. No one knew where he'd gotten to, and, as none of us were exactly buddy buddy with him, no one seemed particularly concerned. To his way of thinking, he'd fucked up. Nothing anyone could say was going to change that. With time, maybe he'd come to see it differently. Oh, and that dinner Geary had promised that would include our families and friends, it never came off. That was fine. We had moved on.

I was certain we had, but Wit's phone call put a dent in that notion.

"Hey, Wit," I picked up, actually happy to hear his voice, "what's up?"

"I . . . I thought you might want to know," he said in a sort of odd monotone.

"Know what?"

"It just came across the wire. Spivack's dead."

"Shit! How?"

"He ate his .357 Magnum for breakfast yesterday."

Neither one of us was shocked by what he'd done or how he'd done it. There was a few seconds of silence between us.

"Where was he?" I asked.

"Up in the Adirondacks someplace. Apparently, he owned a cabin up there."

"Anything about a note?"

"Nothing in the wire story, no," Wit said, sounding a bit distracted. "I'll find out about the funeral arrangements and get back to you."

So, Spivack had taken his own forgiveness out of the equation. Some people are just more comfortable with punishment than forgiveness. Forgiveness is always a messy proposition; complicated, ambiguous, hard to accept. Sometimes a bullet is easier to take. I'd never put a barrel in my mouth, not in jest or in the depths of despair, but I'd been a cop. Cops understand punishment. They believe in it. On the job, they live by it. Some die by it too.

* * *

The coroner's report was straightforward enough. Joseph Spivack had consumed nearly a liter of 100-proof vodka before pressing the tip of his big handgun to the underside of his jaw above his Adam's apple and dispensing a single round. He had left no note, but even the most devout conspiracy theorist couldn't have spun much of a tale out of Spivack's death. Since closing down his firm, he'd spent most of his time drinking alone in his cabin. Still, his suicide made me uneasy.

He was afforded the honor of a pretty nice military funeral out at the Calverton National Cemetery on Long Island. There was no twenty-one-gun salute or anything like that, but there was a small honor guard and a flag-draped coffin. No family showed that I could tell. Some of his old marshal buddies and a few ex-employees came. Wit, Pete, and I were there. Rob Gloria and Larry Mac couldn't get out of work. Neither Geary nor Brightman was anywhere in sight.

When the honor guard finished folding the flag that had draped Spivack's casket into a taut triangle, an officer asked if there was a Mr. Moses Prager in attendance.

"That's me."

The officer approached. "Sir," he said, placing the flag in my hands, "I've been instructed to deliver this to you. On behalf of the United States Army, my condolences."

I was utterly and completely stunned. Though this must have been either a mistake or a very bad joke, the grave site was not the place to delve into it. As they began lowering his coffin, a Navy F-14 passed directly overhead on its way to the nearby Grumman plant. It was purely coincidental, of course, but we chose to ignore that fact and saluted the roaring jet.

We retired to a local bar. Kilroy's Place uniquely reflected the bulk of its clientele. The decor was an interesting mixture of Grumman and military paraphernalia ranging from fighter group patches to helmets to bayonets to a piece of a lunar module mock-up. In a place of honor above the bar sat a wood-and-glass framed flag just like the one I cradled in my arms.

"What do you think the flag thing is all about?" Pete Parson was curious to know.

"Fuck if I know. His life must've been sadder than we thought for him to have left this to me."

Wit was noncommittal, staring into his Wild Turkey as if it were a crystal ball. "He obviously respected you and the work you did for Brightman, Mr. Prager. You should be honored."

"Wit, I think the time has come for you to call me Moe. You think, Pete?"

"I suppose you two have dated long enough."

Wit liked that. "Okay, Moe it is."

Maybe because I had been ceded the flag, all the other attendees stopped by to reminisce. Two consistent themes emerged: Joe Spivack was one tough motherfucker and loyal as any man who'd ever lived.

"Even last year when the company started taking on water, he wouldn't let any of us go," Ralph Barto, a fellow ex-marshal and former Spivack employee, wanted me to know. "Anybody else would have started throwing anything that wasn't nailed down overboard, but not Joe Spivack. Somehow, he pulled us through. Even when he shut us down, we all got two weeks' severance. I bet you it came out of his own pocket. I don't know what you did to deserve that flag, mister, but it must've been something special."

"Hey, do you know why he rated such a nice funeral?" I wondered.

"No. I know he was early in Nam, even before Kennedy was shot, but that's about it. Listen, I'm out on my own now," Barto said. "Here's my card. If you ever need backup, I'm there."

On the way back into the city I asked Wit if he thought there might be a story in Spivack's suicide.

"No story for me," he said, "but there might be one for you."

He didn't volunteer a further explanation and I didn't ask him for one. I had a comfortable life that needed getting back to.

CHAPTER TWELVE

SARAH'S THIRD BIRTHDAY HAD COME AND GONE WHEN THE package from Florida arrived at the Brooklyn store. At first, I was as surprised by it as I had been by Joe Spivack's flag. Then I remembered that I had asked Moira's mother to send it up to me. Inside was a hodgepodge of the personal effects her mother had held on to during the nineteen months of her daughter's disappearance: pictures, a college ID, a ring of keys, her checkbook, some mail. Her mother had attached a handwritten note which included her good wishes that I find whatever it was I was looking for.

Although I considered it a blessing to have finally been involved in a case that I could hold at arm's length, I was daunted by my inability to make any emotional connection with Moira Heaton. I suppose I was saddened, too, by her inability to connect with people in life as she had in death. She would be remembered now, if only through the scholarship that bore her name. It had seemed painfully important at the time, just after the case had come to a head, to somehow discover the essence of Moira Heaton. Six or so weeks had surely numbed the ache, but I flipped through her things anyway.

I don't know what I had expected to find when I asked to see these things. Whatever it was, it continued to elude me. Flipping through her checkbook ledger, I did find one entry from a few weeks prior to her murder that got my attention:

CK NO.	DATE	CODE	TRANSACTION	PAYMENT/DEBIT
426	11/7/81	HNJ 1956	Headlines Search, Inc.	115.00

It stuck out for several reasons, not the least of which was the size of the check. After her rent, this was the biggest check she'd written in months. What could be so important to a woman making barely ten grand a year, I wondered, that she'd be willing to spend almost half a month's rent on it? Second, Moira was nothing if not consistent. She wrote the same checks for roughly the same amounts in the same order for months at a time. There was her rent, her phone bill, her electric, her student loan, and an occasional check written to the local supermarket. Page after page had the same entries, then, a few weeks before she disappears, bang! Naturally, I was curious about exactly what goods and/or services Headlines Search, Inc., had provided to Moira for her money. I didn't waste the time guessing and let my fingers do the walking.

"Media Search, Inc.," a woman answered, "how can we help you?"

"Was your firm once known as—"

"—Headlines Search, Inc.?" she completed the question. "Yes, sir. We are in the process of making the changeover, but unfortunately some of our ads continue to display our former name."

"What is it you do, exactly?"

"Why, are you from Dun and Bradstreet or something?"

"No, no, nothing like that. I'm actually a private investigator and I'm looking into a missing-wife thing," I lied casually. "I'm going through her financial records and I see she wrote a check to you guys about twenty months ago. I guess I'm just curious."

"Oh, you're an investigator. We do a lot of work with you guys."

"That's great, but it doesn't tell me what kinda work that is," I said, letting her hear a hint of impatience.

"Sorry. My name's Judith Resnick, by the way."

"Moe Prager."

"Well, Moe, as our name implies, we do searches. You give us a locale, a date, a subject, any sort of reference, and we'll look through the search area's media and collect related materials. Let's say a freelance reporter is relocating from out of state and he has to do catch-up on local politics. He names some names and we search available archives for his info. It saves him a lot of time and leg-work. For years after my dad founded the company, we only did newspaper searches. These days we've expanded to include radio and television as well. We even have computer hookups to libraries and a few police departments. Only public-record stuff, of course."

"Hence the name change."

"You got it, Moe."

"Sounds fascinating."

"Sometimes. Sometimes it could bore you to tears. Depends on the search."

"Makes sense," I agreed. "How comprehensive are your searches?"

"Again, that depends."

"On?"

"The parameters the client sets and the depth of his or her pockets."

"How'd I know you were going to say that?"

"Because you're a perceptive man," she said with a bit of flirt in her voice.

"Which only an obviously perceptive woman would spot. How big a search would a hundred and fifteen bucks have bought me two years ago?"

"Sounds like a limited-area-old-newspaper search. Something like a search for stories about how the influenza epidemic in the teens affected Des Moines, Iowa. See what I mean?"

"I get it. Listen, Judith, if I give you a reference number, could you—"

"Sorry, Moe, no can do. Confidentiality is as important to us as to you. And even if I were inclined to break the rules, I couldn't help you. The warehouse we store our old records in was gutted by fire about a year ago."

"Fair enough, but can you at least tell me if the reference number is one of yours or not?"

"Sure."

"HNJ1956."

"It's not one of ours. We don't use letters in our system, and our file numbers all have at least six digits. Sounds more like a license plate number. I wish I could be more helpful."

"Thanks anyway. One more question before I let you go, okay? And it's kind of goofy."

"Sure."

"What would a package from your firm look like?"

"That's not so goofy," Judith assured me. "You'd get a tasteful brown envelope stuffed with dated newspaper clippings and/or photocopies thereof. It's that simple. We don't do any analysis. We just provide source material."

I thanked her and asked that she mail me some material about her company. I thought I might have use for her services someday, and if not, I knew a journalist or two who might be interested. Okay, I had some answers, but they were the kinds of answers which led only to more questions. Moira Heaton had spent a chunk of money to have a company search old newspapers. What about and where those newspapers were located were still unknown to me. And what on earth did that reference number on the notation line in Moira's checkbook mean? Was Judith Resnick right? Was it a tag number? If so, from where? The biggest question of all remained: Did the search, whatever it was for, have the slightest significance in the scheme of things? Moira was dead, and nothing was going to change that.

I called Rob Gloria over at One Police Plaza and asked him to run HNJ1956 in all fifty states. I was careful not to mention the connection to Moira Heaton. Cops like their beer cold and their cases closed. They want nothing to do with poking around in the past, especially when their promotions are based on old, closed cases. I needed to be very careful with Larry Mac and Rob, so I lied to Gloria about this being a liability case. He said he was glad to run the tag number for me, but that it would take a while. I knew it would.

My next call went to Sandra Sotomayor at Senator Brightman's community affairs office. She was in a very upbeat mood these days, and why not? She'd hitched her cart to a man whose potential could now finally be realized. When Brightman moved into the governor's mansion in Albany or the Senate Office Building in D.C., there was bound to be a high-level position and a fat paycheck waiting with Sandra's name on it.

"Mr. Prager, how good to hear from you."

"Thank you. Things pretty busy these days in the Brightman camp?"

"Busy, yes, but good busy. If you know what I mean?"

"I do. Listen, Sandra, Moira's family has asked me to do a little research on her. You know, they're curious about how she spent her last few months, what kind of stuff she was working on. I guess they want to feel she wasn't wasting her time. I'm sure you understand."

"Absolutely, Mr. Prager. I'll be happy to help you any way I can."

"Does the reference number HNJ1956 mean anything to you? Could it be a file number related to Moira's work?"

"Sorry. That number don't match anything in our office. Sounds like a license plate, no?"

Well, we were building a consensus on the license plate theory, but not much else.

"Sandra, what kind of work was Moira doing before—Was it anything that required her to do private research?"

"I'm not sure I understand. All research we do is for the people who live in our district and is funded through our budget. Now if Moira was doing some related research on her own, I would have no way of knowing that."

"Okay, Sandra, thanks a lot. Do you think if I needed to, I could come down one day and look over the stuff Moira was working on when she disappeared?"

"It's pretty boring stuff, but sure. Anything for you, Mr. Prager. You're a big hero around here."

Sandra was nice enough, but she needed a major priority readjustment. I was no hero. Heroes rescued people, not political careers.

Two pitches, two strikes. I was way behind in the count. I tried Moira's mom down in Florida. She, too, was glad to hear from me and asked if the package she'd sent had done me any good. I told her it was too soon to tell. I asked about Moira's apartment in the months after she disappeared. I wondered who cleaned it, who picked up her mail. She explained that she could never bring herself to clean the place. She thought it bad luck.

"We paid Moira's rent for the first year," she said, her voice quivering. "John and I took turns with the other stuff like collecting her mail. Why, is there something in particular you're interested in?"

"A large brown envelope from a company called Headlines Search, Inc. I know it's a long shot, but—"

"Would it have been filled with newspaper clippings?"

I couldn't believe my luck. "That's the one."

"What about it?"

"Do you remember what the clippings were about or where they were from?" I asked, gripping the phone hard enough to crack it.

"I'm sorry, but no, Mr. Prager. I don't think I even looked at them when I saw what they were. They were just old newspapers to me."

"That's okay. You had a lot on your mind."

"Is it important?"

"To tell you the truth," I confessed, "I don't know. I guess I'm just really curious about Moira and maybe those clippings could have told me something. That's all."

"Maybe you should talk to John. He might know what happened to that envelope. I don't remember throwing it out or anything."

I tried the reference number on her and she voted for the license plate theory as well. We said our good-byes, each wishing the other well.

Well, I hadn't struck out. Not yet, anyway. There *was* a package. It had clippings in it. Where it had gotten to, however, was now to be added to the mystery list. I picked up the phone to call Brightman and put it immediately back in its cradle. Maybe Moira was working on a special project for him, but Brightman, I realized, would be even less interested in me stirring up the ashes of this case than either Rob Gloria and Larry Mac. The cops had only been promoted in rank, while Brightman was on the threshold of political beatification.

* * *

Katy was intrigued as to why I was begging off dinner, but she knew not to press me on it. I promised to fill her in when I got home. Aaron, on the other hand, would not be so easily placated. It was one thing to have me miss work in order to save the business. It was something else again to have me blow off work to go chasing mysteries of my own creation. And that's what this was, a creation of my own curiosity. Moira's confessed murderer would be safely behind bars until the Second Coming. Ivan Alfonseca had been meticulously detailed about the whys and hows of his crimes against Moira. So there was nothing about this missing package of news clippings that would shine any new light on Moira's death. Enough light had been shined there, anyway. I guess I was hoping the package would shine a little light on her life.

Adonis was back at the door at Glitters. He remembered my face, waving me in without even bothering to ask for the ten-buck cover. I'm not sure I liked that. It's one thing to get a free pass at

Madison Square Garden or the Metropolitan Opera. It's quite another to get one at a third-rate strip joint in Times Square. Hopefully, I wouldn't be making any more return trips and I'd be removed from the most-favored-clientele list.

John Heaton was at the bar, and one didn't need blood work to tell he was hammered. Either the rules about drinking on the clock had changed or he was done with his shift. Under almost any other set of circumstances, I would have avoided further contact with him. Frankly, I didn't much like him, and my distaste for the man had only worsened since the confession. Whereas the news about Moira had come as a sad relief to Moira's mother and given her some sense of closure, it had had quite the opposite effect on John Heaton's already charming personality. If anything, it had shortened his fuse and made his drinking worse—not a good thing for him or anyone else. He'd shown up to Moira's memorial plastered out of his gourd with Domino in tow, nearly coming to blows with a reporter.

"Well, look who it is," he sneered, waving his scotch at me. "Tawny, pour the man a Dewar's."

My initial reaction was to refuse the offer, but if I was going to get him to talk to me, I couldn't afford to piss him off, at least not right away. I noticed Heaton kept looking at the empty stool to his right. There was an unfinished beer and a half-smoked cigarette burning in an ashtray in front of the empty stool. Domino's stuff, I supposed.

"Thanks for the drink." I accepted it with a smile and a nod.

"So what the fuck are you doing here?"

"I wanted to—"

"You wanted to what?" He raised his voice, edging forward on his stool.

"To ask you—"

Now he was up and in my face. "Ask me what?"

"Why don't you sit back down, John?"

"Fuck you. You and your fuckin' friends all made fistfuls a cash off my daughter's bones. What, you come sniffin' around to see if you could pick up some spare change?"

"Why don't you shut your mouth and look in the mirror, Heaton? I just came here to ask you a question about a package Moira re—"

He grabbed my shirt, balling my collar inside his fists. "See, I fuckin' knew it. You and your buddies—"

"This has nothing to do with my buddies, John, so leave them out of it. Now if you don't take your fuckin' hands off me, I'm gonna have to—"

He didn't wait to hear the end of my threat and let go of my collar with his right hand. That wasn't necessarily a good thing given he still had hold of me with his left. He cocked his right arm, but because most of his red blood cells had been replaced by scotch, his movements were slow and cumbersome. The punch, however, was quick enough, his knuckles grazing my cheek as I forced my head against his restraining hand. If he hadn't still been holding on to my collar, I might have been able to avoid the punch altogether. The near miss just pissed him off, rage twisting his face into something ugly and barely recognizable as human. He reared back, but never got the second punch off. The cavalry had arrived in the body of Preacher "the Creature" Simmons.

"What the fuck you think you doin', John?" Simmons's voice cut a wide swath through the din and darkness. His massive hands locked on to John Heaton's shoulders. Heaton, no shrimp himself, looked like a scale-model human against the backdrop of

Preacher's six-eight frame. I was suddenly very happy the empty barstool hadn't belonged to Domino.

"Thanks," I said, rubbing my neck where Heaton's left fist had dug into my flesh.

"What you want?" Preacher asked impassively.

"To ask your friend a question."

"Ask it," Heaton spoke up.

"Your ex-wife says you received a package of newspaper clippings just after Moira disappeared."

"Yeah, what about it?" he wondered, shaking free of Simmons's grasp to reach for his drink.

"You remember it?"

"Yeah, so . . . Why you wanna know?"

"Your ex sent me some of Moira's things because I was interested in getting to know who she was," I confessed, figuring the truth might be worth a try. "It's not any more complicated than that."

"I threw it out. It was just a bunch of old newspaper shit, nothing at all to do with my girl."

"Can you remember where the clippings were from or what they were about?"

"I don't know. You'll have to forgive me," he mocked, swigging the remainder of his scotch, "but I wasn't paying much attention."

"Anything, do you remember anything?"

"Something about a bike, I think, a kid and a bike. That's all. Something like that, a kid and a bike. I'm not sure. Now if you don't fuckin' mind . . ."

I left, nodding good-bye to Preacher Simmons.

If that drunk asshole was right, and the clippings were about some kid's bicycle, I really was just chasing my own tail around for no good reason. On the other hand, Heaton was currently so liquored up, it was impossible to know if he had been telling me the truth in there or if he even knew what the truth was. Walking to the car, I found myself wishing John Heaton was correct. I was way too distracted by this, and even my industrial-strength curiosity couldn't build much of a mystery out of old newspaper stories about a kid and his bike.

CHAPTER THIRTEEN

IF THE LICENSE PLATE THEORY WASN'T DEAD, IT WAS PROBABLY a dead end. HNJ1956 was indeed a current tag number in six states, but five of the states were west of the Mississippi, three of the plates had been issued since Moira's death, and two of the plates were assigned to cars owned by women over sixty years of age. Even if I had been inclined to look into it any further, I couldn't see how a license plate issued to a sixty-year-old grandmother in Wyoming or Utah related to old newspaper clippings about a kid and a bicycle.

Klaus came back to the office to take his lunch break. As he was clearing off the desk, he noticed the pad on which I'd written down the information about the license plates.

"Utah, huh?" he kind of mumbled to himself.

"What about Utah?"

"If there was any *what* in Utah, boss, I wouldn't be living in New York," he said, his turned-down lips hinting at the pain behind his flippancy. "What's this, HNJ1956?"

"I thought it might be a license plate number."

"Well, 1956 was the year my brother Kirk was born. Maybe

it's somebody's birthday. You know, Harold Nance Jacobson, born 1956. Or maybe it was the year someone died."

Bells didn't quite go off in my head, but Klaus had a point. It's an amazing thing how the human mind works, how different minds process the same information to divergent ends. I'd been focused on HNJ1956 for over twenty-four hours, yet it had never occurred to me that HNJ could be somebody's initials, nor had I seen 1956 as anything other than the individual numbers 1–9–5–6. Once Judith Resnick had suggested it was a tag number, my mind seemingly closed off other interpretations. I'd have to be careful to keep that lesson in mind.

There was more to recommend Klaus's analysis beyond its simply being different from mine. It resonated. I didn't have to perform mental gymnastics to see the potential connection between someone's birthday and newspaper stories about a kid and a bike. But what kid? What bike? Whose birthday? Like everything else since I'd first flipped through Moira's checkbook ledger, each possible answer gave rise to more questions.

As I walked the aisles of the store, distractedly dusting and straightening bottles, I tried imagining how I might be able to replicate the newspaper search Moira had paid for a few weeks before Ivan Alfonseca had strangled the life out of her. Even if Klaus was exactly right that HNJ1956 was a group of initials followed by a year, it wasn't enough. Or as my old philosophy professor was fond of saying, it was necessary but not sufficient. I tried anyway.

Judith Resnick, though happy to hear from me, wasn't very encouraging. Even if I could tie the initials HNJ to the year 1956 and could further tie those two elements to newspaper articles written about a kid and a bike, it probably wouldn't do me any good, not as far as her company was concerned. Not only would it take an eternity to search through all the archives, but it would cost a fortune. "Certainly more than a hundred and fifteen bucks," she said.

The bottom line was this: I needed to come up with a specific name or geographic region in order to replicate or approximate the search Moira had paid for. Until then, I was just spinning my wheels.

The other line started ringing before I hung up with Judith. I told her I had to go. She apologized for not being more helpful and let me know she'd already mailed out that brochure I'd asked for.

I picked up line 2: "Bordeaux in Brooklyn."

"Hey, you gimpy Jew fuck, how you doing these days?" It was Larry Mac.

"Don't tell me you got promoted again. What is it now, chief of the Sioux Nation or grand wizard of the Klu Klux Klan?"

"Shut up or I won't take you and Katy to dinner this evening."

"Call 911."

"Why?"

"Because I'm suffering from auditory hallucinations. I could swear you just said you were inviting Katy and me to dinner."

"Asshole, that's what I said."

"Then call 911 anyway, because now I'm gonna have a heart attack."

* * *

The Blind Steer, located only a few blocks away from 10-9-8, was one of the oldest steak houses in New York City. I suppose, like 10-9-8, it had been trendy once, probably around the time Lincoln was giving the Gettysburg Address. Even if you didn't know its exact address, you could spot the life-size red, white, and blue neon steer swinging above its front door from all the way down Ninth Avenue.

Larry Mac was waiting for us at the bar when we arrived. I was surprised to see him alone. I had just assumed his wife, Margaret, would be joining us. When Katy asked after Marge, Larry was kind of vague about the reasons for her absence. Now I *was* suspicious. Earlier, on the phone, Larry had said he had been meaning to take us to dinner since his promotion, that it was the least he could do for me. He explained how the promotion had come so swiftly and as such a shock to him that he hadn't even had time to arrange for the time-honored tradition of a promotion party. That was true. Rob Gloria hadn't thrown his yet either.

Larry signaled to the maître d' that his guests had arrived, and we were shown to a prime table in a private corner of the dining room. While Katy and Larry studied the menu, I studied Larry. As was the norm, he was impeccably dressed in a black linen suit over a gauzy white shirt. I always admired that about Larry—he had an abundance of substance and style. That he had taken us here to celebrate was another indication of that. Yet, there was an unfamiliar tension in his expression that I could not decipher. He seemed to be working too hard at his usual easy charm.

Without a sign, verbal or otherwise, a waiter in a long white apron came to the table carrying a bottle of Mumm Cordon Rouge. Larry offered toasts to me, to Katy. We toasted his successes, current and future. All the toasting out of our systems, we ordered dinner. The food was excellent, the aged beef melting like butter in our mouths. The meal was all so splendid, but there was also that tension Larry had brought with him as an escort. It held tight on to Larry's arm, whispered in his ear even as he ate and made small talk. I wondered if Katy noticed it too. Tonight was about more than just saying thanks. There was definitely some-thing besides steak on my old friend's plate.

After dessert, Larry ordered cigars and three Grand Marniers in heated snifters. Katy excused herself as a darkly attractive young woman in a black satin cocktail dress came to the table tot-ing a humidor. Though not her equal, her looks were reminiscent of Steven Brightman's wife. She placed the humidor before Larry and opened the mahogany box in a very formal, almost ritualistic manner. I half expected her to recite some ancient incantation. When the high priest had selected two cigars, he pressed a folded bill neatly into the woman's right palm. She closed the box.

Larry ran a cigar under his nose, taking in an exaggerated breath.

"All right, Larry, what's going on?"

He laughed a little self-satisfied laugh, clipping the end off a cigar and handing it to me. He repeated the motion and used the out-side of his pinkie to sweep loose bits of tobacco off the white table-cloth. Katy and the waiter arrived back at our table simultaneously.

The drinks served, the cigars lit, I noticed Larry's escort had seemingly vanished in a haze of smoke. The tension was gone. Larry reached into his pocket and placed a small, unwrapped box on the table in front of him.

"This," he said, sliding the box toward me, "is yours if you want it. No strings attached."

Though it was nauseatingly clichéd, I picked up the box, plac-ing it to my ear. Then, almost involuntarily, I shook it. I think I knew exactly what it was the second I felt its weight. I had a replica of one in my sock drawer at home.

"Open it, for chrissakes!" Larry prodded, cigar smoke gush-ing from his mouth.

My hand trembled. I immediately put the box on the table and hid my hands beneath the tablecloth.

"Open it, Moe," Katy urged, curiosity getting the better of her.

My hands somewhat settled, I placed one on the box and slid it to Katy. "You go ahead."

She removed the lid without a moment's hesitation and gasped. Katy's too-thin lips formed a smile fraught with a sense of deep-seated satisfaction. It was the kind of smile you smile not for yourself, but for your kids, or for your team when they pull off an impossible comeback. Katy slid the box back in front of me.

Inside was a hunk of gold-plated metal in the shape of a glittering nine-pointed star. Within the rim of the star was a field of cobalt blue enamel. At the center of the rich blue enamel was more gold in the guise of a Dutchman and an Indian standing on either side of an eagle perched atop a coat of arms. The words CITY OF NEW YORK POLICE formed a gilt-lettered horseshoe around the central symbol. Beneath the symbol was another word: DETECTIVE. In a rectangle below was the number 353.

"The pay ain't great and the hours suck, but it's yours for the asking," Larry rephrased his earlier offer. "You can take Gloria's spot in Missing Persons. If that doesn't move you, you can work a precinct or inside with me. It's your call. In me, you got a rabbi and a Dutch uncle all wrapped up into one."

I heard a voice that sounded like mine say: "Thanks, Larry. I . . . I don't know what to—"

"Don't give me an answer now," he said, squeezing my shoulders. "There's no rush. I know it's a surprise and you're running a successful business and everything. I'm sure you and Katy and you and that brother of yours got a lot to talk about. Call me in the next few days and we'll discuss pay and grade and benefits and that crap."

"This on the up-and-up, Larry?"

"Just as if you got that promotion they fucked you out of in '72 when you found the little girl."

"But my knee, the pension stuff."

"Hey, didn't Rabbi Larry just tell you he'd take care of it? If you didn't notice, schmuck—sorry, Katy—you solved a case involving a cop's daughter. A case no one in this town wanted to touch with a ten-foot pole. You made a lot of people happy, Moe, a lot of people. Forget Geary and Brightman, everybody from the Queens DA to the mayor got mileage off this. Why shouldn't you get what you've always wanted? Believe me, buddy, I had no problem smoothing out the bumps to get you that shield."

"Thank you, Larry," Katy said, reaching for my hand. "You're right. We have a lot to talk about."

I pushed the box toward Larry Mac.

He winked, pushing it back. "You hold on to that. Try it on for size."

We finished our drinks in a sort of peculiar silence. Standing up to leave, I noticed that my barely smoked cigar had put itself to sleep. Larry had meant it to be a kind of victory cigar to celebrate my return to the job. It was good, I thought, that I hadn't smoked it. There was nothing to celebrate, not yet.

* * *

The silence followed us from the Blind Steer home to Sheepshead Bay. Katy understood without needing to be told that there was nothing simple or easy about the decision with which I was now faced.

To the casual observer, even to some participants, all silences can seem equal. But there are differences in silence as there are in darkness. The absence of sound or light reveals little about what has caused the silence or the dark. There is a difference between a broken bulb and a moonless night, no? So it was with my silence. Katy understood one piece of it, the piece I gave her access to. There were, however, layers and textures in my silence to which she was not privy. Once before, in 1978, at a restaurant in Bay Ridge, I'd been offered a detective's shield. And though there was much about the current offer that bore no relation to that situation, there were certain undeniable similarities impossible for me to ignore.

Rico Tripoli, the closest friend I ever had or was ever likely to have, had brought me into the case of Katy's missing brother. At the time, it seemed like a perfect fit. Both parties, the Maloneys and myself, were just desperate enough to take a chance on each other. The Maloneys had exhausted all conventional options in the search for their son. As for me, I was just retired, in terrible pain from my second surgery, and flat out of ideas on how to raise the money for my share of the business. I think I would have tried almost anything. But Rico, as it happened, hadn't brought me in to find Patrick at all. No, I had been brought in to play the fool, to be used as a conduit to leak information that would ruin my father-in-law. Ultimately, I managed to both find Patrick and ruin his father's career, accomplishing the latter without exposing his family to the pain and embarrassment my users had intended for me to unleash.

Understand this, I despise my father-in-law, Francis Maloney Sr. He is a cruel, calculating bastard who, through God's mysterious grace, helped create my wife. I haven't lost a second's sleep in five years over his loss of political sway, nor would I shed a tear on the day of his death. But the notion that my best friend, a man whom I had trusted with my life, had set me up and betrayed our friendship for career advancement has plagued me every day since. Rico's handlers had wanted to gift me with a shield for my keeping my mouth shut and a job well done, kind of like rewarding a dog with a treat for giving his paw and rolling over. I took a pass. I didn't do tricks.

In spite of the quiet in the car, it was noisy in my head. I kept telling myself that this time it was different, that Larry wasn't like our old precinct mate, Rico, that he was high enough on the totem pole not to sell me out. I told myself that it was different this time because I had done good for the right reasons, like when I found Marina Conseco. Not because I felt guilty or threatened, but in spite of those things. Sure, luck had played a part. It always does.

It wasn't luck I was worried about. I was worried about me. That, I decided, was what this apprehension and jitteriness was all about, not the past, not betrayal. Was I up to it? Could I handle the job after so long away? For years I had wanted that shield so badly I could taste it. Now, with all that had gone on, the miscarriage, the second store, did I really want it anymore? My father-in-law, of all people, had once warned me to watch out what I wished for. Did wishes, I wondered, have a shelf life? How long after you stopped wishing could they come true?

CHAPTER FOURTEEN

I SLEPT LIKE A BABY. THERE WERE NO OMINOUS DREAMS IN which Larry morphed into Rico or the cigar girl into Brightman's wife. There were no dueling pistols in the humidor, nor was my father-in-law dressed like a jester. He did not cackle or forewarn. I don't think I dreamed at all.

When I got up, Katy talked around Larry's offer. Eventually we'd get around to discussing it, but there was little doubt she would tell me to follow my heart. As it had once led me to her, she knew to trust it. She also understood I needed to speak to Aaron first of all. Dealing with my big brother would be a more complicated affair. Beyond the obvious issue of our business partnership, he had never really approved of my being a cop. It was Aaron who breathed the biggest sigh of relief when I was put out to pasture. I had every reason in the world to believe he would not be so accommodating as my wife if I chose to go back.

"I'm going to—"

"I know where you're going, Moe. Kiss your brother for me."

I was around the corner from City on the Vine when fire engine sirens began blaring. I pulled to the right. So did the guy behind me, but instead of pressing his brake pedal he used my back bumper to slow his forward momentum. Several decades past the age when I considered cars something worth fighting over, I got out of the driver's seat calm as could be. Besides, it had only been a hard tap. Unfortunately, the guy who hit me was in his early twenties and in no mood to deal with reality or responsibility.

"Why the fuck you stop so short? What the fuck you—"

I put my palms up. "Whoa. Take it easy."

"Don't fucking tell me to take it easy," he barked, leaning over the nose of his car. "Look at this shit."

Frankly, I didn't see what shit he was talking about. Beyond the old dings and dents in my bumper, there didn't seem to be any fresh damage. His bumper, though pretty well flush to mine, did not appear any the worse for wear.

"I'll pull up a few feet," I said, turning toward the front of my car.

He grabbed my arm. "Wait a second, motherfucker. You ain't running on me."

He had just taken two big steps over my patience threshold. I yanked my arm toward the point where his thumb and index finger met, easily freeing myself, grabbed my old badge out of my back pocket, and shoved it into his face.

"How's your eyesight, asshole? Can you seen that well enough?"

"Yeah, yeah, yeah. I'm sorry. I'm sorry. I—"

"This moment here is when you shut up. Like I said, I'm going to pull up a few feet so we can see if there was any real damage done."

This time, he didn't grab me. Even if he was so inclined, he was too busy rubbing his face to make sure my badge hadn't left a permanent impression. I inched the car forward. When I returned to the back of my car, the other guy was on his knees now rubbing his front bumper instead of his face.

"Everything looks okay," he said sheepishly. "Why don't we just forget about this, okay?"

Then he mumbled some other words that seemed to run together. Something funky was going on with my ears. It was just like that day in Joe Spivack's office. I noticed distinct sounds rising out of the din: a jackhammer, the squeal of truck brakes, a guy begging quarters and cursing people when they said no. Then it all fused together.

"Hey, hey, Officer," he prodded, gently shaking my arm. "You okay?"

"Yeah, fine," I said.

"What you staring at? Your eyes look kinda weird. You bang your coconut or something? You sure you don't want me to call an ambulance?"

"Your license plate," I mumbled.

"What about it?"

"The Garden State," I read aloud.

"New Jersey, yeah. So what?"

"NJ. Do me a favor, name some towns in Jersey."

"Look, Officer, I said I was sorry. There's no need to fuck with me. I—"

"Do it!" I shouted.

"Paterson, Marlboro, Newark, Trenton, Camden, Cherry Hill, Hoboken, Alp—"

"Hoboken, HNJ. Thanks, buddy." I shook his hand and gave him a business card. "You ever need a favor, you gimme a call."

He looked at the card. "I thought you were a cop."

"I can't make up my mind."

I got back in my car and found the parking lot Aaron and I kept reserved spots in.

Aaron tilted his head at me like a confused dog. "It's your day off. What the hell are you doing here?"

"I have to make a call."

"You feeling all right, Moe? You came all the way to the Upper West Side on your day off to make a call? Everything okay with you and Katy?"

I took the box that held NYPD detective shield 353 out of my jacket pocket and handed it to my big brother. "I came to talk to you about that, but just at the moment I need to make a call."

"Don't let me stop you. You own half the place."

Instead of continuing to the office, I stopped to look around. Sure, I still came to this store once or twice a month, but in some sense I had moved on. Bordeaux in Brooklyn was my store now. I walked back up front and brushed my fingertips against the five-and ten-dollar bills from our first sales. And mounted just below the bills, a picture of our dad, his tentative smile an impossibly inadequate armor against the pain of his failures.

"He'd be proud, wouldn't he? Of us, I mean." I turned to Aaron.

"Of course he would."

Certainly more proud than he was of my career as a cop. Like Aaron, my dad had disapproved. I always suspected the watch my parents gave me when I graduated the academy was mostly my mother's doing.

Now Aaron was completely perplexed. "Are you sure you're okay?"

"That's a popular question today."

"And what am I supposed to do with *this*?" He held up the shield.

"Hold on to it while I make that call. I'll be in the back."

Judith Resnick was surprised, but not at all displeased to hear my voice. If nothing else, she joked, I deserved a commendation for persistence.

"How would you like some work?" I asked.

"Work's what we're here for. Believe it or not, Moe, I don't sit around here all day just waiting for your calls. What you got?"

"Finally something besides questions. I think I know what HNJ1956 stands for. H is the first letter of the name of a town and the NJ stands for New Jersey. The 1956 is self-explanatory. At least, I hope it is."

"Now that's information I can do something with," she said, brightening. "How'd you figure it out?"

"A license plate."

"But I thought you said—"

"Judith, it's a long story not worth telling. Take my word for it." Then I reminded her about the kid and the bicycle, how that might help narrow the search.

"There's a lot of towns in New Jersey that start with an H, Moe: Hackensack, Hoboken, Hasbrouck Heights, Ho-ho-kus, Hillside. . . . Even if I were to charge you rates from ten years ago, it would still cost a lot more than a hundred and fifteen bucks. So where does that leave your theory?"

"There's a big difference. The woman who paid for the initial search knew what town she was looking for. I don't."

"Good point."

"I can send you a check right now to get the search going and pay the balance when you're done. Does that work for you?"

"That's fine, Moe. I'm going to get some of my people started on it immediately."

"How much of a deposit do you want?"

"To start off, a hundred and fifteen bucks sounds about right."

I liked Judith. She sounded almost as into this as I did, and all she had was money at stake. I didn't even have that. All I had was curiosity. I hoped that would be worth something in the end.

There was a knock on the office door.

It was my brother. "You off the phone yet?"

"Yeah, who wants to know?"

"NYPD, Detective Prager," Aaron burst in, holding up the shield like on TV. "Confess, punk."

"Or what, you gonna start discussing the relative merits of varietal grapes?"

"Exactly."

"Okay," I said, "I did it."

He sat opposite me. "So, little brother, I guess this means good-bye." He tossed the shield onto the desk. "It's not like I thought this day might not come, but shoving that thing in my hand wasn't exactly the most subtle approach. Why didn't you just pay a guy to skywrite it over Brooklyn? It would have saved you the trip."

"Sorry about that. Besides, I haven't made up my mind yet. Right now, it's just an offer."

"Don't take me for a *yutz*, Moses. You're going back, because you have to. It's unfinished business for you. You wanna be like Daddy, always wondering what could have been? I won't let you do that."

"You won't let me, huh?"

"That's right. What, you think you're the only insightful one in the family, that Miriam and me are brain-dead?"

"Not Miriam."

"Fuck you." He raised his hand playfully. "I know that you only got involved in the business for my sake. This was never your dream. Christ, Moe, it's only even half mine. A lot of this is for Daddy. Your share of the business will be here when you get back. I suppose you know this means we're gonna have to hire new help and give Her Royal Highness, Klaus, a raise."

"I know. Thank you, big brother." I stood, walked around the desk, and hugged Aaron. I hugged and kissed him.

"What was that for?"

"For Katy. She told me to kiss you. I guess maybe she knows you better than I thought."

"Make us proud, Detective Prager," he said.

CHAPTER
FIFTEEN

AND SO IT WAS DONE. IF I COULD STILL SHOOT STRAIGHT, I WAS to be reinstated as of September 26, 1983. My physical exam had already been seen to, the doctor conveniently neglecting to examine my knees. I would be a detective third grade. In the interim, I'd be back at the academy a few days a week brushing up on changes in the law and procedure. To get a feel for where I might want to be assigned and to get my feet wet, I would also be doing ride-alongs with different detective units. As Larry Mac kept reminding me, this wasn't just like getting back up on the horse. I'd grown used to regular hours and the easy life. Five years away from the street had taken the edge off.

If Katy had any mixed feelings about my return to duty, she hid them well. Like Aaron, she understood that this was an opportunity that would not come again. She knew this wasn't going to last forever. I was going to hit forty in a few years, and unlike Larry McDonald, I had no ambition beyond detective. Katy also got that detective work tended not to be very dangerous stuff. I think if they had offered to put me back on the street, Katy wouldn't have been nearly so gung ho. Nor would I.

Aaron was as good in deed as in word. Maybe even a little too good. Initially, he resisted the notion that I take a cut in my share of the business. In the end, though, he saw the wisdom in doing it my way. He was taking on a huge burden and deserved to be compensated for it. A wise man once said you can't have a fifty-fifty partnership if one of the partners does one hundred percent of the work. So he gave Klaus a raise, began interviewing new people, and elevated my old buddy Kosta to manager. Kosta, whose previous claim to fame had been managing failed punk bands, nearly fainted at the prospect of earning a substantial income.

Then the envelope came. I recognized it the moment the mailman pulled it out of his pouch. It had been ten days since I had spoken to Judith Resnick that last time. The check was mailed, and in all the fuss surrounding my return to the job, I'd nearly forgotten HNJ1956. It had receded to that place where curiosities go when left immediately unfulfilled. I remembered back to the first time I'd heard Moira Heaton's name. Thomas Geary had spoken it to me at his daughter's wedding. A wedding that now seemed long long ago. I had been so curious the next day, that Sunday, when I went to Pete's place. Then the curiosity had faded. If Geary and Brightman had not elected to rekindle my interest, Moira would have been forgotten like a windblown leaf tumbling across my path.

The envelope was the shade of a paper grocery bag. I held it in my hand for what seemed like a half hour but was probably no more than twenty seconds. It was both thick and light, as one would expect an envelope stuffed with newspaper clippings to be. Walking to the office, I wondered whether I should bother opening it, or just let the past be. Moira was dead. Her murderer was behind bars. Nothing in this packet was going to change that.

Looking back, I felt almost stupid for having pursued the matter with such fervor in the first place. In some ways it had all been about my ego. I thought I owed John Heaton an apology. Maybe I'd get around to it someday.

I tossed the envelope in the trash, but realized there was a balance due. If I didn't open up the envelope . . . Screw that. I'd call Judith and get the tab and thank her personally.

"Hello," a younger, unfamiliar female voice answered, "Media Search, what's up?"

"Is Judith Resnick there?"

"She's not in. Her dad passed away yesterday."

"I'm sorry to hear that. Do you have an address I can send—"

"Hold on, yeah, here it is. Twenty-four Montrose Place, Melville, New York 11747."

"Thanks," I said distractedly as I jotted the zip down. "If you don't mind me asking, to whom am I speaking?"

"Janey."

"Are you an employee, Janey?"

"Nope. They're all at the funeral. I'm a temp, just here to answer the phones today."

"So I guess you wouldn't be able to help—"

"Mister, if it don't involve picking up the phone, I can't help you."

"Thanks again, Janey."

I had a basket of fruits and chocolates sent to the house at 24 Montrose Place and then fished the Media Search, Inc., package out of the trash. The least I could do was to pay the bill and get on with the newest chapter in my life.

I dumped the contents of the envelope out onto my desk. There was less inside than I had thought, about forty photocopies of newspaper stories and an invoice. Most of the girth of the envelope, as it happened, resulted from a thick layer of protective stuffing. Ignoring the clippings, I plucked out the invoice. The balance was a tidy one hundred dollars. Attached to the invoice was a note from Judith.

Moe—

Sorry, but this is all we came up with. Though you asked for only 1956, we found one story in particular that reappeared for several years hence. We included those articles at no extra charge to you. Hope this is what you were searching for. Maybe we can have a drink sometime.

Regards,

Jude

It turned out that 1956 was a big year for bicycle giveaways in New Jersey towns that began with the letter H. I suspect that was true in many towns across the country. Nineteen fifty-six was a prosperous year, a good year unless you were a Communist or a Brooklyn Dodger fan. In Washington, D.C., those two disparate affiliations were often seen as one.

In Hackensack, a boy named Jeffrey Bigelow won a Schwinn for his eleventh birthday by simply entering his name in a drawing. Annie Gault won a pink Huffy in Hobbs End and Calvin Brown, a bright Negro student at St. Mallory's, as the *Hoboken Journal* described him, won a Raleigh English Racer. The saddest story, and the only one I thought might have interested Moira, was about Hildie Steen, an eight-year-old girl who was dying of an incurable childhood disease. These days we call that cancer, but back then you didn't write the words "child" and "cancer" in the same sentence. Hildie had been given a two-wheeler by Hasbrouck Bicycles for her birthday, but died before it was delivered to the hospital. I put that story aside.

The remainder of the clippings referred to the story Judith had mentioned in her note. It had nothing to do with promotional give-aways or little girls with incurable diseases. It had to do with homicide. The stories were in chronological order. The first one, dated October 17, 1956, was from the *Hallworth Herald*.

MAYOR STIPE'S BOY MURDERED

Hallworth, N.J.—Carl Stipe, the nine-year-old son of Mayor Michael James Stipe, was found murdered last evening in the woods near the reservoir. The boy had been reported missing by his mother earlier in the afternoon when he failed to return home from school at the expected time. The case has already been turned over to the New Jersey State Police, who have thus far refused comment. No details about the condition of the body or cause of death have been released. One member of the search team that combed the woods did say the boy's bicycle seemed to be missing. The mayor and his wife are . . .

Other, more detailed stories, from bigger area newspapers, appeared with headlines like **STIPE'S SON SUFFOCATED BY STICKS, STOLEN BIKE STILL MISSING, STATE POLICE STUMPED. DRIFTER PICKED-UP, DRIFTER RELEASED, STIPE DRIFTER DROWNS.**
Even couched in the less graphic language of the day, the pa-

pers detailed a rather gruesome murder. The police theorized that Carl Stipe had been attacked while taking a popular shortcut home from a friend's house. His attacker had knocked Carl off his bicycle and had tried to molest the boy. The cops pointed to the boy's torn clothes as proof of this. But the boy must have struggled and started to scream. In order to keep his victim quiet or to satisfy some deviant fetish, the attacker grabbed a stick and shoved it down the boy's throat. That first stick snapped and the attacker shoved in another stick, then another. The sticks blocked his trachea, and the Stipe boy quickly suffocated.

The attacker panicked and, using the boy's bicycle, fled. Unfortunately, the leaves and pine needles that covered the ground near the crime scene and the windy weather made it impossible for the police to retrieve any tread or footprint evidence. The only lead the cops had concerned a "drifter" two town kids had spotted leaving the vicinity on a bicycle. The boys, acquaintances of the victim, could not say for sure if the bicycle was Carl Stipe's.

About a week later, a man named Andrew Martz was picked up for questioning in the nearby town of Closter. Martz, with no current address and a history of psychiatric problems, seemed like a good fit to the state police. However, the town's boys could not positively identify him, nor did the state police have any physical evidence tying Martz to the victim or the crime scene. They were forced to release him. Some weeks later, Martz's body washed up on the New York side of the Hudson. He had drowned, but whether it was homicide, suicide, or an accident, no one could say.

After Martz had turned up dead, the interest in the story faded. Most folks in the area simply accepted that Martz had been the guilty party and got on with their lives. The following October an article appeared in the *Hallworth Herald* marking the one-year anniversary of the as yet unsolved murder of Carl Stipe. Articles just like it appeared every year until 1968. By then, Vietnam, the civil rights movement, the assassinations, the space program, the Beatles, and free love had squeezed out the memory of a murdered little boy.

Then in 1974, articles of a completely different nature began appearing. Carl Stipe's murder had apparently given rise to a peculiar Halloween ritual. Teenagers, most not yet born when Carl Stipe had been murdered, would dress like either Carl Stipe or Andrew Martz, meet in the woods by the reservoir, and reenact the murder. They'd light a bonfire and hold a séance, trying to contact the dead boy's spirit. By '76, the local cops had put an end to the macabre ceremony. The last mention of the murder came in a 1980 obit for the former mayor of Hallworth, Michael James Stipe.

It was all very interesting and terribly sad, but not any more connected to Moira Heaton than Annie Gault or Calvin Brown or Hildie Steen. Maybe John Heaton, drunk as a skunk most of the time, had gotten it wrong about the kid and the bicycle. Maybe he was just fucking with me. Whatever HNJ1956 might have been, it was no longer of concern to me. I wrote out a check to Media Search, Inc., for the balance, attached a note of condolence, and stuffed it into an envelope for tomorrow's mail. And if I had any lingering doubts, they were put to rest by Sandra Sotomayor when she rang me up later that afternoon.

"Hey, Sandra, what can I do for you?"

"It bothered me for a long time after you called about Moira and that file, so I went back to look over all of Moira's work. I found a file where she was helping a woman try and locate a man she had immigrated with in the fifties. I see here that the man's name was Hernando N. Javier"—enunciated with the perfection of a native speaker—"and Moira made a notation, HNJ1956. There are copies of notes from Moira to the INS and from the INS saying they needed more information to locate the man. I think Moira was doing this thing for the woman on her own."

"You're probably right, Sandra. Thank you very much."

So I had been sent on a wild goose chase by John Heaton and spent two hundred bucks to read sad, old newspaper clippings. My maternal grandmother, Bubbeh, we called her, never read a newspaper or listened to the news a day in her life. Aaron once asked her about it.

"Jews, ve got tsuris enough of our own. Ve don't need to borrow from strangers."

She had a point.

CHAPTER SIXTEEN

NEVER THE BEST SHOT ON EARTH, I STILL MANAGED TO QUAL-ify at the range. Up to that point, I had been reluctant to let Katy start inviting people to the reinstatement/promotion party she, Aaron, and my sister, Miriam, had planned. I'd just finished doing a ride-along with detectives from Midtown South and I was pretty well wired. Oh God, how I remembered that feeling, the bizarre combination of elation and exhaustion. I wanted a drink, but the detectives who'd been saddled with me all shift long had families on Long Island that needed getting home to. I decided to kill two wild turkeys with one call.

Wit was glad to hear from me and even more pleased to share a drink. Although he had not profited directly from the solution of Moira's murder, his exposé on Brightman in this month's *Esquire* had thrust him squarely into the limelight, a place he rather much enjoyed. He was now the subject of nearly as many interviews as Steven Brightman.

He offered to have me to the Yale Club again, but I declined. I thought we might do the Yale Club for dinner another time. Katy, I told him, was a bit of an Ivy League wannabe and would just be thrilled to enter the realm of the Elis. He told me to consider it done. I decided Pooty's, Pete Parson's soon-to-be former bar, would be a good place to meet. I could get that drink and invite both of them to the party.

Pooty's was doing brisk business. Pete, wearing a rather sour puss, was working up front with a bartender who made Joey Ramone look tan and healthy. Not only was this guy sickly looking, but he moved at a pace somewhere between super slo-mo and catatonic. He aspired to lethargy. Pete's face brightened when he noticed his two newest customers.

"You want me to jump back there and give you a hand?"

"Thanks, Moe, but don't worry about it. Hey, Wit." Pete reached over and shook our hands. "One Wild Turkey rocks, one Dewar's rocks coming up." Pete placed them on the bar and took a moment to share a Bud with us.

"Can that guy move any slower?" I asked.

"Are you kiddin'? This fucking guy's so slow we have to scrape the moss and barnacles off him after every shift."

Wit liked that. "Can I steal that line, Pete?"

"You, Mr. Fenn, can take anything you'd like. It's because of you this joint is so crowded."

"How's that?" Wit wondered.

"Your *Esquire* article," Pete said. "Look around and behold. This ain't our regular crowd. When you mentioned me and my kid and this place . . . And it was perfect timing, too," he chortled. "My buyout from my partners is based partially on this month's sales."

That got my attention. "You mentioned Pooty's?"

"I'm crushed," Wit said, putting a hand to his heart. "You haven't read the piece?"

"Oops! Sorry, Wit. I've been a little preoccupied lately. By the way, I wanted to talk to both of you about that. Katy and my brother and sister are throwing a little party for me on September 28 at Sonny's in Brooklyn."

Pete squinted suspiciously. "A party?"

"To celebrate your what, exactly?" Wit was curious too.

I pulled out shield number 353. "On the Monday following the party, you two will have to refer to me as Detective Prager."

"Holy shit! Congratulations, Moe." Pete reached across the bar and patted my back. "I know it's what you always wanted. Okay, everybody, listen up!" Pete shouted the barroom to a hush. "Your next round is on the house. We're celebrating." He leaned over to Wit and me. "Excuse me, guys. I gotta help Mr. Inertia over here. I'll join you in a few."

Wit's reaction was more reserved, his journalistic skepticism switch-locked in the on position. "Yes, Moe, congratulations. This detective thing is sudden, isn't it?"

I gave him a brief rundown on the offer. "I guess it was Larry Mac's way of saying thanks. He owes me from way back and he knows how much it means to me."

"Yes, exactly. He knows how much this means."

"Look, Wit, I got screwed out of a shield a long time ago. Then I turned it down once. I'm a big believer in the rule of threes. If I turn it down now—"

"I'm sorry, Moe. Please forgive me. It's just the reporter in me. I see conspiracies hidden in every good intention. An occupational hazard, I suppose."

"That's okay, Wit. Cops suffer from a similar syndrome. Just ask Pete."

Wit didn't ask Pete. Instead, he led a toast to me with the free round of drinks our host had provided. He was rather eloquent in his praise and hope for my future success, yet his skepticism had put a damper on things. Not that you could tell by how we were acting. By ten that night, Pete had performed "Danny Boy" three times, once as Donald Duck. Wit had done several card tricks and regaled the bar with stories of the rich and the dead. Not so talented as my friends, I simply drank myself silly.

* * *

Dry-mouthed and nearly sober, I found myself pacing the kitchen floor at four in the morning. I would have given anything for the house to not be so quiet. When paranoia and suspicion are toying with your head, a quiet house can be your worst enemy. It wasn't so much what Wit had said that bothered me, it was more the way he'd said it. And his face! It was evident he thought I was somehow being bought off. Now I regretted not having discussed it with him further.

I guess I shouldn't have cared about what Wit thought. He drank a little too much and was too attracted to the sound of his own voice, but he did have good instincts. You didn't achieve his level of success without them. I'd gotten pretty far in my life by attaching myself to people with Wit's feel for things. Whether it was Katy or Aaron or the cops I'd worked with who could sense trouble coming around blind corners, my attraction to these people had put me in good stead. So I was unable to dismiss Wit's reaction.

As I was about to find out, I was right not to dismiss it. But not even Yancy Whittle Fenn could have conceived how right he had been or why. When, after my third glass of water and second dose of aspirin, I found I still couldn't sleep, I finally opened the copy of

Esquire Wit had sent me weeks ago. Although I was awake and nearly sober, my focus was severely lacking. I found myself drifting off, rereading the same sentences over and over again. Two things kept me at it: a picture of Joe Spivack, and something I had scanned but not processed. Then I relocated the sentence and realized my world was about to change again, forever. Just making sense of the words had changed it.

It was a throwaway sentence, a simple biographical fact that Wit or his editor might just as easily have omitted as included. This was the sentence:

Then, in June of 1957, Steven Brightman's family moved across the Hudson to New York from the bucolic little town of Hallworth, New Jersey.

Suddenly, every assumption I had made over the past few months was called into question. Not only were those assumptions suspect, but the facts upon which they were based had, in the course of a few seconds, turned from granite to quicksand.

CHAPTER SEVENTEEN

I HAD SPENT THE REST OF THAT EARLY MORNING PIECING together a rough chronology. Although a little unclear about some of the exact dates, I was confident my time line was accurate enough. Having things written out really helped me see certain causal relationships that had earlier escaped my notice. For instance, Larry Mac's offering me my shield followed closely on the heels of my initial conversation with Sandra Sotomayor about HNJ1956. And wasn't it convenient of Sandra to supply me with a perfectly reasonable explanation of Moira's connection to HNJ1956 on the very same day I received my package from Media Search, Inc. This, in spite of the fact that I hadn't asked her about it for weeks. I believe in coincidences as much as the next guy. To swallow these, however, would require more faith than I currently had on account.

There were other, far more disturbing conveniences and coincidences, but to make any sense of them I would need help. Problem was, the people I would usually go to for assistance had been compromised. They were now all so invested in keeping the stench of scandal off Steven Brightman, I couldn't be absolutely sure I'd be able to trust them. An outsider looking at this set of circumstances might well make the same judgment about me. If I pretended to have never read Wit's piece and forgot all about HNJ1956, I'd have my dream fulfilled. Unfortunately for the guilty party, no dream of mine or anyone else's was worth two murders and a suicide.

I was about to attempt quite a precarious balancing act. The challenge was picking my stage assistant. There was only one candidate I could count on for the job, one who would not give me away, intentionally or otherwise. This trust was not based on something so facile or unsavory as self-interest or personal gain, but on the death of a man's grandson. I dialed Wit's number for the second time in two days.

* * *

The ride out to Hallworth from Manhattan took less than half an hour. Before picking Wit up at his hotel, I'd stopped at the Brooklyn store to retrieve the clippings from Media Search, Inc. Just as on our trips to and from Long Island, we rode in near silence. Wit looked through the clippings as I drove and scanned the map. We had already discussed strategy on the phone, and what was there to say, really?

Coming into Hallworth, we crossed over a tiny one-lane bridge, the wood plank roadway sighing from the strain. Beneath us, an endless freight train lazily clanked its way along lonely tracks, blowing its mournful horn as if to announce our arrival. We were here, after all, to unbury the dead. I pictured Carl Stipe, his bicycle leaning against his hip, tossing rocks off the tiny bridge at passing trains.

Hallworth was a town of big hills, green carpet lawns, and lush, gnarly trees. Beyond the big Victorian manses scattered about the little hamlet, there was something palpably old-fashioned about this place. If you hid the cars parked in the driveways along Main Street, a time traveler might say he'd landed in 1935 instead of 1983. There was a comfortable feel to a place where bulldozers and wood chippers had yet to lay waste to vast tracts of land. Everything was grown in, grown up, or grown over. I liked that. I also liked how the asymmetry of the streets actually depended more on topography than on some greedy developer's vision. There wasn't an artificial cul-de-sac as far as the eye could see. Wit and I agreed that it much resembled the town we'd seen glimpses of in the clippings about Carl Stipe's murder. It wasn't hard to fathom how traumatic such a crime had been in a place like this.

We parked out in front of the *Hallworth Herald* offices on Terrace Street. Terrace Street seemed to be the only street in town dedicated to commerce, and that dedication was halfhearted at best. It wasn't Rodeo Drive, not by a long shot. There was a quick mart, a pizzeria, a video store, a dentist's office, a shrink's, and a druggist's.

The *Herald* was a storefront operation with green linoleum floors, a pressed tin ceiling, and desk legs held together with nails and adhesive tape. There was a beat-up TV in one corner, and a radio, too. Each of the five desks in the office was covered in mountains of paper under which typewriters and telephones were the only recognizable features. Curled and yellowed ads and articles were thumbtacked to the walls in between framed front pages from past editions. Stories about Carl Stipe's murder were conspicuous by their absence.

Only two of the desks were currently occupied. Seated closest to the door was a mousy woman of indistinct age. She had stooped shoulders and pale skin, and smoked a cigarette that seemed surgically attached to her lower lip. Toward the rear of the place was a real old-timer. He was bald on top and gray on the sides, and looked like he hadn't eaten since a week ago last August. Maybe he was too busy sucking on his pipe to be bothered with food. Neither the cigarette nor the pipe seemed anxious to help us. I cleared my throat loudly enough to get their attention.

"Can I do something for you gentlemen?" the old guy spoke up.

We walked back to his desk, the mousy woman paying us no mind at all. When we got closer to the ancient mariner, he slipped on a pair of wire-frame glasses.

"I'm Y. W. Fenn," Wit announced with the proper blend of conceit and humility. "This is my driver, Moe."

"Micah Farr," the old man stuck out his right hand, "editor in chief, reporter, copyboy, and dishwasher. To what do we owe the pleasure of a visit from the great Yancy Whittle Fenn?"

Wit and I exchanged knowing glances. We recognized Farr's name from the Stipe murder coverage. Farr had done all the local reporting, some of his stuff getting picked up by bigger papers.

"Call me Wit."

"Everybody calls him Wit," I chimed in.

"Okay, Wit, what brings you to our fair hamlet?"

"Steven Brightman. I did a piece on him—"

"—in *Esquire*. Yeah, I read it. Good work."

"Indeed. Thank you. My concept is to do a follow-up about what shaped and influenced Brightman, a sort of prequel to my *Esquire* exposé. In it, I'd delve into his early years here in Hallworth and then across the river."

"Nice idea," Farr agreed. "No doubt now that he's been

cleared of suspicion in that poor woman's murder, the ambitious little bastard's set his sights on the next Senate race. When he announces, you'll have your piece all set to go."

Wit winked at the reporter. "Why, how cynical of you, Mr. Farr."

"Yeah, I guess so. By the way, call me Mike."

"Everybody call you Mike?" I wondered.

"Nah, everybody who knows me calls me an old prick, but since we're just getting acquainted, Mike'll do for now."

We all had a good laugh at that. Mike explained that the girl at the front desk was his niece and how she'd had the misfortune of catching the journalism bug early in life.

"Learned at her uncle's knee, I'm afraid. Too bad. She'll end up like me," Farr bemoaned, "old, lonely, and forgotten."

Wit changed subjects. "We were curious if you could take a few hours to show us around. You know, point out the old Brightman house, where he went to school. If you have any old anecdotes about him or could introduce us to some people who knew him. I'll credit you in the piece."

"Love to. We haven't had a juicy story of our own since . . . well, not in a long long time. Not much happens around here. Which is a good thing, I suppose. Annie can hold down the fort. Can't you, dear?" he shouted to her.

She just waved.

We put Farr in the front seat next to me. Wit sat in the back. The old reporter guided us through a series of lefts and rights, pointing out houses that he thought were particularly pretty or that had been designed by famous architects.

"These are the greenest lawns I've ever seen," I said without really meaning to.

"Yeah," Farr agreed, "the town is patrolled by lawn police. If they find any brown spots, a truck comes by that night and sprays it to match your grass."

He took us by a country club that was rimmed by beautifully trimmed hedges. Besides their meticulous upkeep, the hedges were remarkable in that they were of varying heights, widths, and lengths. Yet from our vantage point it was impossible to discern a coherent pattern.

"They're pretty amazing, aren't they?" Micah Farr was almost boastful. "Word is, they're even nicer in an aerial view. The rumor is that from above they spell out 'No Jews.' "

"How pleasant," Wit remarked.

"We got other country clubs let everybody in, but the hedges ain't as pretty. Brightman's old man used to be a member here. That's why I showed it to you."

"A lot of anti-Semitism in Hallworth?" I asked.

"Not really, no. Even here, it's not true anymore. The town's changed over the years, but not very much. That's the glory of this place, people don't really change it. It changes them, almost always for the better." Farr was wistful. "It's why I've stayed all my life."

Finally, the old reporter took us to the woods by the reservoir where Carl Stipe had been murdered.

"That's the reservoir over there." He pointed. "There's the pool club. That house over there, you see it? Just through the woods. That's where Brightman lived as a kid."

Wit spoke on cue. "You know, Mike, in the course of my background research on Brightman, I came across some rather disturbing stories about a child being—"

"Carl Stipe was his name. He was the mayor's kid," Farr interrupted, a mixture of dread and excitement in his voice. "He was found not five feet from where we're standing. In fact, his house was right over there." He pointed in the opposite direction from the old Brightman house.

"He was tortured or something as I recall, wasn't he?" Wit played it cool.

"Sticks shoved down his throat. It was horrible."

"You saw the body, then?" I asked.

"I did. By the time they found him, all his blood had settled. He was white as a sheet, his eyes frozen open, staring up at the canopy." Farr looked up at the trees. "I'm not likely to forget that."

"If I remember correctly, a drifter did it," Wit said.

"Nah," Farr pooh-poohed. "That guy Martz had nothing to do with it."

"But—"

"But nothing, Wit," Farr insisted. "People believe stuff sometimes because it's what they want to believe. You know that. And the people around here wanted to believe Martz did it more than anything. They wanted to get on with their lives, and that would have been impossible if they thought the killer was still roaming around out there somewhere. Or worse still, if the killer was living among them. No sirree, everybody around here was pretty well interested in hanging it on that poor sick bastard Martz."

"Everyone except you," I said, remembering the follow-up articles which had appeared in the *Herald* marking the anniversary of the murder.

"I didn't buy it then and I don't buy it now."

"Did the police ever have any other suspects beside this Martz fellow?" Wit was curious to know.

"If they did, they weren't saying."

"And you?" I asked.

"Me? I'm a reporter. I don't have theories."

"Did they ever recover the bicycle?" Wit wanted to know.

Micah Farr squinted at us suspiciously. "You two fellows seem awfully more interested in the Stipe murder than Brightman. What's going on, boys?"

"You're a sharp newspaperman," Wit complimented. "I am interested in the murder, because I think it's why the Brightmans moved to New York. I think the murder had a profound effect in shaping Steven Brightman. I think it's an angle that will work for me in the piece."

Farr bought it. "You're right. A few families moved away soon after the murder. If you want more info on the murder, I'd talk to Phil Malloy over at the municipal building. He's mayor now, but back then he was a local cop. When we get back to the *Herald*, I'll put a call in to him if you'd like."

Wit clapped Farr on the shoulder. "That would be great. Thank you. May I just ask you one or two more questions, Mike?"

"Shoot, Wit."

"The stories said Carl Stipe was coming from a friend's house and using these woods as a shortcut. From whose house was he coming?"

Farr pointed again. "See that house right there, the one next door to where the Brightmans lived?"

Wit and I both said that we did.

"That was Ronny Bishop's house. That's where the kid was coming home from. They were one of the families that left after the murder. I guess I couldn't blame them."

There really wasn't very much more for us to do there in the woods between the pool club and the reservoir. We took a ride past the houses the Brightmans, Stipes, and Bishops had lived in. Carl

Stipe's mother still lived in the big Tudor on Reservoir Road. We saw her outside, collecting her mail. I stopped the car and watched her retreat back into her home. My heart ached for her. I wondered what she believed about her son's death.

Wit treated us to lunch at a pub in a neighboring town. Here Farr gave us as much background on Brightman as he could. Which, frankly, wasn't much. Reporters, he said, weren't in the habit of researching eleven- and twelve-year-old kids. Steven Brightman, as it happened, had been a good student, a friendly kid who played Little League. The reporter seemed to know a great deal more about Brightman's dad, the big-time lawyer. I asked if Farr remembered the other families who had moved away in the wake of the murder. He wrote out a list of four or five names.

As we drove the old reporter back to the *Herald,* I couldn't help but feel disappointed. Although the proximity of Brightman's house to the crime scene and the Bishop kid's home was interesting, there was nothing in what Farr had told us to tie Brightman closer to the murder itself. Without something more substantial, all the intricate scenarios I had constructed would collapse under their own weight.

Micah Farr was good to his word and rang up the mayor on our behalf. The mayor was thrilled at the prospect of speaking to someone like Wit. Any good press for Steven Brightman was good press for him and his town. Three months ago, when Brightman's name was still tainted by Moira Heaton's disappearance, the mayor would probably have hung up on Farr. How quickly things change. Farr did warn the mayor that we might ask about the Stipe murder, but downplayed our interest. He told us to come ahead just the same.

The municipal building was a converted school building

around the corner from the *Herald*. The mayor's office was up on the second floor. Like the rest of Hallworth, the mayor's office was clean, well appointed, but unpretentious. Flags, portraits of past mayors, and all manner of certificates and medals were on display. After the introductions, I found my eyes searching out Mayor Stipe's portrait. He was a handsome man with distant eyes. My guess was he'd sat for the painting while the pain of his boy's death was still quite fresh. I thought of his wife, retrieving the mail. I felt much more sorry for her. I joined Wit across from the mayor's desk.

Phil Malloy was a loquacious fellow in his late forties who sported a thick gray mustache and a spare tire at what had once been his waistline. He was glad we were in town, glad to be mayor, glad to help. Phil was glad about most things. Unfortunately, gladness wasn't much of a replacement for substance. He had very little to tell us about Steven Brightman, but he would be glad to dig up his junior high school yearbook, glad to put us in touch with his old teachers, glad to give us another tour of the town.

He was slightly more informative about the Stipe murder, but not much. Within hours of finding the boy's body, the local cops had handed off to the state police. Unlike Farr, the mayor thought Martz had done it. What else would he think? This was his town now. If he had doubts about Martz's guilt, he wasn't saying. He didn't know if the state police ever considered other suspects or if they had alternate theories, but, he assured us, he would have been glad to share them if he'd known of any.

As the mayor rambled, Wit trying to seem interested, I found myself losing hope. We couldn't afford to walk out of Hallworth empty-handed. In a town this size, word of Wit's visit would spread fast. Even if we could count on Micah Farr not to mention it in the *Herald,* Malloy struck me as the kind of guy to spend the rest of the afternoon on the phone telling everyone he knew. And once word spread through town, it would spread out of town. Then we were finished. We had a one-day head start and we were on the verge of blowing it. The time for caution, I decided without consulting Wit, had passed. There was one fact about the Stipe murder that no one had mentioned: the two boys who'd seen the man ride out of the woods on a bicycle. I had a hunch and took my shot.

"Excuse me, Mr. Mayor," I interrupted, pulling out the detective's shield which would never actually be mine, "I'm Detective Prager from the NYPD and I need your help."

I'm not sure who looked more surprised, Wit or Malloy. Wit kept quiet and let me play my hand. He, too, recognized that we needed to come away from today's visit with something tangible beyond scenarios and suspicions.

"I'm a little confused," Malloy confessed, "but I'll be glad to help any way I can."

Gee, what a surprise.

"I'm afraid I've enlisted Mr. Fenn in a bit of deception, and I hope you won't hold that against him," I continued. "I work cold cases, Mr. Mayor. And we've just had a very cold case heat up— two, actually. About the time of the Stipe homicide here, we had two similar cases in the Bronx. They've gone unsolved all these years, but recently, we received an anonymous tip that led us to a likely suspect. The thing of it is, we don't have anyone who can eyeball this guy. So what I was hoping was I could tie our cases to your case and clear them all up."

"Anything I can do, I will." Malloy was so pumped up at that moment, I think he could have chewed through steel plate.

"You had two witnesses see a man leave the wooded area around the reservoir on bicycle, right?"

The mayor was impressed. "You did your homework, I see."

"So, if they can ID our suspect as the man they saw that day . . ."

Malloy fairly jumped out of his seat. "Holy cow!" Then, almost immediately, he deflated. "I really can't tell you who they—"

"I understand," I said, empathetic as hell. "The kids were minors, and to protect them, their identities were kept secret. I admire you, Mr. Mayor, for keeping your oath as a cop, but we're talking three dead little boys here. Now, I don't need you to go all the way. I know that one of the boys who saw the man that day was Steven Brightman. I've already talked to him about it and he's agreed to view a lineup."

"How'd you find out?" The mayor was flabbergasted.

I made it up, putz! "We have our ways," I answered. "But what I need from you is the other kid's name. If we can get him to positively ID our suspect, we're—"

"I'm sorry, Detective Prager, but—"

"Listen, Phil, I understand about giving your word."

"It's not that. Kyle Lawrence was the other kid's name," Malloy said without hesitation. "It's just that he's dead."

"When?"

"About two years ago. Some weird disease. He was a heroin junkie."

"Two years ago, you say," I repeated almost unconsciously. There was another one of those coincidences.

"Yup, Detective Prager, two years. Micah'll have the exact date. I'm sorry if I ruined your case for you."

"That's okay," I assured him, shaking his hand. "Brightman

might be enough. But now I need something else from you, Mr. Mayor."

"Name it."

"You've kept those names secret all these years and now I need you to keep the subject of our little conversation a secret. Now that we're down to one witness, we can't afford to have Steven Brightman compromised in any way. I'm sure you understand. So, if anyone should ask, please say Mr. Fenn was here asking only about the wholesomeness of Hallworth and how it might have helped shape Steven Brightman's life. Please don't even mention the Stipe case."

"You have my word."

"Again, Mr. Mayor, thanks for the help."

"Glad to do it."

*　*　*

Wit didn't say a word until we had exited the converted schoolhouse. He realized the risk I had taken. The stakes of the game had just been raised. It wasn't until we got back to my car that he spoke up.

"That was quite an improvisation. My compliments. But that little act in there, it could blow up in your face. You understand that?"

"Next to murder, what does it matter?"

"Murder! Moe, yes we will leave town with a little bit more information than we arrived with, but we're a million miles away from murder."

"We'll see. Do you have that list Farr gave us with the names of the families who moved out of town after Carl Stipe's death? Read off the names."

Wit complied: "Kenworth, Hitner, Lawrence—"

"Curiouser and curiouser," I said.

"It proves nothing."

"I'm sure Kyle Lawrence's death started the chain of events that led me here. It's a place to start."

"Start what, Moe? That was twenty-seven years ago. Lawrence is dead. The case is closed to almost everyone's satisfaction."

"Is it? Let's go ask Carl Stipe's mother."

"Point well taken. However, I would be remiss not to alert you to the fact that in spite of your rousing speech in the mayor's office, word is going to leak back to Brightman."

"I'm not an idiot, Wit. I know that. When it leaks back to him, we'll just have to figure out how to use it."

It was turning dusk when we plopped ourselves back in my car parked in front of the *Hallworth Herald*. I turned the ignition and pulled the transmission into drive, but Wit clamped his hand around my right forearm.

"Wait! Farr's niece is waving us into the office."

I put it back in park and left the car running. "You stay here, okay?"

Wit didn't protest. He was tired and badly in need of a drink. In any case, after the little coup I'd pulled off in the mayor's office, I think he trusted me to deal with Annie.

She was alone in the smoky office, a new cigarette dangling from her lower lip. Sitting across from her, I noticed that she was actually attractive in a bohemian sort of way. She wore no makeup, and her washed-out brown hair was just drooped over her rounded shoulders. The limp hair disguised sparkly brown eyes, a pleasantly sloped nose, and a strong jaw. As close as I was, I now figured Annie to be in her early forties.

"My uncle treats me like I'm not here, and I guess sometimes I let him," she said. "I should have introduced myself before."

"That's okay. My name's Moe Prager."

"I know who you are and so does my uncle Micah. You didn't let that aw-shucks small-town-reporter act fool you, did you? You're that investigator from the city that cleared Steven Brightman."

"How'd—"

"I know this is Jersey, Mr. Prager, but we get the same TV stations as you. That was big news in this town. My uncle and I watched the news conference when they announced that you had found that woman's killer. It was front page of the *Herald* the following day."

"Is that what you wanted to tell me, that my trying to keep a low profile didn't work?"

"No, I wanted to tell you some things about Steven Brightman."

I tried not to react, but in trying, I gave myself away. I went with it. "What about him? To hear the people around here tell it, he was a nice boy who got good marks and played Little League."

"That's because you talked to people who were adults when we were kids. Not that Steven was public enemy number one or anything, but he was a fourteen-year-old boy once."

I recalled what her uncle had said to us earlier in the day about how reporters were ill-equipped to research the lives of kids.

"Surprise me, Annie," I challenged her.

"Steven was in a gang."

My first reaction was to laugh at her, but I didn't. I had been a fourteen-year-old boy once myself. I remembered the intense desire to belong. It almost didn't matter to what, as long as my friends belonged too, and I was accepted. The intensity dimmed after I grew out of my awkwardness and girls appeared on the horizon.

Annie misread my silence. "Not a gang like in the city. There were no Sharks and Jets in Hallworth. It wasn't the Episcopalians rumbling with the Lutherans on Railroad Avenue at midnight. Maybe 'gang' isn't the right word. It was more of an 'us' and 'them' thing."

"Did they have a name, this gang?"

"The James Deans. The JDs for short."

"Juvenile delinquents. How perfectly fifties."

"But it was the fifties, Mr. Prager, and James Dean was a Hallworth kind of antihero. The boys in an affluent town like this couldn't relate to guys who played it tough like Brando or Lee Marvin or even Vic Morrow, but James Dean . . . And when he died in a car crash, it just sealed the deal. You're probably a little too young to remember the stir he caused. In college, I wrote a paper comparing his career to that of the Romantic poets. I mean 'romantic' in the sense of the long ago—"

"—and the far away. Byron, Shelley, Keats, and company. Some cops go to college, Annie."

She apologized. "I didn't mean to condescend. Forgive me."

"Forget it. So Brightman was in this club or gang or whatever. Do you remember any of the other kids who were in the JDs?"

"There weren't many," she said, lighting up another cigarette. "Let's see, there was Jeffrey Anderson, Michael Day, Kyle Lawrence, and Pete Ryder."

"So few. Why?"

"Even in the midst of the baby boom, Hallworth was a small town. And like you said, Mr. Prager, it *was* the fifties. Conformity was still like everyone's second religion."

"Do any of the other James Deans still live in town?"

"Kyle died a few years back. Pete Ryder went to West Point and was killed during the Tet offensive. Jeff Anderson left years ago, California someplace, but I'm pretty sure Mike Day's still around."

"How sure?"

"I used to be married to the prick."

*　*　*

The houses on Conover Street were the smallest houses in Hallworth, but their lawns were just as green and their hedges as trim as in the rest of town. Maybe Micah Farr wasn't kidding about the lawn police. I wouldn't know. Local code enforcement isn't a huge deal in Brooklyn. There's such a mishmash of tastelessness and beauty in the County of Kings, it's hard to discern where the one started and the other one ended.

Number 23 Conover was a clapboarded saltbox set on a little bluff. Darkness had come in force, and climbing the steps up from the street was a bit of a challenge for Wit and me. Wit looked haggard, his age and addiction to alcohol showing in his face and posture. I wasn't too sure I would have withstood a close inspection myself. It had been a tiring day, long on hints and traces, but short on substance. Mike Day met us at the front door. Annie had called ahead.

He didn't look anything like I'd expected he would, given the appearance of his ex-wife. Mike stood an inch above six feet. He was still quite tan, athletic, good-looking, dressed in chinos and a golf shirt embroidered with the name of a big Wall Street brokerage. He welcomed us in and offered us drinks. I thought Wit might click his heels and scream, "Hallelujah, praise the Lord." I took a beer. Wit made due with a few fingers of Maker's Mark.

"So, gentlemen, Annie tells me you think I might be able to help you," he said, showing us into his living room.

"Maybe. Wit's doing a follow-up piece for *Esquire* on an old friend of yours."

Day's face brightened. "Stevie's going places now that that ugliness has been cleared up. I always knew he would. He has some set of balls on him."

"Does he?" Wit, now feeling his oats, joined the conversation.

Day proceeded to regale us with tales of the young Steven Brightman's bravery and daring. He swam across the reservoir at the age of nine even though it was illegal and most adults wouldn't have dared. He jumped off the rocks at Indian Falls into Iron Creek although the creek was only a few feet deep at most points.

"You see, the thing about Stevie was, *he* did it, but didn't expect the rest of us to follow. It was okay if we did and okay if we didn't. What he did was to challenge himself, not us. I always knew he had big things ahead of him."

Wit and I let Day go on as long as he wanted, hoping that he'd arrive at a natural segue into the subject of the James Deans. Unfortunately, we had let that opportunity slip by. We were forced instead to listen to an interminable sermon on the glories of junk bonds, the torturous saga of his marriage to Annie, and his take on the failures of the football Giants.

"You know, Mike," I interrupted, "Annie mentioned something to me about a group you and Brightman and a few other guys were in that I found pretty intriguing."

He seemed surprised, if not upset. "Oh, yeah, what group was that?"

"The James Deans."

"The James fucking Deans." He laughed quietly, a smile that was part joy, part embarrassment washing over his handsome face.

"I haven't thought about the James Deans in twenty-five yea
Man, we thought we were so cool."

"Who were the James Deans, exactly? Annie wasn't sure,"
I lied.

"There was me and Stevie, of course, and Kyle Lawrence and
Pete Ryder. Oh, yeah, and Jeff Anderson, too."

He repeated the sad particulars of the tragedies that had be-
fallen the group. Day, too, said they thought of themselves as a
gang, but really weren't. His riffs on being a fourteen-year-old boy
sounded awfully like my own thoughts.

"We only ever had to do one thing that even remotely resembled a gang," he said, completely without guile.

"What was that?" I asked.

For the first time Mike Day hesitated. "To get into the gang,
you had to . . . um . . . take a scalp."

"A scalp!" Wit started.

"Not a scalp scalp, not a real scalp."

I could see Day regretted having brought it up, but I couldn't
let that get in the way. "Explain that scalp thing or it's gonna end
up in some national magazine and that won't be good for anybody.
You know what'll happen if you don't tell us. You were married to
a reporter, for chrissakes!"

"Don't remind me. Well, the scalp thing is what we called it,
but what it meant was you had to steal something to get into the
James Deans. You know, committing an act of defiance. I hope this
isn't going to cause Stevie any trouble."

Wit reassured him. "Not at all, Mr. Day. It's just background
information. I won't use it in my piece, so feel free to continue.
You'll notice, I'm not taking any notes."

Mike Day breathed a big sigh of relief.

s. "Do you remember what each member stole?"

ght about it. Giggled. Flushed red. "I stole a box of

apkins from Wiggman's Pharmacy on Terrace Street.

k his father's watch. I didn't think that should count."

"Too easy," I said.

"Exactly," Day seconded. "Jeff always was a bit of a pussy, but Stevie said it counted."

"The others?" Wit prompted.

"Pete stole Mr. Hart's glasses right off the rostrum at band practice. Stevie took the school mascot, the Hallworth Harrier, from the hallway outside the gym. It wasn't a real hawk, just a statue of one."

"That leaves Kyle," I reminded him. "What did he take?"

"You know, I don't know. That's funny, I forgot that. We never did find out what Kyle took, but Stevie vouched for him. He said that he was there and saw Kyle do it and that was good enough for us. Stevie's word was always good enough for us."

Wit and I exchanged sick, knowing glances. Mike Day, Pete Ryder, and Jeffrey Anderson might not have had a clue as to what Kyle Lawrence had stolen in the presence of Steven Brightman, but Wit did, and so did I. Knowing and proving, however, are not synonymous. We were still a long way from proving.

CHAPTER
EIGHTEEN

I DIDN'T WANT HIM TO DO IT, BUT WIT VOLUNTEERED. THE TRUTH of it was, we needed to buy more time, and unless we threw one of us to the wolves, we weren't going to get it. Wit was the logical choice. He was less vulnerable to outside pressures than I. As a member of the press, he was fairly insulated from most physical threats. He was a long time divorced. His children lived well out of state. And in spite of what Thomas Geary thought of Wit's inheritance, Wit assured me Geary was wrong.

"Poor sods don't live at the Pierre," he chortled.

So I had to turn rat. Before doing so, I made sure to finally get some sleep. The hangover I had skillfully avoided the night before through a combination of adrenaline and outrage had only been postponed, not canceled. By the time I dropped Wit off and pulled into my driveway at home, my head was tearing itself in two and my body literally ached from exhaustion.

Katy was still awake and was horrified by the look of me. "You didn't come to bed last night and you were gone this morning before I got up. What's going on, Moses? You're not acting like a man on the verge of getting what he's always wanted."

le of aspirin and we'll talk about it."

shower and a handful of aspirin, I sat Katy down

why a little boy's murder in 1956 meant I was never

get any detective's shield beside the replica she had

t for me two Christmases ago. She did not try to undo any of

reasoning. I was glad, because I had no more energy to fight, only to sleep.

"I might be going away for a few days," I said before closing my eyes.

"Where?"

"It's better if you don't know. It's better if no one knows. We'll all be safer that way. Can you take Sarah up to your parents' for a while?"

"I guess. Is it that serious?"

I didn't answer. I couldn't do another thing. Thankfully, sleep came crashing in before I could make sense of the look on Katy's face.

* * *

They were gone by the time I got up. I was never so glad to have my family away from me. I didn't know how much physical danger any of us were in, but I wasn't going to take chances with Katy and Sarah. There had been enough loss in our lives. There had been enough loss in the lives of too many people connected to this business. No one but Wit would be in any danger if I could pull off the rat routine. First I had to find Ralph Barto's card.

Barto, whom I'd met at Joe Spivack's funeral, was someone I needed to talk to. Not only had he been a U.S. marshal, he'd also worked for Spivack. He had offered his services to me, and I was about to take him up on that offer.

He picked up on the first ring. "Barto Investigations."

"My name's Moe Prager, Mr. Barto. We met at—"

"—Joe's burial. I wouldn't forget you. You got Joe's flag. What can I do for you?"

"I'm not sure yet, but can we meet?"

"Name the time and the place," he said.

I gave him the address of the Brooklyn store. Although it was unlikely I was being watched, I thought it wise not to draw undue attention by going to Barto's office. I instructed him to stroll into the store in the early afternoon just like any customer and that we'd take it from there. He didn't question the arrangements.

The phone rang nearly before I put it back down. It was Larry McDonald. It was unnecessary for him to say anything more than my name for me to know word of our visit to Hallworth had already leaked back to Brightman. In a way, his call was a relief. There would be less guessing involved from here on out, and I could act preemptively.

"Fuck, Larry, I'm glad you called. There's something we need to talk about."

"What?"

"I think I may have to postpone my reinstatement for a week or two. I think Wit's out to cause us all a lot of grief."

That was met with silence. Good. I couldn't be sure how much Larry knew of the details of what was really going on or even if he was taking his directives straight from Brightman. The further he was from the truth, the better I liked it. First, it made him an easier target for my manipulations. Second, it let me believe my old friend's integrity was still intact. And I very badly wanted to believe that.

"What's this nonsense about Wit?" he asked. "I was calling to

...at they're considering reinstating you as a detective sec-
de."

That's great, Larry, but this other thing's more important.
st me, okay?"

"I've always trusted you, Moe."

"Good, but we gotta talk. Maybe tonight. The Hound's Tooth?"
He did not pause. "Seven o'clock."

"Seven."

Wit answered on the first ring. He sounded bright and alive,
as if he'd been waiting by the phone all morning for my call. I had
no trouble understanding how pumped he must have felt. He was
on the hunt, but in danger himself. It was all very primal stuff.

"Word's back to Brightman already," I said. "I just got off the
phone with Larry Mac. He was calling to let me know they'd up
the stakes for my keeping my mouth shut. They're thinking of reinstating me as a detective second grade. It's amazing. In the seventies, I couldn't make detective no matter what I did. Now I've
made detective and gotten a bump in grade without even being reinstated. At this rate, I'll make chief by November."

"And what did you say?"

"That there was something more important going on. That
you were out to cause us all a world of trouble. I didn't mention
Brightman by name."

"And . . . ?"

"We're meeting this evening to discuss it. I think it's time to
buy those two plane tickets to California, Wit. Don't forget, book
them with a layover in St. Louis or Chicago. Leave a message on
my machine with the details."

"I'll have them booked for us so the information is out there if
anyone is interested. I've also called a few people at *Esquire* and let

the name Jeffrey Anderson slip out of my mouth in connection to Steven Brightman."

"Good. I'll see you at the airport tomorrow."

* * *

Klaus was a bit confused by my showing up at the store when I was supposed to be preparing for my return to the job. I assured him that it had nothing to do with a lack of confidence in him. Beyond that, I was unwilling to say much else. Wit and I had to strike a proper balance in setting things in motion. While leaving enough of a bread crumb trail for interested parties to follow, we could not afford to leave whole loaves on the ground behind us.

Barto strolled in about a quarter past one and asked Klaus if he could help him select a red wine to have with dinner. I told Klaus to take his lunch break and that I'd be happy to help the gentleman. Klaus rolled his eyes at me and mouthed the word "Cop." I guess Barto did look a little out of place. He was strictly a scotch and beer man.

"So what can I do for you, Mr. Prager? You were kinda vague on the phone."

"No, I was very vague on the phone. The truth is I think I have an idea why Joe Spivack committed suicide. It's why he left me the flag. He wanted me to wonder about that. It was a sort of challenge."

"That don't sound like Joe. He wasn't a subtle kinda guy. If he had something to say, he'd just come out and say it."

"Even if he was ashamed of himself?"

Now Barto hesitated. "Maybe then. So why do you think he—"

"I don't want to say anything about it now, because I would just be guessing. I think I owe him more than a guess. But I'm not going to bullshit you, Ralph, if it turns out I'm right, it won't be pretty."

"Joe's dead. It'll take more than sticks and stones to do him any harm. And if what you say is true about him leaving you the flag and all, then he wanted you to find out."

"Okay, so you're not gonna get squeamish on me?"

"I can't afford to," he confessed. "I got ex-wives in two states to support."

"You said something to me at the bar that day after Joe was buried about Spivack and Associates having financial trouble, but that he refused to let anybody go. Do you remember telling me that?"

"I do."

Barto went on to explain how last year had been a financial nightmare at Spivack and Associates. Most of Spivack's staff were old-school investigators, either ex-marshals or ex-cops. They had been slow to adapt to the use of computers and other electronics. They were seat-of-the-pants types of guys, and Joe Spivack had an aversion to taking divorce work. He felt it was beneath him.

"The Moira Heaton thing," Barto continued, "now that was the kind of thing Joe loved. But those kinda cases are few and far between. That case kept us going for a time, but by last year even that had petered out."

"Do you know where Joe got the money to prop up the company after things went south?"

"To tell you the truth, Mr. Prager, I didn't give a shit where he got it from. When I went to the bank with my paycheck, they cashed it."

"When you were a marshal, where were you stationed?"

"Vegas, Miami, but mostly New York. Why," he asked, "is that important?"

"Maybe. You met Spivack in Miami?"

"No. Up here, but we had mutual acquaintances down in Florida."

"How would you like a job, Ralph?"

"What's it pay?"

"Five hundred retainer against your regular daily rates plus all expenses. But you might have to do a little traveling."

"When I was eighteen, I joined the navy to see the world. There's plenty I ain't seen yet and a lot of places I'd like to see again."

We went back to the office and I wrote him an eight-hundred-dollar check. Five hundred was the retainer. Three hundred was for the trip to Miami.

*　*　*

I had to be careful with Larry McDonald. For one thing, he was a good cop. He'd been a real detective while I'd only played one in my head. He'd sat across from some of the world's most accomplished liars. Now I was going to sit across from him and feed him a plate of bullshit while trying to convince him it was caviar.

"What's going on, Moe? You called in today and you're not even back on the job yet."

I kept reminding myself not to overexplain. "It couldn't be helped."

"So what are we doing here? What could Wit possibly do to give us shit? We haven't done a fucking thing—"

"Whose idea was my reinstatement?"

Larry's face went blank.

"Come on, Larry," I prodded, not wanting to give him too much time to think. "Who came to you with it?"

"My chief."

"And do you think your chief snatched this idea out of midair? Somebody with juice whispered in his ear."

"I didn't give it much thought, Moe. I was just happy for you."

"I'm happy for me too, but Wit's gonna fuck it up for all of us." I appealed to Larry's healthy sense of self-interest.

"How?"

"He thinks he has a line on something Brightman did as a kid that will ruin his political career. I was with him in Jersey yesterday checking it out. That was no coincidence today that someone mentioned me getting the bump to second grade. You're too smart a man not to see the connection."

Larry got down to business. "Tell me what's going on."

"Wit got a lead about some bombshell shit Brightman and this guy Jeffrey Anderson did as kids. We went to Jersey yesterday to talk to this Anderson, but he's moved out to California somewhere. Wit's flying to California tomorrow to look for this guy, and I'm going with him. I gotta keep an eye on him. Can you clear a few days for me, postpone my reinstatement for a while?"

"Don't worry about it, but to tell you the truth, Moe, it sounds like you're talking outta your ass. What could this guy possibly have on Brightman?"

"That's what I'm going to find out." I stood to leave.

"Don't you want your drink?"

"No time. Gotta go home and pack. I have a long trip ahead of me."

He didn't know the half of it.

CHAPTER NINETEEN

THE FLIGHT FROM LA GUARDIA TO O'HARE HAD BEEN UNEVENT-
ful if not exactly enjoyable. Wit was a nervous flier and had trouble keeping still. The Wild Turkeys didn't do anything but exacerbate his jitters, and frankly I was glad that we'd made the second legs of our journeys to separate locations. Actually, only one of us had taken that second flight. By the time Wit got to L.A., I was already in Miami.

Miami was a funny place. In some ways it was like the Catskills south. Once *the* hot vacation destination, it had fallen on hard times in the seventies. Unlike the Catskills, however, Miami was enjoying a renaissance of sorts, but not one built on art and enlightenment. No, the rebirth of Miami was driven by the ultimate cash crop of the decade, cocaine. Miami was the most desirable transshipment point for the bulk of cocaine smuggled into the States from the Caribbean and Central and South America. Florida's seemingly endless coastline made it a smugglers' paradise, as the coastline of Long Island had been a boon to bootleggers and rumrunners half a century before. But I wasn't here about cocaine. I was here about another kind of smuggling, the human kind.

Barto had gotten a good head start and had a fair amount of information by the time I checked into my motel. He'd left a message for me at the front desk. It was dark here just as it would be back in New York, but the harbingers of autumn, the crispness in the night air and the hints of gold in the leaves, were absent. By the feel of the hot, damp night on the skin of my face, it might as well have been mid-July. The dankness that lurked in the peach and teal green corners of my cheap room did nothing to argue me out of the illusion of summer.

There was a knock at my door. It was Barto. During our previous two meetings, I hadn't bothered taking much notice of him. Until yesterday, he'd been more of a what than a who. He was built like a fireplug, short and squatty. Gravity and years of eating bad food had given him a prominent gut. He had a chubby, almost boyish face. He'd also lost most of the hair on top of his head, though he hadn't yet faced up to the fact. I'm certain Barto fancied himself quite the miracle worker with how he parlayed the few strands of top hair he had left into a sort of spiderweb covering his bald pate. He probably hadn't seen himself on videotape recently. It was one thing to look in a mirror and fool yourself. It was something else to see yourself on film.

"You were right," he said, barely able to contain his enthusiasm. "Spivack flew down here at least three times in the last year. I had some old contacts do a little checking. He spent most of his time in Little Havana, just like you predicted. You want a beer?" he asked, holding up the six-pack he held in his right hand.

"Sure."

"It's from some country in Central America, El Salvador or some shit, " he warned, twisting off two caps. "It's yellow as cartoon piss, but it's pretty good stuff. Here."

"Don't go into advertising, Ralph."

Not understanding, he shrugged his shoulders. We drank in relative quiet.

"So, Joe was down here that much, huh? Three times."

"At least," Barto answered. "Maybe more. I can find out for sure if I go to the field office and have them check."

"That won't be necessary. How often's not really that important. All I needed to know was that he was here. What about Alfonseca?"

That enthusiasm once again spread itself across Barto's boyish face. "Ivan was one bad little puppy, even back in Cuba. He was in jail by the time he was eleven and came over when Fidel cleaned out his jail cells in the seventies. Florida's still paying the price for that bullshit. Criminals are the one commodity we don't need to import, but that didn't stop his assholiness Jimmy Carter from taking the bastards in like they was fucking engineers and rocket scientists."

"Maybe President Carter just wanted to keep the U.S. marshals busy."

"Did he ever. We earned our pay down here, let me tell you."

"But did Ivan and Spivack ever cross paths?"

"I won't be able to tell you that until tomorrow or maybe the day after that."

"And the middleman," I wondered, "any luck there?"

"I got my feelers out on that. I got a friend or two still works down here. There's plenty of ways to funnel money back to families left behind in Cuba, but a big amount like you're talking requires someone with contacts inside the government there and the community here. Those kinda people don't grow on trees, Mr. Prager. Little Havana's bigger than it used to be, but it's still a tight community. We'll find the middleman."

"Okay, Ralph, I'm pretty beat. We'll talk tomorrow."

"You want another beer?"

"No thanks. *Buenas noches,*" I wished him in my grade-school Spanish.

"*Viva la revolución. Viva Fidel. Viva—*"

"Good night, Ralph."

*   *   *

Rain was tap-tap-tapping on the glass-slat-and-aluminum windows when I got up the next morning. It was a gray tropical rain, heavy and fast with a sun chaser. I ate breakfast across the street from the motel in a waffle house. I was in the mood for a waffle. I hadn't eaten one in years. But when I noticed that the waffle irons hadn't been cleaned since the Bay of Pigs, I opted for eggs. There wasn't anything for me to do now until I heard from Barto, so I asked the woman behind the counter where the closest car rental was. I had a friend who lived not too terribly far away, a friend I hadn't seen in quite some time.

The ride up to Boca Raton was pleasant enough, and finding the Millennium Village retirement complex was easy. I'd asked directions at the supermarket when I stopped to buy a bottle of vodka and some pastries. The problem was, I hadn't called ahead. I don't know. I guess I really wanted to see the look on Israel Roth's face when I strolled into his condo unannounced.

"Who's there?" he screamed impatiently as I knocked at his door. "What, you trying to take the door off the hinges?"

I kept knocking. "Special delivery."

"Stop already with the knocking. Nothing's that special." He flung back the door.

"Hey, Mr. Roth."

"Mr. Moe!" He might have been in his seventies, but he hugged like a college wrestler.

"Izzy, you're crushing the rugelach."

"Come in. Come in."

I put the goods down on the coffee table and gave him back a proper hug. He had reminded me of my father when we'd met two years before in the Catskills. Time had done little to change that, but I liked Israel Roth for who he was, not for who he wasn't. We exchanged the expected small talk about his health and my family, carefully avoiding any discussion of the incident that had brought us together in the first place. He wanted to know if Katy was still depressed over the miscarriage. He was thrilled to hear the answer.

"So, Mr. Moe, you came an awfully long way to bring me a box of Publix rugelach, which, to tell you the truth, taste like rolled-up cardboard with jelly filling."

"I notice you're not complaining about the vodka."

"Complaining! Who's complaining?"

Though it was early afternoon, we had a shot or two of the vodka.

"So, you didn't answer my question about this unexpected visit, Mr. Moe."

"What question? I didn't hear a question."

"What is this, *Jeopardy,* for chrissakes? You have to put things in the form of a question or you get the buzzer?"

There was no avoiding it, so I told him. He took it calmly, if not gladly. No amount of cruelty or calculation surprised him. He had seen firsthand the very worst of man. He had witnessed the systematic slaughter of his family and friends and breathed their ashes into his lungs. Though no longer capable of tears, he was not

unmoved by the suffering of others. He had not let the inhumani-
ties he'd suffered turn him dead inside. It was one of the things I
admired about Mr. Roth. I didn't know if I was that strong.

"You're going to meet with the man who funneled the money
back to Cuba?"

"I hope so. This ex-marshal I hired seems to know his way
around down here. Apparently, Joe Spivack—"

"The one that killed himself?"

"Him. He didn't cover his tracks that well. Within hours of
getting in himself, Barto found out Joe'd flown down to Miami at
least three times in the last year. I guess Spivack never thought
anyone would connect the dots."

"Maybe." Mr. Roth was skeptical. "It doesn't seem a little
odd to you that such a man would be so obvious? Would a man, a
professional at his job, be so sloppy? Look at what you say about
the flag, that it was a hint or a challenge. It seems inconsistent, no,
to be so subtle on one hand and obvious on the other?"

My first instinct was to argue with him, but I could see Izzy's
point. I didn't know Joe Spivack all that well. He was, as Izzy had
so aptly put it, a professional. Now that I stepped back and gave it
some thought, it did seem a little odd that he had taken so little
care to cover his own tracks. Only if he had contemplated suicide
all along, which was possible, would his sloppiness have made
sense. Then why all the secrecy? Why no suicide note? Why the
flag? On the other hand, if he had meant not to get caught and
hadn't contemplated suicide, why hadn't he traveled under an assumed name? Why hadn't he driven or taken the train? There
would have been no paper trail. But Barto had been specific about
Spivack flying in.

"You make some sense, Mr. Roth."

"We *alter kockers* occasionally do, you know. I'm goin' to ask you a question and I don't want you should get mad. Okay?"

"Go ahead."

"You have with you your gun?" he asked sheepishly.

"No. I flew down, remember? I'm not licensed to carry on aircraft. Guns and aircraft don't mix."

"Wait here a second."

He stood up and went into his bedroom. I used the time to consider what he had said about Spivack. Mr. Roth had definitely planted the seed of doubt and it had quickly taken root. Something wasn't right, but I couldn't yet see what it was.

Israel Roth stepped back into the living room of his neatly kept condo. He held a rectangular plastic case in his right hand.

"Here, Mr. Moe." He handed me the case. "I want you to take this for while you're here. Then, before you go home, you can give it back."

I opened the case. Inside was a little .25-caliber automatic in pristine condition. I took it out, clicked off the safety, and ejected the bullet that was in the chamber.

"You should never leave a loaded weapon around, Mr. Roth, especially ones with chambered rounds."

"What, so I should tell the burglar to wait until I put the clip in and put a bullet in the chamber? I got no small children here, Moe, and I keep it well hidden. I'm not a reckless man."

"I know, Mr. Roth. I didn't mean to lecture. It's just that guns are funny things. If you hesitate or are afraid to use them, they'll get taken away from you and used on you."

"I wouldn't hesitate, believe me. In my clothing store on Flatbush Avenue I used to keep a big .38. More than once I had to stick it in somebody's *kishkes* when they tried to stick me up."

"But why do you need a gun down here?"

"I sell a little jewelry on the side, nothing too fancy. Everybody's got some little side business in this place. The money is nice, but it's not so much the money as it keeps you sharp, awake. Retired people don't so much die as they let themselves fall asleep a bit at a time. They become passive and inactive and they forget they're alive."

"I understand."

"So I keep the little pistol when I go to the bank or pick up inventory. That's all. It makes me feel safer. There are people who prey on the old. I've been prey once in my life. Never again. Now it'll make me feel safer if you keep it for a few days. All right?"

I didn't hesitate. He'd sufficiently spooked me. Everything had been falling so neatly in line. Maybe too neatly. Mr. Roth had done me a tremendous favor, not necessarily by giving me the gun, but by calling attention to a blind spot.

We chatted for a little while longer. I was glad of it. I wouldn't have wanted to leave with the pistol being the last business between us. It really was good to see him. My grandparents had been very old when I was a boy and my parents had both died relatively young, so I'd never formed much of a relationship with a man of Mr. Roth's age. I found his calm demeanor and his perspective a great comfort. Although he didn't talk about it much, I knew he was estranged from his son. I guess we both filled a niche in each other's lives.

He went back into his bedroom to put away the gun case, then reemerged with three smaller jewelry boxes.

"I had meant to send these to you for Hanukkah, but I prefer to let you take them home with you. This one we'll open here. It's for you," he said, a proud smile washing over his face as he raised up the lid of the blue velveteen box.

Inside was a Star of David. It was lovely, the points of the star formed by overlapping pieces of gold that were shaped like the number 7.

"When we were up in the Catskills, Mr. Moe, I noticed you didn't wear one. I hope you don't think it is presumptuous of me to—"

"Not at all. Will you help me put it on?"

We were quite a sight there, the two of us with our hands shaking, trying to get the clasp open.

"Thank you, Israel. I don't know what to say."

"The look on your face is thanks enough. There's one there for Katy and for Sarah, too. I only hope they are as pleased as you look."

"They will be. I better get going," I said, tapping my watch.

We wished each other well. He promised to come visit in November during his biyearly pilgrimage to the Catskills. I told him Katy would never forgive him if he didn't show.

"I promise. I promise!" he shouted as I retreated down the hall.

During the drive back to Miami, I couldn't help touching the star. It had been so long since I'd worn one that it felt odd against my chest, even a little uncomfortable. A little discomfort was a good thing, I thought. It made you pay attention. On the other hand, I had almost forgotten about the pistol tucked in my jacket pocket. Strange, the things you get used to.

*　　*　　*

The red message light on my motel-room phone was flashing madly when I reentered the dank world of peach and teal. The calls were all from Barto, each successive message more feverish than the last. Where was I? He'd found the middleman. It hadn't been easy to arrange a meeting, but the meeting was set. It would be just me, the middleman, and Barto.

"You show up on your own. I'm gonna get there ahead of you just to make sure the coast is clear and that he ain't fucking with us. I'm pretty sure this guy's on the up-and-up. My sources tell me not to sweat it," he said in his fifth and final message. "This guy's a pro, a moneyman. He's got no use for violence. Bad for business, he says. I'll see you later."

*   *   *

I was ten minutes early. The Black Flamingo was an abandoned art deco hotel on the wrong end of Miami Beach. There was nothing unusual in that. The most prominent design features in this part of town seemed to be foreclosure signs. Apparently, the cocaine economy had yet to trickle down to this end of the beach. As seedy as it was, there was a kind of decadent charm to the area, an echo of great things that once were. And the ambient sound of the ocean only added to its down-at-the-heels allure.

There was a gap in the plywood at the back of the old hotel, as Barto had said there would be. In spite of the ex-marshal's assurances about the remoteness of violence, I felt better for having Mr. Roth's little .25 in my pocket. There was no getting around it. I'd carried a firearm strapped to some part of my body almost every day going on fifteen years. Although I'd never had occasion to fire a single shot in anger, I felt naked without a gun. Unfortunately, Mr. Roth's .25 had about as much stopping power as a spitball.

I snapped on my flashlight and stepped through the hole at the back of the hotel into what had been the kitchen. I could see the flickering shadows of candlelight beneath the doors that led out of the kitchen into what I assumed was the dining room. I made my way ahead around the dusty stainless-steel kitchen fixtures. With a flashlight in one hand and my other hand nestled around the .25, I used my right shoulder to push through the double doors.

I used a little too much nervous energy and spilled sideways through the doors. Before I could regain my balance, I stumbled over an old bundle of linens left carelessly in the middle of the floor. Except it wasn't a bundle of linens at all. I think I knew that even before I hit the ground. The candle blew out.

"Fuck! Barto!" I scrambled to the body, clenching madly at the flashlight. In one panicked motion I flicked the flashlight back on and rolled the body onto its back. "Barto, are you all right?"

Only it wasn't Barto, and he was as far away from all right as I was from Singapore.

"You're a little early, Prager. I see you've met Gedalia Morenos." Barto's voice bounced off the tile floor and plaster walls in the darkness. "He was a big man in Little Havana. He had a spe-cial talent for getting *dinero* back to Cuba to help out the families left behind."

"Like the Alfonsecas, for instance," I said, trying to keep Barto talking.

"Oh yeah, just like them."

"So it was you who arranged for Alfonseca to take the fall for Moira's murder."

"Too bad you figured that out so late in the game, Prager."

It was no good. The source of his voice was impossible to lo-cate. But as long as the place stayed dark, I would keep breathing. I pulled the .25 out of my pocket and undid the safety. If I could buy a little more time to calm myself down, I might have one chance.

"So I was wrong about Spivack," I called out, pressing my belly to the ground next to Morenos's body.

"Not completely," Barto answered in a lower voice that didn't bounce around the room quite as much. "Using a guy like Alfonseca to take the fall was Joe's idea, only he wouldn't go through with it all the way. It was such a good idea, too good to let go to waste."

"You had no such qualms. Two ex-wives to take care of, right?"

"No problems at all," he answered. "The bitch was already dead."

Good. If my guess was right, Morenos's body was between me and Barto. My showing up early had prevented Barto from getting the body out of the way and lining up a clear shot.

"So you went through with it without Spivack. He didn't know about it until it was too late. And by then, he had to play along or risk being exposed himself."

"Yeah, something like that."

"If you kill me," I shouted, "they'll tie you to me through the checks I paid you with."

"What checks? I got rid of those ten minutes after you gave 'em to me. Anyway, why don't you let me worry about that. Your troubles are all over."

A blinding light flashed, there was a loud crack, and Morenos's lifeless body jumped. It jumped again, again. I couldn't afford to hesitate. I aimed the little .25 into the beam of light and emptied the clip, each shot aimed slightly higher or lower, further left or right than the last. Something clanged against the tile floor. Glass broke. The room went dark again. Barto moaned, but I didn't hear him fall. I didn't wait around to see how badly he was hurt. I picked up my flashlight and ran, banging through the kitchen doors, into the sharp corners of the kitchen fixtures and out into the night.

I scrambled to my rented car, fumbling for my keys as I went. I forced my hand to steady and turned the ignition. It caught immediately and I was off. It was all I could do not to floor the gas pedal, but I couldn't risk getting pulled over, not with Irving Roth's empty pistol in my lap. I could also feel blood begin seeping out of the cuts the kitchen fixtures had gifted me with as I ran for my life. When I was several blocks away and sure I heard no sirens, I pulled to the curb and disassembled the .25. I wiped the individual pieces clean with the sleeve of my jacket. I threw part of the automatic off a bridge as I crossed. I tossed another piece down a storm drain. I dumped the empty clip in a garbage can near the motel.

If Barto was in any kind of traveling shape at all, I didn't figure to have much time before he showed up at my motel. But I had something to do even before I cleaned up and got out. I put in a call to Israel Roth.

"Mr. Moe"—his voice was happy and a little boozy—"it was a joy to see you today."

"You too, Izzy. I hear in your voice that you're still enjoying the vodka."

"Guilty as charged."

"Listen, Mr. Roth, I need you to do something for me and I need you to not question me about it."

"What's wrong? Are you all right?" The airiness went right out of his voice. "Where are you?"

"I'm okay. I'm okay, but I need you to do this for me."

"What?"

"Go to the local police station and report your gun missing. Don't overdo it. Be apologetic. You're an old man, they won't be too rough on you. Tell them you had it with you this afternoon when you went to the store and when you checked for it, it was gone. Tell them something like that. Will you do that for me?"

"Are you hurt?"

"Izzy, please. I'm fine. Just do it. Do it now!"

"I'm doing it. I'm doing it."

"I'll call you tomorrow and we'll talk about it then. Just to let you know, you saved my life today. Thanks. Bye, Mr. Roth."

I hung up. I knew it would be better for me to check out immediately and get out of town, or to another motel at least. But I couldn't risk the desk clerk at this motel or the next seeing me in the disheveled state I was in. I tore off my clothes and took a fast shower, scrubbing my hands almost raw. Luckily, none of the cuts I'd accrued were either deep or on my face. None were readily visible. I packed in a hurry, careful to keep the clothes I had just removed in a separate pillowcase.

The desk clerk was too busy with hourly customers to pay me much mind. I paid my bill in cash and asked for directions to Cocoa Beach. I had no intentions of going there, I just remembered the name from I Dream of Jeannie. It's weird what you think about. It was an obvious ploy, but anything I could do to put some space between Barto and me was worth a try. In any case, the desk clerk didn't have a clue how to get to Cocoa Beach. He had just moved to Florida from Madras.

I drove all night, fueled by a sick kind of elation. I was alive. A man had actually tried to murder me and I was still alive. But was he? I'd done it, finally. I'd shot a man. Or had I? I guess I'd find out one way or another. I'd never bought into that crap about violence begetting violence. I believed it now. There was a direct line from Carl Stipe's murder to Moira's to Spivack's suicide to what I'd done tonight. What I failed to recognize was that a chain of violence, unlike basketball, did not come with a twenty-four-second clock. It didn't matter that Carl Stipe had died almost thirty years ago. Once he was killed, more violence was inevitable.

I dumped the pillowcase containing the clothes I'd worn during the exchange of gunfire in the rear end of a garbage truck parked at a rest stop outside Tampa. A little farther north, I turned in my rental car and took a bus up into Georgia. I flew from Savannah, Georgia, to Charlotte, North Carolina, and from there into La Guardia. I called Katy to tell her I was all right, but lied about where I was. I called Wit's hotel room in L.A. He wasn't in. I left a message for him to come home. The second I had hired Barto, our carefully thought out charade was over. I wished I hadn't found out the hard way.

If, in my exhaustion, I had begun having second thoughts about the chain of violence, they vanished the moment I scanned the headlines at a newspaper stand outside the arrival gate.

The Post: **IVAN THE TERMINAL**
The News: **IVAN TERRIBLE NO MORE**
Newsday: **RIKERS REVENGE**

Anthony Murano, the brother of one of Ivan Alfonseca's victims, had several weeks ago gotten himself purposely arrested. Yesterday, while both men were preparing to be bused to court, Murano attacked Alfonseca. Witnesses said it was all over in a flash, that Murano, a recently discharged army ranger, snapped Ivan's neck like a twig. No one was shedding any tears. Lawyers from as far away as California were tripping over themselves volunteering to defend Murano. Did I think this was part of the master plan? No, not this. This was revenge, pure and simple. If anything about revenge can be pure and simple. Whatever it was, pure or not, it had made my task nearly impossible.

I took a cab to a hotel across the Grand Central Parkway. Inside my room, I called my brother. There are times when only family will do, and this was one of them.

CHAPTER
TWENTY

AARON HAD DONE AS I ASKED, MADE THE PHONE CALLS, DELIV-
ered the messages. He was an awfully efficient messenger. Everyone I had asked to call had called. Everyone I had asked to see had
come. But I did not fool myself that it was all Aaron's considerable
salesmanship which had produced these remarkable results. It was
as if the sense of inevitability which now dominated my waking
hours had seeped into the lives of all the people connected to this
case, from the perpetrators of the crimes to their accomplices to the
people on the periphery. This case, which, in the end, was not
about kidnapping or rape or even murder, but about a bicycle and
a silly gang of wealthy boys who called themselves the James
Deans. I clipped my old .38 to my belt, clicked off the room light,
and checked the door handle behind me. Today, I had determined,
the chain was to be broken. The violence that began twenty-six
years and eleven months ago was going to come to an end.

*   *   *

You had to admire Steven Brightman. He was out and ready for
jogging early, the sun barely hinting at its arrival. Far enough away

that he wouldn't notice me, but close enough to see his face, I watched him stretch for five minutes on the steps of his brownstone. Although he could not have anticipated what was about to happen, he had to have some idea that the things he had so skillfully manipulated for so many years were about to spin wildly out of control. Yet his calm expression never changed. If he was frightened or worried, he didn't show it. I could not make the same boast.

When he started down the block toward me, I was almost tempted to stay hidden and let him pass. I couldn't. Like with Barto, I would probably get only one chance. In spite of his cool, collected demeanor, he wouldn't be expecting this, not here, not now. I needed him off balance, but also feeling he had the upper hand. He struck me as the type of man who would always feel he had the upper hand. As he ran past, I stepped out from behind some brownstone steps.

He startled. "For chrissakes, what the fuck—Prager?"

"We need to talk."

"You look like shit. Go home. Shave and shower, then call me later. We can talk about anything you want then."

"Now!" I whispered angrily, letting him see the barrel of my gun pointing at his belly.

"Okay. What's this about?"

"I just got back from Florida."

"How nice for you." He sneered. "You don't look like you got much of a tan."

"Barto tried to kill me."

"Who?"

"Look, Brightman, we can do this a few ways."

"And they would be . . . ?"

"One is I hand you my pistol, let you pat me down to see I'm not wearing a wire, and we have a talk out here in the nice empty street about compensation."

"I'm listening."

"The other is I stick this gun in your ribs and take you for a ride."

"You won't kill me."

"You're right, I won't, but John Heaton'll be happy to. You ever meet his friends Rocky and Preacher Simmons? They won't need much encouragement, Brightman, and I bet you I can be awfully fucking convincing."

That put a chink in his armor. Though he was still smiling at me with his mouth, his eyes had withdrawn from the performance. They were too busy sizing me up.

"Tick . . . tick . . . tick . . ." I waved the .38 from side to side. "Clock's running."

"What is it you think you know?"

Good. Good. He'd given me an opening. I held my revolver out to him, flat in my palm, my finger nowhere near the trigger.

"It's one or the other, Brightman, no free samples. It's a limited menu. We talk or you die; those are your choices."

He swiped the .38 out of my hand and stuffed it in the waist band of his shorts. Without him asking, I removed my shirt and spun around slowly. I put the shirt back on. I spread my legs and let him run his hands and up and down both legs, inside my socks.

"Check under my balls," I instructed.

He laughed, but did it anyway. I moved to the car parked closest to us, sat on the fender, and removed my shoes and socks.

"Okay?" I asked.

"Not yet." He looked down the block in either direction,

stepped into the street to see if he could spot anyone lurking about. The early Sunday sky was a bit brighter now, and the new light afforded him a pretty good view. Satisfied that we were alone, he said: "Talk."

"I want you to know that I think you're a piece of shit and if I was able to prove anything I was about to say, we wouldn't be having this little chitchat. I'd throw the proof up in the air between the DA and John Heaton and let them fight for it like a jump ball. Fortunately for you, all I got is a bag full of circumstance and supposition."

"Why not open the bag and let me have a look?" he said, his eyes still locked on my face. "Then maybe we can determine the value of your assets."

"Let's start with the James Deans."

"The James Deans . . . You're very good, Prager. What a bunch of jerks we were. You know, one other person's mentioned them to me in twenty-seven years."

"Yes, I know. Kyle Lawrence, the boy who helped you murder Carl Stipe. He's one of the missing pieces. Something happened around the time of his death that caught Moira's attention. That's why you had to kill her. But I'm getting ahead of myself."

There was no denial. Brightman said nothing. He didn't have to. The cocky smile he'd been showing me for the last several minutes slid off his face. He noticed me notice.

"As you were saying . . ."

"Okay, so to get into the James Deans you had to take a scalp, steal something, right? You had balls, so you took the Hallworth Harrier. Mike stole a box of sanitary napkins from Wiggman's. Pete grabbed Mr. Hart's glasses. Jeff was a pussy and stole his father's watch. That leaves Kyle. What did Kyle steal? Mike Day told me that no one but you knew and you vouched for him. What did he steal, Senator?"

"It's impolite to ask questions you think you know the answers to, Mr. Prager. Didn't your mama ever teach you that?"

"She was too busy teaching me not to steal and murder. The way I figure it, you and Kyle saw Carl Stipe's bike outside Ronny Bishop's house. You knew he would take the shortcut through the woods to get to his house. What a scalp that bike would be, and from the mayor's kid, no less. It was close to Halloween, right? So you two got your masks and went into the woods to wait for him. How'm I doing."

"It's all very fascinating, so far."

"So Carl comes riding by and one of you shoves a stick through his front wheel and he topples over, headfirst. You should've just taken the bike and split, but, of all things, one of you is worried the kid might really be hurt. So Kyle or you go to check on him. A fatal mistake. When you get close, he rips off your mask and sees who you are. Then he starts screaming and struggling. He threatens to tell. You threaten him back. If he doesn't shut up, you're going to kill him. Now he's panicked and struggles harder, screams louder. You ask Kyle to help hold him down, but the kid still won't shut up. One of you reaches for something to shove into his mouth to quiet him—the stick you used to knock him off the bike.

"You shove it in to scare him, but it's gone too deep. It snaps. Now the kid's gasping for breath, struggling even harder because you *are* going to kill him. You're panicked too. You *have* to kill him. You ram the stick in again and again. Then the kid's dead. You take the bike and split. I think maybe you weighted it down and threw it into the reservoir. I don't know. Why don't you tell me where the bike is?"

He actually started laughing. "If you knew where the bicycle was, you'd have more than supposition and circumstance, wouldn't you? We couldn't have that."

"Okay, all right," I relented, "you can't give me any physical proof. I didn't suppose you would. But I want to know who killed the Stipe kid. You don't have to say a word. Was it you?"

He shook his head no. He was shrewd. He knew that if he asked me the same question, my reaction would be much the same. It would hold no water in court, but I wasn't worried about the rules of evidence at the moment.

"I know you were a bright and ballsy kid, Brightman," I moved on, "but I was confused about the statement you and Kyle made to the cops afterward. Even if you had thought to do it, to go to the cops and feed them a story about a drifter leaving the woods on a bicycle, I couldn't picture any fourteen-year-old clever enough to know just exactly what to say. Most kids would have given themselves away, saying too much or too little. You and Kyle, though, gave just the proper amount of detail to throw suspicion away from you, but not enough to point at any one person in particular. Then I realized that had to be your father's doing. He would know what to say, how to say it, and to whom. He would know how to keep your names out of it, how to get the cops to shield your identities. He knew, huh? All these years, he knew."

Again, Brightman was silent, but his fists were clenched so tightly I thought his nails must be biting into the skin of his palms.

"Then that poor schmuck Martz got picked up by the cops. You and Kyle would probably have gotten away with it without him, but he made it a done deal. When he was unlucky enough to drown, you guys were home free. Your dad waited a respectful amount of time and then got you the hell out of Hallworth. I'm curious, did you and Kyle ever talk about that day? Did you two keep in touch?"

"So you don't know everything," he chided. "There's holes in that bag of yours."

I ignored him. "Well, did you two talk?"

"Not ever, not once from the day I moved. I put Hallworth behind me."

"You mean you thought you did, until about two years ago. Then something happened. And here I'm only guessing, but I think I'm pretty close. Kyle must've found out he was dying. That fucks with a man's mind, you know, knowing he's about to die. It's bad for a young man, especially one who has murdered a little boy. Maybe that's why he turned to a life of drugs in the first place. Who knows these things?

"Then I remembered how weird my mom started acting when she found out how sick she was. Suddenly, she remembered the shitty things she'd done to people over the years. There weren't many, but what few there were ate her like the cancer. She made a list of people she felt she needed to apologize to and either called or wrote to everyone on the list who was still alive. But when you've committed murder, who do you apologize to?"

Brightman looked a bit puzzled. "Are you asking me?"

It was my turn to laugh. "Don't waste your energy on it now. You'll have to ask yourself that question eventually, unless you plan on living forever."

"Get on with this or I'm leaving."

"So Kyle knows he's dying," I picked up. "He writes you a letter. Something about how guilty he's felt all these years since what happened in Hallworth in '56 and how he needs to unburden himself before he dies. When people find out they're dying, they get religion chop-chop. He suggests you do the same before it's too late. But you two were close when you were kids, so he says he'll keep your name out of it. You don't panic. You did that once and it cost a kid his life. No, you're working on some sort of plan to prevent or delay Kyle from going to the authorities. Then Kyle has the good form to drop dead a little sooner than expected. You think you're off the hook. Unfortunately, Moira Heaton's seen the letter or overheard the phone call. I know this for a fact."

"How would you know that?"

"HNJ1956. It's a notation I found in Moira's checkbook under a check she'd written to a research firm. You know that already. Sandra Sotomayor told you all about it. It's why I got offered reinstatement. It's why you had Sandra call me up and offer me some bullshit story about the meaning of HNJ1956."

"She'll never testify against me."

"No one's asking her to testify to anything," I said. "This is between you and me, remember?"

"Yes, a little chat about compensation."

"Exactly. You know the funny thing about Moira, Brightman?"

"Was there something funny about her? I hadn't noticed."

"That's my point. By all accounts, she was unfunny, unattractive, and unexciting. But she was a bulldog. When she was curious about something, she wouldn't let it go. The way I see it, Moira didn't confront you about the letter. She figured she'd do a little research first. She probably made the mistake of confiding in someone like Sandra, or maybe she asked one too many questions and word got back to you. Once again, you didn't panic. This time, however, the person on your ass didn't have a terminal disease.

You waited her out, hoping she'd lose interest. Eventually, though, she forced your hand. She was making progress, getting close. That's why she started asking around about the statute of limitations. You had to get rid of her."

"Did I?" he said smugly.

"I have to admit, this is the thing I had the most trouble with and the thing I'm still most iffy about. At first, I thought you might actually have paid Alfonseca or somebody else to do it, but that would have been too risky. You would have been far too exposed. No, you did it yourself. You were the only one you could trust to do it right."

"And how did I accomplish this miraculous feat? Through the use of prestidigitation? There's the issue of my alibi, you remember."

"That alibi works only if you accept other facts. Once you open up your mind to alternative notions, you, Senator, become a very obvious suspect. The cops assumed all along that it was Moira that witnesses saw leaving the office that night. But I looked at those witness statements very carefully. Eyewitness testimony is notoriously inaccurate. None of the witnesses got a look at Moira's face that night. The closest witness was in a passing car. The others were fifty to a hundred yards away. And by the time these witnesses came forward, the papers had already tainted the information.

"Witnesses are suggestible. If you tell them they should have seen a five-foot-seven woman leaving an office at around eight p.m. that's what they see. That wasn't Moira leaving at all. It was either you wearing her coat or someone like Sandra or maybe even your wife. Moira was already dead by then, neatly wrapped in plastic. Then early on that Thanksgiving morning, you went jogging before the sun came up. No one would question that. You do it every day. You got in your car, drove to the alley behind the office, loaded Moira's body into the trunk, and disposed of her. You got home when you were expected, sweaty as usual, but not for the usual reason. Dead weight is always harder to handle than people expect."

"Bravo! Bravo!" Brightman applauded. "You're wasting your time in the wine business. You should take up writing fiction. You have quite a flair for it."

Again, I ignored him. "One problem solved. But for every problem solved, there are two lurking. You underestimated the press reaction. You see, you knew Moira. To you she was some boring, plain-Jane, forgettable drip who no one would be interested in. To the press, the disappearance of a young woman under mysterious circumstances is like blood in the water to sharks. It doesn't matter to them if the woman looks like Quasimodo and has the personality of a brick. They turn her into the Black Dahlia and sell papers. So you'd gotten away with two homicides, but your political career was fucked."

"Yes," he agreed, "fucked is the word."

"But things began breaking your way. Spivack and Associates was floundering, and Joe, who probably assumed you were innocent in Moira's disappearance, came to you with an idea of how to save his company and your career at the same time. You prop up Spivack and Associates and he'd find you some shithead to take the fall for Moira. He probably convinced himself he wasn't doing anything wrong, really. After all, you hadn't done it and you wouldn't be free to run for higher office until the crime was solved. For his part, he'd be saving his company and a lot of people's jobs. You didn't have to be asked twice and gave him the money. But he got cold feet. I don't know why. Maybe he started taking a good look at you for the crime and arrived at the same conclusion as me. In any case, you refused to take the money back. He may not even have offered. He knew he'd already been compromised."

Brightman looked impatiently at his Swatch. "Now the clock's running on you, Mr. Prager."

"I'm almost finished."

"Thank God!"

"I'd watch that if I were you. You're already into him pretty deep."

"Look—"

"Did Barto come to you or was it the other way around? Doesn't matter. Barto sees that Ivan Alfonseca's been arrested for all these rapes in the boroughs. He remembers Alfonseca from when he worked as a marshal in South Florida. He waits for Alfonseca to get convicted on enough counts so he'd have nothing to lose by confessing to Moira's murder. Barto arranges to have the family back in Cuba paid off. During trips to Rikers, his lawyers bring him the office sign-in sheets to fill out. He is given a story to remember about how he killed Moira and where he planted the jewelry. Now all you need is a patsy to think he's discovering all this on his own. That's where I come in. The timing was just too perfect. After two years, you just had to have me now. Why? I kept asking myself. Why?"

"It certainly wasn't your charm," Brightman said. "I shall have to have a talking-to with the man who recommended you. He assured me you'd be adequately incompetent."

"Really, and who was that?"

"Let's get on with this, Prager."

"I'm curious about how you handled Spivack. My instinct is you and Barto kept him in the dark. Although he'd already been compromised, there was no need to involve him until he couldn't do anything about it. On the other hand, he might have been a part of it as long as he thought you were innocent. Or you might've had more on him than I'm aware of. I guess I'll never know."

"The man did kill himself. I don't think he did that because he was depressed over his wardrobe."

"You did almost everything right, even lying about having slept with Moira. That was brilliant. It took my attention away from any other reason you might have to do away with her. Once I was convinced it wasn't about an affair, I stopped thinking of you as a suspect. And you deserve a lot of credit for having the foresight to keep some of Moira's jewelry. That's what sold everyone on Alfonseca. Almost everything broke your way. Spivack killed himself. Alfonseca's dead. I don't know where Barto is. The thing is, if you'd only hired some other poor schmuck besides me, you'd have gotten away with it."

"Oh, but I have, Moe. Like you said, your brilliant oratory is just so much smoke. It's completely valueless. None of it would stand up in court, and if your pal Wit ever tries to print a word of this, he knows I'd sue and win."

"I don't suppose I could appeal to your humanity and ask you to come with me and turn yourself in?"

"Humanity! Are you nuts? I'm a politician."

"Then just tell me where Moira's body really is and the bicycle, too. These families have suffered enough." I raised my right hand. "I give you my word, I won't mention you at all."

"Sorry. I have no idea what you're talking about."

"Okay, how's about you take my revolver and blow the back of your head off."

"Once again, I must disappoint you," he said as calmly as if I'd asked him to pick up some flour for me at the store.

"How about I go to your brownstone and tell your wife what you've done?"

"Be my guest. Unfortunately, she's away with friends, but I'll have her call you when she gets back. She wouldn't believe a word of this."

I ripped my .38 out of his waistband and pressed the barrel to his head. "How about I blow your brains all over the street?"

He didn't look scared until I pulled back the hammer.

"All right, Prager, what is it you want?"

"Nothing," I said. "You've already given me what I wanted."

"What?"

I pulled the trigger. Click. The front of Brightman's running shorts got dark with moisture and a stream of urine ran down his bare leg.

"You fuck. It was empty."

"Old cop rule: Never give a murderer a loaded weapon."

He twisted up his face into a mass of red distortion. "You're not getting a fucking penny from me now, you asshole."

"How's it feel, thinking you're gonna die? I bet you Moira and Carl didn't piss themselves."

"Carl shit himself, the little screaming bastard. What a fucking baby. All he cared about was what his father would say if he didn't fight for that stupid fucking bicycle."

"He was a little boy, for chrissakes!"

"Not a penny, you hear me?"

"Like I said, you've already given me what I want."

"What is that supposed to mean?" he demanded.

I didn't answer, but walked up the brownstone steps and rapped on the front door. "Come out, come out, wherever you are."

It took a few seconds, but the door swung back. Brightman's wife, Katerina, was first out. Her eyes were rimmed in red, silent tears staining her perfect face. Her presence wasn't strictly necessary, but I had wanted so much to punish Brightman. His career would be over. Geary would see to that. Somehow, that wasn't enough. I wanted him to hurt, to suffer, to lose someone he loved the way the Stipes and Heatons had.

Thomas Geary was next through the door, his rugged good looks intact. He shed no tears over Brightman. There were always other horses, other races to run. If not exactly responsible for Moira's death, he was not guiltless, either. His money had helped finance Moira's execution. Though no pauper, Brightman could never have afforded to pay off Spivack, Barto, Alfonseca, Morenos, and the like without raising an eyebrow. Geary didn't ask where the money was going, because he didn't want to know. He had admitted as much to me in my noisy hotel room across the way from La Guardia.

"Looking back," he confessed, "there were a thousand questions I should have asked. It was the same about hiring you. Though we both trusted the man who recommended you, I was quite skeptical. You had no track record to speak of, and frankly, Constance thought you were a bit of a pushover as a boss. Your brother sounded more qualified. Now, in all honesty, I wish I had hired him."

"That makes two of us."

Brightman's face, red with fury, went starkly white and blank. He was naked before the world for the first time since his birth. He stared at the open windows on the first floor of the brownstone, realizing Katerina and Geary had heard every word. Still, none of it would hold up in a court of law. But there are other courts in which to try a man, and places in the cosmos where the statute of limitations never ever applies.

EPILOGUE
MY SHIELD

IF THE LAST FIFTEEN YEARS HAD TAUGHT ME ANYTHING, IT WAS that there was no justice in this world. There's nothing particularly original or profound in coming to that conclusion. All grown-ups come to it in the end. Coming to it, however, has set me free. It lets me sleep at night while men like Steven Brightman walk unfettered among us. Actually, I'm not sure where he's walking these days. I lost track of him when he disappeared from the headlines.

Within a week of our bit of street theater, Brightman made big news when he resigned his office and withdrew from politics altogether. He and Katerina flew to the Caribbean shortly thereafter and got a divorce. Hurting her that way is the only regret I have about how I handled that day. Sometimes I think it would have been enough to have had only Geary there to hear. In formulating my plan, I had convinced myself that I was protecting Katerina, that I could not let her continue to sleep in the same bed with a man who had, in the course of his life, murdered a nine-year-old boy and a twenty-three-year-old woman. Now I find myself wondering if I hadn't just wanted to punish Brightman. Had I punished Katerina instead?

Thomas Geary was good to his word. As long as I didn't go public with what I knew, he would make sure none of us suffered from the truth. Larrry Mac and Rob Gloria kept their promotions. Though we have never discussed it, I suspect Larry McDonald has figured out what actually happened, or a version of it. Like I said, Larry was a good cop, a very good cop. But in his way he was as ambitious as Steven Brightman had been, and could not be bothered with the details of how he got to where he wanted to go. Rob Gloria wasn't a gift-horse-looking kind of guy and probably never gave a second thought to Brightman's resignation. We don't talk much, Gloria and I.

Pete Parson's kid has flourished on the job and has already traded in his sergeant stripes—the NYPD equivalent to the rank of captain in corrections—for lieutenant bars. Pete made a killing on the sale of his share in Pooty's. Though he hasn't yet moved south, he and his wife have taken several exploratory trips to the Outer Banks, Hilton Head Island, and Myrtle Beach. I think he enjoys thinking about and planning the move more than he will the moving. When he finally gets around to leaving he'll do what all good New Yorkers do when they relocate. He'll pine away for good pizza, kosher deli, and the type of energy that doesn't exist anywhere else on earth.

Wit never wrote that follow-up piece on Brightman. He said that working with me on the case changed him forever, though I think it has precious little to do with me. While he hasn't stopped drinking altogether, he has cut back severely. Whether it's enough to save his liver, it's too soon to say. But the biggest change has come in his writing. He has given up doing those celebrity exposés and now devotes his time to writing about people the world usually ignores or has forgotten.

His first book after the dust settled was entitled *A Lonely*

Death: The Times of Susan Leigh Posner. It was Susan's remains
in the marsh across from Lake Ronkonkoma that the Suffolk
County cops had thought might be those of Moira Heaton. Wit
hired me to help do the background investigation into what had
driven Susan to suicide. My name's first on the acknowledg-
ments page. I'm very proud of that. I would have been equally as
proud had the book not won the Pulitzer. It's dedicated to Carl,
Moira, and Little Man. Little Man is what Wit used to call his
grandson.

Wit took Katy and me to the Yale Club for dinner as promised.
It was very cute how impressed Katy was by the place and by a
sober Wit's charm. I remembered my first time there and Wit's
slide into nastiness greased by three double bourbons. We both
had come a long way in a very very short time. Homicide changes
everything for the killer and the victim, but like an earthquake its
effects can be felt by everyone for miles around.

After Brightman had faded into obscurity, Wit and I took a
drive into Hallworth. We parked across the street from the big
Tudor on Reservoir Road. We watched Carl Stipe's mother raking
late-autumn leaves into plastic bags. Though she was only in her
late fifties, she seemed much much older. She moved with a robotic
deliberateness that was painful to watch. There were tears in my
eyes and Wit's, too.

I started to get out.

"Are you sure you want to do this?" he asked.

"No."

I got out of the car. The noise of the closing door got Mrs.
Stipe's attention. She stopped raking and turned to face me.

"Can I help?"

I froze for a second, looking for a sign in her face that would tell me she wanted to hear what I had to say. When I didn't answer her immediately, she just sort of shook her head.

"Sorry, ma'am, wrong house."

She didn't say a word and went back to the task at hand. In that second of hesitation, I thought of Katerina Brightman and how my not thinking things all the way through had made an unintended victim of her. What would the truth, I wondered, really do for Mrs. Stipe? I certainly wasn't smart enough to do the permutations.

Judith Resnick sent a lovely thank-you card to me, though she said she was having trouble coming to terms with her dad's death. We have spoken on the phone a few times since. She hasn't asked me about HNJ1956. I don't know what I'd tell her if she did.

* * *

Aaron has started searching for a location for our next store. He says I'm to blame for our rapid expansion.

"With all your *meshugas,* we made new managers and hired new people. We have to have someplace to put them all."

Of course, the fact that we were doing amazingly well didn't have a thing to do with it.

In early November I received the most unexpected call at the Brooklyn store I think I've ever gotten. It was my father-in-law, Francis Maloney Sr., the old political hack, inviting me to lunch. He knew that in spite of my antipathy against him I would never turn him down. On the ride over I realized I was more frightened than I'd been in the Black Flamingo. The worst Ralph Barto could have done was kill me. My father-in-law had the ammunition to do much worse. He could ruin my marriage with a few words whispered in Katy's ear. It was just like him to do it this way, to tell me first so he could enjoy watching me squirm.

Thin Tim McGuinn's was an old cop hangout in the shadows of the Brooklyn and Manhattan bridges that served a lunch buffet of boiled meats and bleached vegetables. I forgot sometimes that Francis had been a cop. I didn't like to think of him that way. What he had done on the job tarnished the badge I carried in my pocket.

Though my father-in-law was short and thick, he was easy to spot in a crowded room. And there he was, seated in the third booth from the door with a glass of Bushmills on the rocks on the table before him. He actually stood up and smiled when he spotted me. I was nauseated with fear and he must have seen it in my expression.

"You'll get yours someday, but not today. Relax, son-in-law." He said it like a curse. "Sit down and have a drink. You look as if you need one."

"Dewar's rocks."

"Jimmy," Francis called to the bar, "Dewar's rocks for the lad."

He waited to bring my drink over from the bar before talking. When I lifted the glass, he warned me not to.

"I'd offer you food, but you don't look as if you could keep it down, boyo. Haven't you figured out why you're here?"

"No, Francis, I haven't. If it's not to tell me you're going to ruin my life, then—"

"So the tough Jew hasn't gotten it all figured out. I'll be damned."

"That's beside the point."

He didn't like that. "There's no call for that, especially as I'm here to toast you for a job well done. To you, Moses Prager, and a job well done."

"A job well—" Then it hit me. "You son of a bitch. You're the one. You're the one who recommended me to Geary and Brightman."

He smiled. "Ah, the joy of it. It was Joe Donohue and Thomas Geary who five years ago pushed to have me squeezed out of the party. Geary didn't think I knew, but I did. That bastard Donohue died before I could pay him back. I couldn't believe my luck when Geary and Brightman came sniffing around about you. I knew they wanted a patsy. I may hate that I have to breathe in the air you breathe out, but I know you're no patsy. Fucking Jews are all troublemakers to begin with, never happy to leave well enough alone. And with what you did to me and my family, I had every confidence you would ruin their plans. I don't know what you did to force Brightman to resign and I don't care, but here's to you! There is justice in this world."

I didn't explain why I was laughing when I walked out of Thin Tim McGuinn's.

Two weeks later, Israel Roth showed up in Sheepshead Bay. We had spoken several times after my return to New York, but I had been purposely vague about what had transpired during my time in Florida. He hadn't gotten in any trouble with the Boca cops. They had scolded him like a child and suggested he take a gun-safety course offered by the local NRA. I apologized for what I'd put him through.

"Don't worry, Mr. Moses, you'll see. For being an ass when you're young, the punishment is getting old."

One night, when Katy and Sarah had gone to bed, we sat up drinking scotch and vodka. I explained to him about how his offering me his automatic had saved my life. He looked very perturbed at me when I suggested that our meeting in the Catskills and our reconnecting in Florida must have been a part of some great plan.

"I've seen too close the results of some of God's great plans. It's better you think of things as luck or misfortune," he advised.

"To luck and misfortune!"

That cheered him up. He said that there had been nothing in the papers about either Morenos or Barto, but that he'd keep his eyes open. I wasn't sure I much liked that, but there was nothing to be done about it.

On the day he was to leave, I gave Mr. Roth back the boxes he'd given me. I told him it was only right that he give Katy and Sarah their stars. He almost started crying. Almost. Like he said, he had too closely seen some of God's great plans. As he put their stars around their necks, I too tied the one he'd given me back in Florida. I had gotten quite used to it by now. The strange thing is, I could have been reinstated and gotten my detective's shield in spite of everything. I had turned it down. Somewhere along the way, I'd realized I had my shield, only not the one I'd expected.

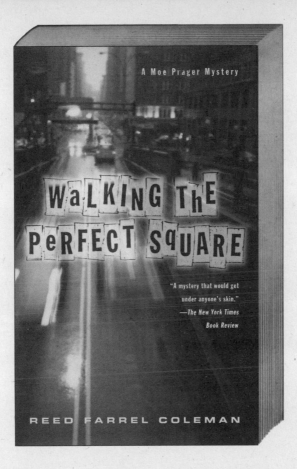